THE BEAST

A WICKED VILLAINS NOVEL

KATEE ROBERT

TRINKETS AND TALES LLC

ALSO BY KATEE ROBERT

Wicked Villains

Book 1: Desperate Measures

Book 2: Learn My Lesson

Book 3: A Worthy Opponent

Book 4: The Beast

Book 5: The Sea Witch

Book 6: Queen Takes Rose

The Island of Ys

Book 1: His Forbidden Desire

Book 2: Her Rival's Touch

Book 3: His Tormented Heart

Book 4: Her Vengeful Embrace

The Thalanian Dynasty Series (MMF)

Book 1: Theirs for the Night

Book 2: Forever Theirs

Book 3: Theirs Ever After

Book 4: Their Second Chance

The Kings Series

Book 1: The Last King

Book 2: The Fearless King

The Hidden Sins Series

Book 1: The Devil's Daughter

Book 2: The Hunting Grounds

Book 3: The Surviving Girls

The Make Me Series

Book 1: Make Me Want

Book 2: Make Me Crave

Book 3: Make Me Yours

Book 4: Make Me Need

The O'Malley Series

Book 1: The Marriage Contract

Book 2: The Wedding Pact

Book 3: An Indecent Proposal

Book 4: Forbidden Promises

Book 5: Undercover Attraction

Book 6: The Bastard's Bargain

The Hot in Hollywood Series

Book 1: Ties that Bind

Book 2: Animal Attraction

The Foolproof Love Series

Book 1: A Foolproof Love

Book 2: Fool Me Once

Book 3: A Fool for You

Out of Uniform Series

Book 1: In Bed with Mr. Wrong

Book 1.5: His to Keep

Book 2: Falling for His Best Friend

Book 3: His Lover to Protect

Book 3.5: His to Take

Serve Series

Book 1: Mistaken by Fate

Book 2: Betting on Fate

Book 3: Protecting Fate

Come Undone Series

Book 1: Wrong Bed, Right Guy

Book 2: Chasing Mrs. Right

Book 3: Two Wrongs, One Right

Book 3.5: Seducing Mr. Right

Other Books

Seducing the Bridesmaid

Meeting His Match

Prom Queen

The Siren's Curse

To readers who prefer their love triangles to end happily for everyone involved.

CONTENT WARNING

This book contains the aftermath of a parental death by cancer (it happens before the beginning of the book), which may be upsetting for some readers.

CHAPTER 1

ISABELLE

We have to do something.
It has to be you, Izzy.
For the good of the family.

My sisters' voices ring in my ears, even hours after our conversation. I stand on the curb and stare up at the building before me. It looks nearly identical to those around it: a nondescript gray square reaching into the sky as if it has every right to be there. It's not remotely the same. No, this place arguably holds the most power Carver City has to offer. Neutral space. Every territory leader has an open invitation to come and go—for a price, of course. My eldest sister has been here a few times, but I'm strictly forbidden from attending.

Or I was before my father died.

It's been months, and the grief still clings to me like a second skin. During my darkest days, I wonder if it won't cling forever. My father was supposed to live for decades yet, to pass power to his daughters and retire to do whatever powerful men do when they're no longer running a territory.

He was fond of saying he'd like to spend his last days surrounded by dogs and grandchildren.

It won't happen now. Cancer took him and there's no getting him back.

I have to close my eyes against the cascade of emotion. I don't want to be here, walking into the devil's den. I'm not the leader like Cordelia. I'm not the genius like Sienna. I am simply the youngest. The woman who never quite grew up, the one who values her personal freedom above all else. My sisters were always destined to hold positions within our father's organization. I was allowed to find my own way. Up until my father's death, I believed that way would lead me on countless adventures and travel across the world. To *freedom*.

That's no longer an option.

The first step is the hardest: to keep moving toward the fate I want nothing to do with, to not turn and run until I'm somewhere far from Carver City and the chains my sisters are asking me to encase myself in.

Inside, the facade of normality continues. I step into the elevator and take slow breaths that do nothing to calm my racing heart. I don't know if I can do this. It seems simple enough from where my sisters sit. Our two most formidable generals have left us and are making no plans to return. It's imperative that they stay, so we will do anything to ensure it happens. *Simple.*

Except it's not simple at all. Not for me.

The elevator doors open and I step into a room that's my first indication I've left the real world, such as it is, behind. The room is uniform marble, giving the impression of being unmoored. The only furniture is a single desk, and a beautiful Black man sits behind it. He looks up as I approach and gifts me with a smile that seems to brighten the room. "Welcome back to the Underworld, Isabelle Belmonte."

Of course he knows who I am, even though this desk sat unmanned the only other time I came to the Underworld. Being the daughter of the so-called Man in Black is enough to make me a strange kind of famous. I give him a practiced smile even though all I want to do is turn around and leave. "Thank you."

He rises gracefully and motions to the large black door dominating the wall behind him. "Since it's officially your first time, Megaera will need to speak with you before you engage in any activities."

Activities. Such a mundane word to encompass a very unmundane topic. I know what goes on here, of course. Everyone in Carver City does. Power and kink and sex. The thought thrills me even as my palms go clammy.

I had wondered if Hades would acknowledge our very short, very ill-fated meeting several weeks ago. From the front desk man's greeting, he is. I don't know if that's a good thing or a bad thing. I came here before looking for some insight into our problem with Beast and Gaeton, but Hades gives nothing away for free and I'm not desperate enough to make one of his infamous deals.

If tonight goes poorly, I might have no other choice.

I nod at the man at the front desk, keeping my expression locked down. "Is Megaera available now?"

Another of those beautiful smiles. "She is. Please go ahead."

"Thank you."

Approaching the giant door feels like approaching the entrance to the Underworld in truth. Once I cross this threshold, there's no going back, which is fitting because there wasn't any going back from the moment my sisters sat me down and laid out what will happen to us if Gaeton and Beast leave permanently. More intense skirmishes with our borders. Maybe even war, if it comes to that.

I've just lost my father. I will do anything to ensure my sisters stay safe. *Anything.*

Even reach out to my exes under these less than ideal circumstances.

The door gives easily beneath my touch and I step through into darkness. I blink, trying to adjust. It's not truly *dark* back here, but the intentionally dim lighting creates a strange intimacy I don't know what to do with. I stop short, trying to take stock of the room. A large oblong bar in the center surrounds a truly overwhelming statue of what appears to be an orgy. Deep booths line the walls on all sides, many of them occupied. A door on the other side of the room has a short white woman standing in front of it—obviously security of some kind. Through there is where the kink happens, where people shed their civilized selves and engage in all manner of things that I can only know about in theory.

Beast and Gaeton may be patrons of this place, but they never brought me here. Neither of them ever—

My brain feels strangely buzzy and detached and I can't decide if I'm relieved or disappointed that I don't see the men in the lounge. Either they're not here yet, or they're already in the back *playing* with other people.

I have no right to the jealousy that stings my chest. None. Gaeton and I haven't been together in over a year; my relationship with Beast ended a mere month after mine and Gaeton's did. They are single and free to do as they wish with whomever they wish.

I rub my hand against my chest, my palm skating over silk. I dressed carefully tonight in a short black dress that clings to my body and teases at what I may or may not be wearing beneath it. I'm still not sure it's the right choice.

I'm not sure of anything any longer.

"Isabelle."

The white woman who approaches seems perfectly at

home here. She wears tailored slacks that nip in at her ankles to display expensive red heels and her equally crimson blouse drapes over her lean body in a way that feels down-right sexual. Dark hair falls to her shoulders in waves and does nothing to soften the sharpness of her features. But then, this woman doesn't look like she's interested in blunting her edges. She gives me a smile that doesn't quite reach her eyes. "I'm Megaera. Come with me."

I fall into step behind her, my body obeying before my mind has a chance to catch up. It's almost enough to make me dig in my heels on principle, but I can't afford to have my entrance to the Underworld barred.

We head down a hallway and through a door into a study. Once again, I stop short and try to process. It's a deep room decorated in grays, with an arrangement of couches on one side and a desk on the other. The lack of color should make it feel cold, but somehow it's welcoming in a distant kind of way.

Megaera moves to perch on the edge of the desk and waves an elegant hand at the chair in front of her. "Sit."

I sit.

She studies me as if she wants to peel apart my skin and poke around inside my head. It's not a comfortable feeling, and I have to force myself to hold her gaze despite every instinct demanding I drop my eyes. Finally, Megaera sits back and props her hands on the desk. It should look casual, but it somehow gives the impression of a predator about to pounce. "I'll admit, I never expected *you*. Not after Hades sent you packing with your tail between your legs." She tilts her head to the side, still studying me. "I should bill you for all the damage Beast and Gaeton have caused this club, all because of your pretty little pussy."

I blink. "Excuse me?"

"You're in the Underworld, sweetheart. There's no point

5

in playing coy. You've never come to play before, which means you have a reason for being here and I highly doubt it's because you've suddenly developed a lust for kinky good times. If that were the case, you would have already indulged with those two fine specimens."

She's making too many jumps. I can barely keep up. "What are you talking about?" Except I know, don't I? Did I truly expect to walk in here with no questions asked? Hades and Megaera don't hold influence over the main players in Carver City by being fools.

"Keep the playacting for the men, Isabelle. That shit doesn't work on me."

At her derisive look, I tense. She's right. Playing innocent won't get me anywhere in here. I should have known better. That role usually works better with men, anyway. I straighten the tiniest bit, though it's still a challenge to hold her gaze. "I need them."

"Now we're getting somewhere. Elaborate."

How much to tell? I decide to stick with what's public knowledge. "They're our generals."

"Mmm. Seems to me like they *were* your generals when your father was still alive." Something like sympathy flickers through her brown eyes. "Sorry for your loss."

"Thank you," I reply automatically, just like I have every other time someone has offered their condolences in the last few months. The words mean nothing, change nothing. Every person in this city could drown in their apologies and sorrow and it still wouldn't bring my father back.

Megaera finally sighs. "Hades has decided to let this little drama play out despite my reservations, so you'll be allowed into both the lounge and the playrooms, provided you follow the club rules. Consent is our god, Isabelle." She gives me another long look. "You have subbie written all over you. I'd say I don't understand how *those* two managed not to drag you in here at one point or another, but I know all too well about how misguided men can be when they put you on a pedestal."

I'm not sure what I'm supposed to say to that. "Thank you for access to the club."

"I doubt you'll be thanking me before this is over." She shakes her head and pushes off the desk. "I can't keep you from approaching them, but if they aren't interested in talking, you don't get to force the issue. You might be the precious princess in your territory, but this is neutral space and our rules prevail over all others here. Do you understand?"

"Yes." If I'd been able to corner Gaeton and Beast in my own territory, I wouldn't need to come here. But they've been slippery. I'm not even sure Gaeton has been home in over a month and he's not taking my calls—any of our calls. And Beast? Even when he was in my bed, he felt like more ghost than man. No one can pin that man down if he's not interested in being pinned down. It was one of the things that drew me so strongly to him initially, a way I thought we were kindred spirits.

Megaera nods again, but not like she likes it. "Do you have a basic understanding of kink?"

"Yes." One could argue that I have more than a basic understanding, but it's all theoretical. My respective relationships with Gaeton and Beast were both vanilla, which is something of a startling revelation now that I know where their tastes lie. They may have attended meetings at the Underworld with my father over the years, but to the best of my knowledge they didn't indulge until our respective relationships had ended. I don't understand it. They must have known what they liked, must have known they weren't being completely fulfilled in my bed. And yet neither of them ever said a single thing about it. I want to know why;

one of the many answers I don't have a right to, but crave all the same.

She motions to the door. "Then by all means. Go play. Mind your manners or you'll be bounced out of here so fast, that pretty head of yours might spin right off your neck."

I rise slowly to my feet. "You know, most of the time when people decide they don't like me, they've actually met me first."

Megaera raises a perfectly shaped dark brow. "I'm not most people, and even if I were, I consider Gaeton my friend. Beast is one of our patrons. I've witnessed the damage you did to them, Isabelle. Some things are unforgivable."

She's wrong, of course. Or, rather, she doesn't have the full story. It's easy to paint me villainous shades for the production, but it takes two to tango—or three, in this case. We did not come to this place on my power alone.

But that's none of Megaera's business.

I channel my middle sister, Sienna, and stare Megaera down. It still doesn't feel natural, but I've been taught how to move amongst big players from the time I first learned how to walk. This woman is powerful, but she's just one of many. Ultimately, she holds no power over *me*. In theory. "If we're done here …"

"Step carefully, sweetheart." She waves me out the door, and I have to concentrate to keep my gait even and unhurried.

In the short time I was closeted up with Megaera, the lounge has gained a number of people. Couples and throuples and people who seem content to talk and ignore the promise of sex in the air. Or maybe it's not sex. It's *power*, the kind sometimes exchanged only for a night, sometimes for a lifetime.

I feel like I'm dying of thirst and someone just shoved me into an ocean. Water everywhere, but none of it for my drinking. All of these people are off-limits to me. They aren't why I'm here.

A couple moves toward the bar, clearing my line of sight to the booth nearest the door back to the playroom. I get a sense of a massive white man, and then he leans forward into the meager light cast over the table. Dark hair that's gone a little shaggy from need of a haircut. Shoulders that will fill any doorway. A surprisingly generous mouth on a face that looks carved from the side of a mountain. He's got freckles, too, though I can't pick them out across this distance.

Gaeton meets my gaze across the room. His dark eyes widen for the barest moment before he locks it all down. There was a time when he didn't try to hide himself from me, but I've long since burned that bridge. I don't deserve his kindness, or that hint of vulnerability that belies his size and strength. He could take me apart at the seams, but he always handled me as if I were made of spun glass.

No longer.

He starts to stand, but goes still halfway through the motion, his attention landing on something over my right shoulder. Or, rather, some*one*. The air shifts in the room, filling with the promise of violence. Just like that, I know who's behind me.

My entire body clenches as Beast's rough voice sounds in my ear. "Hello, Isabelle."

CHAPTER 2

ISABELLE

J twist to see Beast and, as always, his beauty takes my breath away. He looks like the prince in a fairy tale, all sculpted cheekbones and sensual lips. His short dark hair is perfectly styled, and he's wearing his customary jeans and T-shirt. It should make him look underdressed—everyone else in the room is wearing suits and dresses—but Beast simply looks at home in his skin.

One would never know he's one of the deadliest people on my father's payroll.

My breath catches and pain lances my chest. Not my father's payroll. Not any longer. Not ever again. He's gone and there's nothing in heaven or hell that will bring him back again.

Something flickers in Beast's blue eyes, something almost like concern, before he goes icy cold. "What are you doing here, Isabelle?"

I can see Gaeton climbing slowly to his feet out of the corner of my eye. I keep my body slightly turned toward him, an invitation I desperately need him to take me up on. I need both these men in a room, and I can't do that if Gaeton thinks I showed up here with Beast.

I lick my lips, and Beast's attention follows the movement. "I came for you." I glance at Gaeton, now striding toward us with long steps. "Both of you."

Gaeton stops just out of reach. I'm painfully aware of a number of eyes on us. We have the attention of the room. If they shun me now ...

My sisters will pay the price. Our *territory* will pay the price.

I shove down my pride, shove it deep and lock it away. There is no place for it here. I can't demand anything, can't expect them to fall in line. They hold all the power in this interaction and pretending otherwise will only result in ruin. Instead, I let my voice quiver the tiniest bit. I'm not even faking, not really. I'm simply letting my control lapse a small fraction of an inch. "I just want to talk. Please."

Gaeton and Beast exchange a look filled with so much animosity, I have to fight not to take a step back. Beast shrugs. Gaeton gives himself the smallest shake and looks around, seeming to register that we have an audience. "You have five minutes."

"More like two," Beast murmurs.

Not enough time, but I'll make it work. I don't have another choice. "Okay."

Gaeton turns on his heel and stalks to the door leading deeper into the club. I follow, having to work to keep pace with him in my high heels. I can feel Beast at my back, but he makes no move to walk next to me. Impossible not to feel like a prisoner being marched to her execution. These men would never, ever hurt me ... Or at least that used to be true. I don't know what's true anymore. The world stopped making sense when my father died.

It doesn't matter. Whatever their price, I'll pay it to ensure my family remains safe.

The door leads into a large room. There are scatterings of couches grouped together in a way designed to encourage socializing and in between those spaces are all manner of kinky equipment. Spanking benches. Suspension racks. St. Andrew's Crosses. Things I recognize from my internet searches, but can't remember the names of off the top of my head.

"Eyes forward, Isabelle."

I snap my gaze to Gaeton's back and, just as quickly, ignore the command. There is a man with medium-brown skin flogging a plus-sized white woman while another man kneels between her spread thighs, his face buried in her pussy. My skin goes hot and tight at the sight, and then goes even hotter when I recognize her. It's Tink, my clothing designer and now the wife to Hook, one of the other territory leaders. Now that I recognize her, I realize I recognize him, too. *Oh gods.* She's completely helpless, completely on display. Even as part of me cringes at the vulnerability, a small corner of my mind it writhing in jealousy of her experience.

Gaeton leads us out of the room and down a hallway lined with doors. He chooses one seemingly at random, but when we enter the room, it appears to be a generic study. Steeped in understated elegance, but normal in every way that matters. But then I notice the panel on the wall near the door and the cameras situated to ensure no corner of the room is hidden. Not so normal, after all.

Gaeton kicks one of the chairs in front of the desk so it is angled to see the entire room and drops into it. The man doesn't know how to sit without sprawling, and even with fury darkening his expression, this is no exception.

Beast shuts the door and moves to lean against the desk,

unconsciously mirroring the same position Megaera took when I spoke to her. He crosses his arms over his chest and watches me. Waiting.

Gaeton has no such patience. "What the hell are you doing here, Isabelle?"

Now's the time to lay out my argument, but the words dry up in their presence. I lick my lips again, and give him the same answer I gave Beast. "I'm here for you. For both of you."

Gaeton doesn't look impressed. "Yeah, I don't think so. We tried that and it blew up in our faces. I'm not doing it again."

If I don't talk fast, they'll pack me up and send me on my way and this will all be for nothing. Failure is not an option. It can't be. "Come back to the territory. Resume your positions. We need you."

Beast raises an eyebrow, but it's Gaeton's cruel laughter that echoes through the room. "I should have known this is all power and games. It always was with you." He leans forward and braces his elbows on his big thighs. "I don't pretend to speak for this asshole, but there's nothing in that territory for me now."

Nothing.

Including me.

It shouldn't hurt so much to be rejected by a man who already dumped me, but it does. Sweet gods, it does. I turn to Beast, but I might as well seek solace from a glacier for all the warmth he gives me. Hopelessness rises in my chest, threatening to send me to my knees. I can't fail. I *can't*. My bottom lip quivers the tiniest bit before I shut my reaction down. "Please."

Beast studies me a long moment. His lips slowly curve, the barest hint of a cruel smile. I've seen that expression on his face before, always preceding him delivering one of my father's punishments to someone who crossed him. "Get on your knees, Isabelle. If you're going to beg, do it properly."

Gaeton flinches like the other man struck him. "What the fuck, Beast?"

Beast doesn't look away from me. It feels like the intensity of his gaze is a weight across my shoulders and chest, driving me slowly, inexorably, to my knees. "You heard me. How bad do you want us back?"

"You don't speak for me," Gaeton rumbles.

I already left my pride at the door. I can't afford the luxury of it when I'm bargaining for the lives of so many. In the end, it's far simpler than I could have dreamed to give in to Beast's gravity and sink to my knees. The carpet is surprisingly soft against my bare skin and I shiver. "Are you happy now? *Please* come back."

Beast rises and moves slowly around me. It's a struggle not to twist to keep him in sight. Instead, I focus on Gaeton, on the way he watches us so closely, his gaze jumping from me to Beast. "What are you up to, you bastard?"

Beast digs his hand into my hair and tugs sharply, bowing my back and drawing a gasp from my lips. In all our time together, he was always devastatingly gentle, until I thought I'd go out of my mind and scream in his face to *touch* me. Pain flickers to pleasure and back again, and I have to bite back a moan. I stare up into his beautiful face, but he's not looking at me. He's looking at Gaeton. "I propose a bargain."

"You're out of your fucking mind."

"Gaeton." Beast says it almost gently. "*Look* at her." He gives my hair another sharp tug. This time, I can't stop the moan. My body doesn't feel like my own. My skin is too tight, my nipples pebbling and my pussy clenching with an ache only one thing can assuage. What is he *doing* to me?

"Get your fucking hand off her." Gaeton's voice is low and strangled. "Now."

Beast releases me in an instant and I slump forward, barely catching myself before I crumple into a ball on the floor. Dazed, I touch the smarting spot on my scalp. I should be furious he dared handle me like that, but all I can focus on is how much I *need*. I straighten back to kneel with some effort. "What are your terms?"

"No."

Beast ignores Gaeton and resumes his position leaning on the desk. "The three of us for a limited duration. At the end, you make a choice once and for all. Him or me. Regardless of your decision, we will both stay in the territory and resume our roles."

"You want me to pick?" My inability to choose is what caused this catastrophe to begin with. I strive for calm, to stop myself from shoving to my feet and demanding answers. "And then what? We date? You get your bragging rights and dump me? What?"

"Worry about that when we get there." There it is again, his cruel little smile. "For the duration of this little bargain, you will pay penance, little Isabelle."

I shiver. "What does that mean?"

"It means that you played us to your heart's content for years on end. Now it's our turn." He turns to Gaeton. "You're furious about how things fell out."

"Yeah." The word seems almost forced out of him.

Even as I remind myself I don't have any power here, I can't stay silent. "That's not fair. You two are the ones who proposed the idea to date me at the same time." And I was fool enough to agree to it, thinking it a wonderful way to have my cake and eat it, too. I should have known that if I couldn't pick one of them before we dated, I certainly wouldn't be able to once we were in the throes of a relationship.

"We played by her rules and cut off pieces of ourselves to

15

be worthy of her." Beast turns those eerie blue eyes back to me. "Now we drag her down into the dirt with us."

Gaeton folds his hands together and seems to be actually considering it. "Explain what the fuck you mean when you say 'us.'"

"We top her together."

My gaze jumps back and forth between them. Surely they're not saying … *"Together."*

Gaeton doesn't look at me. "Careful there, Beast. Might start to think you're sweet on me."

Beast doesn't blink. "It's an efficient use of time and effort." He's on the move again, but this time he circles Gaeton, coming to a stop behind the big man's chair. He leans down, not touching Gaeton, but near enough that I catch my breath at the sight of him so close to the bigger man. His rough voice is pure sin. "Think of every depraved thing you've wanted to do to that sexy little body. All the times you held back. All the fantasies you kept locked down."

They're both looking at me like a pair of wolves who happened across a lamb in the forest. I can't stop another shiver. I came here with the intention of walking out with both of them. I didn't bargain on *this*. Any of it.

But we need them too much for me to walk away. I clear my throat. "State your terms in explicit detail."

Beast still hasn't moved back from Gaeton. "Gaeton and I dominate you. We fuck you. We are your gods and masters for the duration of two weeks. You will have a safe word and will use it when necessary, but otherwise will obey our every whim. At the end of the timeline, when we've balanced the scales, you will make a decision and stand by it."

The loss of power is staggering. They want me trapped and helpless. A safe word, yes, but we all know I have no choice in this. If I say no and walk out of here without them, there's a very large chance that my territory will fall.

Cordelia is ruthless and a good leader, but the loss of our father and his two top generals at the same time is too high a cost. Already our enemies nip at our borders, testing us. We need Gaeton and Beast back, and we need them back now. "What will you do to me?"

"Anything we want."

"And after?"

Beast's expression doesn't change. "After you choose, you honor that choice in the way you should have from the beginning. Your very own happily-ever-after. Isn't that what all princesses dream of?"

Maybe other princesses. Not me. My dream was always to be free. I feel like I'm watching that future swirl the drain as we speak.

I'd known it would come to this, even if I wasn't willing to admit it to myself. There is always the next power struggle, always the next crisis. My father didn't need me to play a vital role in territory politics, but my sisters do. If I'm in a relationship with one of our most powerful generals, we won't be able to flit away at a moment's notice. I'm not sure we'll be able to travel at all, not when his absence can make the difference between victory and defeat in any given skirmish.

I knew I would have to compromise when I agreed to talk to these men. I didn't realize I'd have to sacrifice everything.

Gaeton shoves to his feet. With me still on my knees, the difference in our sizes is so pronounced, I might as well be kneeling at the base of a mountain. He seems to realize the same thing and stops short as if he's afraid he'll trample me with one wrong step. "I didn't agree to anything."

"But you will." Beast still hasn't moved. "You want to know the answer as much as I do." The answer on who I'd choose. I'd like to know that answer, too. If making a choice between these men was so easy, I would have done it years ago and saved us all the heartache.

Gaeton doesn't deny it. "There has to be a better way."

Beast shrugs. "We've participated in scenes together over the last year. Consider the next two weeks one long scene."

They've participated in scenes together? The jealousy wrapped around my heart digs its thorns in deeper. It's not even necessarily the fact that they fucked other people—or were intimate, since I know enough about kink to know that it doesn't necessarily mean sex. It's that they let others experience parts of themselves that they always held back from me. I got the sweet, vanilla sex. The *making love*. The term makes me cringe.

Gaeton looks down at me, his dark eyes stormy. "You aren't doing this because you want us—either of us. You're doing this because of your family. Out of loyalty."

I open my mouth, but Beast beats me there. "No lies, Isabelle." His growling voice turns my name into a threat and a promise.

I clasp my hands in my lap so neither of them will see me shake. "It doesn't matter why I'm doing this."

"It might not matter to him." Gaeton shoves his hands into his pockets and glowers. "It sure as fuck matters to me."

My throat tries to close. I wish I could go back in time and change things, but I *tried* to change things on my own and look where that left me. Alone. Free, but at what cost? I swallow hard. "I want you. I want both of you. That never changed, even if everything else did." When he doesn't move, I force myself to continue. "But yes, the reason for this timing is because of my sisters." Gaeton looks away and I rush on. "The second you left, the Sea Witch started pressing our borders. I don't know if we can hold without you."

"Ursa won't risk a full-on attack."

I wish I had his confidence. I give a bitter laugh. "Not a

month ago, she wouldn't. My sister might have been my father's right hand for a decade, but to everyone in Carver City, she's untried. Muriel gives them pause, but the fact that Cordelia lost both of you so quickly after my father's death?"

There it is again, that horrible knowledge in the base of my chest. The loss that I don't think I'll ever recover from.

My father wasn't a good man. Not by any stretch of the imagination. But he loved me and my sisters to distraction. He protected us and cherished us and was a good father in every way that counted.

"I miss him, too." Gaeton reaches down and runs a gentle finger across my cheekbone. I'm horrified to see it come away wet. I hadn't even realized I was crying. He turns back to Beast and sucks his finger into his mouth. A challenge, but the other man simply waits. Finally, Gaeton nods. "I accept. Two weeks. We exchange topping her. You don't get to top me."

Wait—what?

I'm still wrapping my head around the implications behind that statement when Beast answers. "Deal, though that's open to negotiation on a case-by-case basis." He turns his attention on me. "Condoms or no? Your choice, princess."

This conversation makes my thoughts churn and dip. He's moving too fast. "I'm on birth control." I have been since I was sixteen and my oldest sister dragged me in to get the prescription. I swallow past a suddenly dry throat. "I'm, uh … I've been tested recently."

"So have I." Beast looks over. "Gaeton?"

The big man crosses his arms over his chest. "Me, too." His dark brows lower. "You don't have to agree to this, Isabelle. The rest, yes, but not this."

I'm not agreeing to no condoms because I feel like I have to. I *want* to. And no matter how tangled the history between us, how much hurt we've heaped on each other over the length of our respective relationships, I trust these two men. I can't help but trust them. "It's what I want."

"So be it." Beast nods. "Pick a safe word, Isabelle."

I blink. "*Now?*"

Beast gives a slow smile that feels more like a threat than an expression of joy. "Did you think we'd agree to the muzzles without a token of your sincerity? Prove you mean what you say tonight and we come back to the territory at the end of the two weeks."

It's happening. Good gods, it's really happening. I stop clenching my hands and press my palms to my bare thighs. There's no going back now. I have their agreement. All that's left is to ensure I don't break the terms.

Ensure I pick one of them to keep forever at the end of this. That I give up any chance at freedom, and accept that no matter how these two weeks end, I lose. I can't think about any of it too hard. Instead, I focus on the here and now. A safe word. Simple, really. I look down at my hands. "Candlestick."

"Good." Beast straightens. "Let's get started."

CHAPTER 3

GAETON

J don't want to do this.

I slouch into the chair I recently vacated, still trying to come to terms that Isabelle Belmonte is *here* and bargaining her body and future away because of some bullshit power struggle her sisters are embarking on. Oh, the power struggles didn't *feel* like bullshit when I was working under the Man in Black. They felt vital and world-ending. Now, I'm not so sure. What the hell is it all *for?* I don't have answers, and I'm not sure anyone in this room does. Isabelle will say it's for the continued safety of her family and the people under their protection. Beast? I have no fucking idea what goes on in that man's head.

Beast stalks around Isabelle like one of the great cats toying with its food. Building anticipation for the strike, enjoying the way she jumps a little every time he moves out of her line of sight.

If I were a better man, I'd call this whole thing off and haul Isabelle out of the Underworld and right back to the safe embrace of her sisters. They might have sent her here to draw us back, but there's no chance in hell that Cordelia and

Sienna approved of us defiling their youngest sister. They'd barely tolerated us before and we treated Isabelle like a queen. I can fault Beast many things, but I can't fault him that.

"Gaeton." The snap in his voice is a hook in my stomach, slamming me into the here and now.

I resent the fuck out of it. He's not my Dom. He's not even my friend. He's a man I used to hate and now am forced to tolerate from time to time. I glare. "Maybe you get off on playing with someone who's just going through the motions, but that's not my kink. *I* like consent, you bastard."

"Mmm." His deep voice rumbles through the room, seeming to wrap around all of us. "Our little Isabelle wants to be punished. It's why you came here, isn't it, princess?"

"Yes," she breathes. She's watching him like she's never seen him before. There's fear there, yes, but there's no missing the way her lips part and her eyes go hazy with need. Just like there's no missing her nipples pressed against the silk of her dress when he pulled her hair.

Or maybe I'm just deluding myself in an attempt to justify taking from her exactly what I want. To fuck her and humiliate her and make her cry from the intoxicating mix of pleasure and pain, her senses so overloaded that she can't do anything but beg for what *I* will give her.

Maybe.

"Gaeton still needs convincing." Beast shakes his head slowly. I can't help watching him as he gathers her hair and lifts it from her neck. We might have scened together in the past, but it was always beneath another's guidance, playing support in someone else's fantasy. I've never seen Beast orchestrate his own scene. When he plays, he plays behind closed doors, and Hades's submissives are too professional to gossip about it afterward.

He twines her hair around his fist, gently but inexorably

bending her back so that she's depending on his strength to keep her off the floor. Her breath comes faster now, her tits shaking a little with each inhale and exhale. Realizing she's not wearing a bra nearly has me groaning aloud. I clench my fists to keep still, to keep myself apart. I might have agreed to Beast's bargain, but I don't trust this. I don't trust *him*.

"Part your thighs, princess." Beast's command might rumble, but he sounds almost like he's sitting down to dinner. Barely affected. If not for the way he devours her with his gaze, I might actually believe it.

Isabelle moves slowly, obeying him in fits and starts until her thighs are splayed wide. Even as I tell myself not to look, my gaze is dragged down, down, down to where she's revealed herself. "Fuck."

"Tell me what you see."

Again, I obey that snapped command even as I tell myself not to. "She's not wearing panties."

"Dirty girl," he murmurs. "You *were* planning on fucking us back into submission."

"No."

"Yes." He reaches down, quick as a snake, and pinches her nipple hard enough that I wince. Isabelle cries out, but she's not arching away from him. She's pressing her chest *into* his touch.

Holy shit, he's right. She does want this.

"Told you." His attention is all on me now. "Tell me what you see, Gaeton," he repeats.

Between one breath and the next, I decide to embrace this. Fuck it. I'm going to regret it, but the temptation of having Isabelle on my cock—in my bed—is too strong to turn away from. I lean back, intentionally adopting a relaxed sprawling pose. "It's dim as fuck in here. I can't see shit."

"Unacceptable." He shakes his head. "Can't have her hiding from us."

My mouth practically waters with anticipation. "She came in here wearing that little tease of a dress and flashing her pussy. Seems she doesn't want to hide."

"I'm inclined to agree." Beast leverages Isabelle to her feet. He keeps one hand in her hair, steering her a few steps toward me, close enough to touch. "Best send a message then."

At that, the hazy lust in her eyes clears. "Don't you dare. This dress is brand new."

I hold her gaze and rip the fucking dress in half. Her body jerks with the movement, but she can only shift so far, because Beast holds her mostly immobile. I pull the straps down her arms and let the ruined fabric flutter to the ground. She stands there in heels and nothing else and, fuck, but Isabelle Belmonte does things for me.

She's built solid, the kind of body that fills out a person's hands. The kind of body that can take a rough fucking, though in the past I would have fallen on a literal sword before I let myself off the leash enough to indulge in dirty play with this woman. She's too good for that, too good for me.

I know better than to scene angry. It's a recipe for disaster. But I am fucking *furious*. I sit back and give myself a moment to study the way her light-brown skin has gone dusky with desire, her brown nipples pebbled and her body shaking. "When I finger your pussy, am I going to find you wet, Isabelle?"

"I don't—" She cries out when Beast gives her hair another pull. "Yes."

As pissed as I am, as light as this is compared to some of the shit I've seen—some of the shit I've *done*—in the Under-world ... "Isabelle, tell me your safe word."

"Candlestick," she gasps.

"You say that word, this stops." I glance at Beast and find

him watching me closely. "It doesn't mean the bargain stops, so don't be a fucking hero. On the other hand, if you lie to us, this whole thing is off. Not using your safe word when you need to is a fucking lie. Do you understand?"

Her mouth moves, those prettily painted red lips gasping for whatever words it will take to ensure we don't back out of this deal. She learned from the best, after all, and she's heavily invested in seeing this through, no matter what it takes. Finally, she whimpers, "Yes, I understand. I won't lie." She shivers, goose bumps rising over her skin in a wave. "I'll use my safe word if I need it."

It's enough. It has to be enough. BDSM only works if there's a measure of trust involved, and if I don't trust her to use her safe word, then I have no business being in this room.

I'd rather cut my cock off than walk out that door.

Beast shifts her closer yet. "Now that we have that out of the way, It's been a year since you had your hands on her, Gaeton. Since either of us did."

The reminder makes me thin my lips; that we were both arrogant enough to date her at the same time. That I put my heart in her hands, foolish enough to think I'd ever be enough for her, that if we just dated long enough, she'd choose *me*, love *me* enough not to need him. I know he's riling me up. I know he's playing us both. But I have a naked, quivering Isabelle nearly in my lap. I'm seeing this through to the end.

I give a low laugh. "Better give her a thorough examination, then." A humiliating play, examining her like she's an animal instead of a person, but that's the intention. Isabelle has enough pride to fuel an army. It's part of what drew me to her in the first place, how fucking untouchable she was, standing there next to her father, perfect and above us all. I just want to carve off a little piece of that pride and get her off in the bargain.

Beast nods and hauls her back, guiding her to resume her place on the floor. "Clasp your arms behind your back. Yes, like that. Now spread your legs. Wider, princess. You can't expect him to see properly if you're playing the shy innocent."

She obeys, each move jerky as if she's fighting herself to do it. Torn between obedience and wanting to tell us where to shove our games.

Obedience wins.

This time.

CHAPTER 4

ISABELLE

I have never felt more exposed in my life. The position of my arms bows my back and thrusts my breasts forward. My thighs are spread so wide, cool air caresses my pussy. Through it all, Beast keeps his unyielding grip on my hair. He's not hurting me, not really, but the promise of it makes me feel needy and hot.

I have no control. I've handed it over willingly.

Gaeton slides easily out of the chair and to his knees. He still towers over me, but I don't think there's a position in existence that won't highlight our size difference. One look at Beast has the other man using his grip on my hair to bend me backward again. Helpless. I am so helpless, and Gaeton's big palm sliding up the inside of my thigh makes me panic and slam my legs shut. A laughable rebellion, as if he can't simply force my thighs open. The thought should scare me. Instead, it makes me damn near pant with desire.

"Do you want to fight me, Isabelle?" He speaks roughly, but he doesn't move his hand, not to retreat and not to slide farther up. Gaeton studies me as if he can't begin to divine what I'm thinking. As if he wants to hear me say it. "Do you want me to shove your legs open and take what I want? Do you want Beast to hold you down while I force you to orgasm again and again?"

No. No, of course I don't want that.

I open my mouth to say it, but stop short. I promised to tell the truth not five minutes ago. I can't go back on my word over something as mundane as a dark desire, no matter how much it feels like he's digging around beneath my skin and exposing me more thoroughly than simply putting my naked body on display.

"Answer the question," Beast breathes in my ear. He's so still behind me, if not for his grip on my hair, I might believe he's left the room.

I don't want to answer. I desperately don't want to.

But I promised.

Anything for family.

I lick my lips. "Yes. I want that."

Gaeton's eyes go wide the barest amount before he assumes his lazy arrogant facade that I both love and hate in equal measures. He twists his hand between my legs to grip one thigh and then wedges his other hand in to grip the other. I fight him. I can't help but fight him. It doesn't matter that it's a lost cause, that I have no hope of winning this struggle.

He spreads my thighs inch by inch, a torturously slow display of strength. He could just yank them wide and take what he wants, but no. He's humiliating me with my inability to stop him.

I could stop him. A single word and it's over.

I don't *want* him to stop. I want him to force me, to take and take and take until need washes me away entirely.

It's not until I'm spread wide again that I realize no one is holding my arms. I start to move them, but Beast catches my wrists and clasps them together in a single hand. "Ah ah."

"Let me go." It's too much and not enough and neither of them have really touched me yet. Not in any real way.

"No," Gaeton rumbles. He glances at Beast. "On the floor. Hold her down."

I struggle harder, but they move me like they would a doll, Beast shifting back and shoving me to the floor. I don't miss the fact that no matter how rough he is, he keeps my head from bouncing on the hardwood. He grabs my wrists and pins them on either side of my head.

I stare up into those blue, blue eyes, and I don't see the man I thought I knew in them. There is no warmth for me, no tenderness. There is only a deep, dark hunger, like I've stumbled into a monster's lair and now he's only too happy to eat me right up.

Shoving against his hold does nothing. Less than nothing. "Stop."

"You know how to stop us." Gaeton gets rougher with my thighs, pressing them up and out, spreading me obscenely. "You're awfully wet, Isabelle. You fight and claw and curse, but your pussy knows who owns it." He spreads my folds with his thumbs. "I could shove my cock into you right now. You're ready for it."

I'm gasping like I've run a marathon. "No." *Yes, yes, yes, fuck me, oh gods, please fuck me, I need you.* I never thought I'd get another chance to be with either of them again. Now that it's here, that it's happening like *this*, in a way I never dared imagine …

It's beyond comprehension.

Beast gives my wrists a squeeze. There's no mercy for me on his face. "You don't get either of our cocks until you earn them." His gaze slashes to Gaeton. "Remind her who she belongs to."

Every part of me balks at the idea of belonging to anyone.

Freedom is the only god I truly worship. It always has been. "You don't own me."

"For the next two weeks we do." Beast tightens his grip on my wrists, nearly grinding the bones together, but that feeling is nowhere near as intense as his gaze drilling into me. Like he's dragging away every protection I've spent years building around myself. "Lick her pussy, Gaeton. Fuck her with your tongue the way I know you're dying to."

Gaeton drags the flat of his tongue over me from top to bottom. I don't know what I expected, but he doesn't rush. He traces every part of my pussy as if reacquainting himself. As if claiming me. I open my mouth, but I can't remember what role I'm supposed to play. Pleasure steals my words, steals my very thoughts, leaving only the animal behind. I try to arch up to bring him closer. "My clit. Suck on my clit."

Just like that, his mouth is gone and he delivers a stinging slap to my clit. I scream more from surprise than pain. "What the hell?"

"You don't give the orders, Isabelle." The words sound almost dragged from Gaeton. "You'd do well to remember that."

I'm still working on coming up with a retort when the door swings open. All three of us freeze as a man walks in. He's beautiful in an old school Hollywood sort of way, all square jaw and fresh face, with the body of a Greek god. He also looks furious and ready to punch something. "You two know better than to play non-con with a newbie. It's not sanctioned."

Neither Beast nor Gaeton move, which means I *can't* move. This man I've never met is seeing every single part of me and I have absolutely no control over it. I wiggle as much as I'm able. "Let me up."

"No," they answer together.

Beast considers this intruder. "She's fine."

The man lifts his chin though he seems to be fighting not to drop his gaze to me. "All the same, the rules are the rules."

I try to shift, but neither man is letting me up. Gaeton finally gives the stranger a lazy smile. "If you're so concerned, Hercules, why don't you sit in and watch? You think it goes too far, you call a stop to it."

The man—Hercules—freezes. "That's not how it works."

If anything, Gaeton's grin widens. "Call Hades. Get permission."

I don't understand what's going on here. I had my warning from Megaera earlier. I don't get why this man is here, why he's calling *Hades* to … get permission to watch whatever Gaeton and Beast have planned for me?

Humiliation sears my skin. I want to curl into a ball and cover myself as best I'm able, and here I am, splayed out at their whim. We all watch Hercules use the phone on the wall to make a call. He doesn't say much, but his conflicted expression tells me everything I need to know.

Hades agreed.

"No." I yank on my arms, but Beast only presses me harder to the floor. "I don't want an audience." *Do I?*

"Too bad, princess." Beast seems to approve of this new development. "Sit on the chair right there, Hercules."

The man obeys, but he's glaring. "You are not my Dom and I am not part of this scene."

"Noted." Beast gives a small smile. "But it'd be a shame if you didn't take a moment to appreciate Isabelle's pussy."

I blink up at Beast. My skin has to be a deep red from the blush coursing through my body, hot and unpleasant. He is so careless with my pride, as if he wants to crush it beneath his heel. I have years of instinct demanding I close my legs, hide from this new experience. "Stop."

"Tell me your safe word, Isabelle." Gaeton slides his hands

up the tops of my thighs and drags this thumbs over my pussy.

Every time he reminds me that I'm choosing this, I get hotter, more confused. I blink down at him. "Candlestick."

"Good girl." He gives my pussy another meandering stroke. "Do you want to use it?"

Do I want this to end? I can't decide. I'm so confused by my body's response, I'm shaking and they've barely touched me. Somehow I'm shaking *more* because we have an audience. I promised them honesty, but I don't even know what the honest answer is.

All I know is that I'm not ready for this to stop. "No, I don't want to use it," I whisper.

"Mmm." Gaeton glances at our audience. "Look, Hercules. She's so pretty and pink and she's practically weeping for my cock." To my endless mortification, the second Hercules's gaze drops to where Gaeton is spreading my pussy with his fingers, I'm certain I can actually *feel* myself get wetter.

"She's been playing the part of the untouchable princess, but it turns out she's a little slut who wants us to force her to the floor and fuck her rough." Beast speaks almost conversationally, as if he's not describing wanton acts. As if he's not trotting out my shame in explicit detail.

"That's not what I want." I'm suddenly sure that's exactly what I want, what I've always wanted.

"Yes, it is." Beast considers me. "I think our princess likes being on display."

Gaeton shoves a single finger into me roughly and makes an approving noise. "I know she does. She's so wet, she's practically dripping."

They're talking about me like I'm not in the room. Like I'm a plaything and not a person. I love it. I hate it. I have to press my lips together hard to keep a moan inside.

Beast strokes my wrists with his thumbs, the barest softness in the midst of his grinding grip. "Let's give Hercules a little show."

"Sounds good." Gaeton releases my thighs, but before I can do more than kick out once, Beast has me up and against his chest. Gaeton lies on the floor and Beast moves me forward. I realize their intent and start struggling in earnest. I don't know why I'm fighting. My body aches from what little Gaeton has tongued me. I desperately want the orgasm they promised. More, I ... like the idea of being put on display like this?

It's for that very reason that I fight the hardest. I don't understand this desire. My body has taken over, and with every inch Beast forces me forward, I get hotter. Gaeton grabs my thighs and lifts me bodily to straddle his face. I stare down at him in shock. "You can't really mean to—"

Beast straddles Gaeton's chest and pins my wrists at the small of my back. His other hand comes up to clasp my throat. His grip isn't rough enough to restrict my breathing, but the faint pressure about makes me come on the spot. And then Gaeton begins eating my pussy and I have to close my eyes. It's too good, too bad, too *everything*.

Beast gives my throat a little squeeze. "Eyes open, princess. It's rude to ignore your audience."

Almost against my will, I obey his command. From the way Hercules came into the room, I expect him to look like he's half a second from wading in and dragging me to safety, but something's changed in the last few minutes. He's relaxed in the chair and he's watching avidly, bright pink spots on his cheeks and a blatant cockstand in his slacks that he makes no move to either cover or do something about. He's merely there to observe and yet he's affected by this scene.

"That's right." Beast is as tempting as a devil on my shoulder. "He likes what he sees. Give him a show, little slut." The words should sound like an insult, but they're almost an endearment in his rough voice. "Ride Gaeton's mouth like you're dying to do."

I shouldn't.

Gaeton gives my hips a squeeze and sucks hard on my clit, making me jump. It's almost as if my body, once in motion, can't stop. Or that's what I tell myself as I rock against his mouth. It feels good. Wet and dirty and oh so wrong.

"What do you think, Hercules? Isn't she a pretty little slut?" Beast releases my hands, but I'm too far gone to remember that I'm supposed to fight this. He catches my right breast and squeezes, offering me up to this stranger's gaze.

"Very nice, Beast." Hercules is affected, yes, but he's not looking at me like he wants to fuck me. He's watching all three of us as if we're a private showing of an art piece that he deeply appreciates. It's strange and yet perfect at the same time.

Gaeton shifts and then his tongue spears inside me. It feels so good that this time I can't stop my moan. I rock my hips harder, grinding down on him. "Yes, please, yes."

"He's got his tongue in your pussy right now, doesn't he?" I can feel Beast's cock against my ass, but he sounds as unaffected as if we just sat down to dinner to talk about our day. "I bet you never rode his face like this when you dated. Gaeton's been at that pussy—he loves oral sex too much to deny it—but I bet it was always sweet and polite and you came quietly."

He's right. I hate that he's right. "Stop it."

Beast doesn't stop. He uses his hold on my throat to keep me pinned to him and works one nipple and then the other, alternating rough pinches with featherlight touches. "Do you even know what Gaeton likes, princess? Or did you believe that knight in shining armor bullshit? The truth is that he's just as much a little slut as you are." His lips brush the shell of my ear. "Did you know that just a few months ago, we fucked a friend, filling her with three cocks, and it still wasn't enough? Gaeton needed her Dom to fuck his mouth while she rode his dick."

There it is again. That barbed jealousy that demands I pull back, protect myself because these men might have loved me once, but they kept *so much* from me. "Fuck you, Beast."

"Not me, princess." His chuckle is raspy and deep. "But we're going to fuck you. Over and over again, in every way possible. I'm going to come all over that pretty pussy of yours…" He barely lets me process his words before he whispers the next part. "And then I'm going to make Gaeton lick it up."

My orgasm hits me with the force of an out-of-control speeding vehicle. One second I'm dazed and trying to process the information Beast is spilling into my ear, and the next I'm coming so hard that a scream slips from my lips. It only seems to spur Gaeton on and he picks up his pace, eating me out sloppily as if he can't get enough, as if he wants to taste every bit of my orgasm. On and on it goes, until my body simply can't handle it any longer.

I slump back against Beast and he catches me in his strong arms. "That's enough, Gaeton."

Gaeton gives me one last long lick and then transfers his attention to my inner thighs, gentling me back down to earth. I don't … I can't … What the hell just happened?

Part of me expects Beast to dump me on the ground and keep the humiliation trend rolling, but he gathers me into his arms and rises easily. He's only a few inches taller than me and built lean, but there's a deceptive amount of strength in his compact body. "Are you satisfied?"

For a second, I think he's talking to me, but Hercules rises and nods. "I stand corrected. Apologies for interrupting your scene. I owe you."

Gaeton does a full body stretch on the floor and rolls easily to his feet. "You ended up heightening the whole experience. Consider us even."

Hercules glances at me and hesitates, but finally shakes his head. He adjusts his slacks, which spectacularly fails to hide his hard-on, and walks out of the room.

Beast jerks his chin at the couch. "Gaeton, sit."

"Woof."

"Bad dog," Beast fires back without hesitation.

Gaeton glares a bit, but he finally moves to the couch and sprawls across it, taking up more than his fair share. Even this is different. When Gaeton and I were together, he moved as if afraid of shattering everything in the room—of shattering me. It felt like he was always trying to compress his big body into a smaller package. He motions with a flick of his fingers. "Hand her here."

Beast's arms tighten around me for half a second before he carefully sets me onto Gaeton's broad lap. The careful way of holding me after he just spilled filth into my ear leaves me feeling like I have whiplash. I blink up at Beast. "I don't understand."

"You will."

I'm not sure if that's a promise or a threat.

Gaeton splays his hand across my lower stomach and pulls me back against his chest, but all his attention is on Beast. "Stay or go?"

"Go. I'm nowhere near finished, but I have no intention of sleeping here tonight." He shoots an arch glance at the cameras situated in each corner. "Or having Hercules burst through the door another time or six."

"Mmm." Gaeton nods. "Agreed. Your place or mine?"

For the first time, Beast looks less than completely in

control. His eyes flare hot as his gaze drags over my body, over both our bodies. He looks at me like he wants to fall on me like a wild thing, to hold me down and fuck me against Gaeton's chest until he's worked out every little bit of anger on my body.

I shiver. There's fear there, yes, but I am not opposed to the promise in those wild eyes. Before I can decide if I want to do something to encourage or discourage him, he snaps his attention to Gaeton's face. "Whichever one is closer."

"Mine it is."

CHAPTER 5

BEAST

*G*etting out of the Underworld has never been complicated. Finish a scene. Clean up. Walk out. After Hercules's interruption, I should have expected things not to be so simple. I retrieve our coats and Gaeton wraps his around Isabelle. She's too drunk off the adrenaline letdown and her orgasm to fight too hard about being naked under it—or his carrying her out of this place.

We almost make it.

We're halfway through the lounge when Aurora appears in front of us as if by magic. She's a tiny little thing, all light-brown skin and big brown eyes, with a penchant for bright hair colors. It's been pink for a long time, but she's edging toward a frosty pastel version instead of the brilliant hue she started with. Aurora is sweet enough that she invokes every Dominant protective instinct I have. She doesn't look particularly sweet right now. She looks furious. "Hades wants to see you."

I feel Gaeton go still at my back. We're staying in Hades's territory right now, renting places in a neutral space while we figure out what the fuck we're doing if we're not generals for the Man in Black any longer. Gaeton and I made our choices separately, but like in all things since I showed up in Carver City, we seem to be endlessly on parallel tracks. We can't afford to ignore a summons from Hades.

I give Aurora a long look. "Since when do you run messages for the old man?"

Her expression goes a little sharp. "Since I took over Tink's old position as Meg's second-in-command."

That, I didn't expect. Tink was mean enough to keep even the Dominants in line when she needed to. Aurora is … not. But Meg isn't the type of woman to make mistakes when it comes to the club, so she must see something I haven't.

Still, it's in my nature to push. "We're a little busy."

Aurora props a hand on her hip. She's wearing a tiny white lace slip that hugs her curves and barely covers her enough to be considered decent. "That wasn't a suggestion, Beast. Not for either of you. Hades wants to see you, and the longer you make him wait, the less likely the conversation is going to go the way you want it to."

I raise my brows. "Someone's been taking lessons from Meg."

She doesn't blink. "Stop patronizing me and get back there, or I'm going to have to get Allecto involved."

"Shit, Aurora." Gaeton huffs out a laugh. "Beast is just being a dick. No need to bring out the big guns." He steps past me, not quite shouldering me aside, but damn close. "Lead the way."

She gives Gaeton a smile. "Hey, big guy."

"Looking good, Aurora. Like the dress thing. It new?" He falls into step beside her, chatting easily as if he's not holding Isabelle in his arms, leaving me to trail behind. It's just as well. Gaeton is better at charming people than I am. Likely because I never bother to try. It's easier to intimidate if you speak less, because it gives your enemy no traction to guess your thoughts. Gaeton prefers a different strategy.

She leads us back to Hades's public study. It's decorated in shades of gray and carefully positioned lights that leave the man behind his massive desk bathed in shadows. Hades doesn't need all the theatrics to intimidate, but he sure as hell seems to like them.

Gaeton doesn't bother to take a chair and I'm content to follow his lead. I glance at Isabelle to find that she's fallen asleep in his arms. My chest gives an uncomfortable pang, but I stifle it. She came here with every intention of doing whatever it took to bring us back. If she accepted the price we laid out, then she has only herself to blame.

Besides, she needs this little catnap. Dawn is a long ways off, and we have a whole hell of a lot to compress into the two-week timeline.

Hades steeples his fingers in front of his mouth, bringing our attention back to him. "You two are dancing a fine line with this one."

I give him my full attention. "That's our business."

He pauses, letting the silence tick out, letting me know exactly who holds the position of power in this place. Him. Not me. It shouldn't irritate me so fucking much, but here we are. He sighs. "War is everyone's business."

Gaeton goes stiff next to me, but I don't look at him. "Say what you mean to say, Hades. You're wasting our time."

"As you wish." Hades, leans forward, bringing himself into the light. "You are living in my territory out of the grace of my goodwill. I highly suggest you do nothing to that woman that will antagonize Cordelia Belmonte. She will go to extreme lengths to protect her youngest sister, and that includes doing the equivalent of cutting off her nose to spite her face. If you both are removed from the equation, it's entirely likely she will lose part—or all—of her territory to Ursa. You know what that means."

It means the carefully balanced ecosystem of Carver City will potentially collapse. War between two territories is the kind of conflict that will send waves through the rest of the city, affecting everyone. I've seen it happen before. It's why I ended up here in the first place, fleeing a losing war in Sabine Valley. Regardless of what happens with Isabelle, I refuse to repeat history. We'll ensure she's safe and the territory is stabilized. It's held this long. It will hold for two more weeks.

I exchange a look with Gaeton. He nods, letting me lead this conversation. A fucking first, though I suppose that's not strictly true any longer. Since our respective relationships with Isabelle detonated, some of the animosity between us collapsed with it. Not all, not by a long shot, but I can stand next to him without wanting to cut his fucking throat. An improvement.

I meet Hades's gaze. "Two weeks won't make a difference one way or another. Beyond that, I wouldn't worry too much about Cordelia seeking revenge since she's the one who sent her baby sister here tonight in the first place."

Hades doesn't blink. "I highly doubt she envisioned the terms of the bargain you struck with Isabelle Belmonte."

Heat courses through my body, but I muscle back my physical response. All in good time. Because we *do* have time now. Two weeks is more than long enough to play out every filthy fantasy I never let myself contemplate with Isabelle. The fact that Gaeton will be doing the same concurrently feels strangely right. We began this journey at the same time, and we'll finish at the same time as well. "That's our business."

"See that it doesn't become my business." He glances at

Isabelle, gaze cold. "She's playing in deep waters. Don't let her drown and bring ruin upon us all."

I cross my arms over my chest. "If you're done …"

"I am. For now."

I turn and lead the way out of Hades's office. Aurora is nowhere in sight, which is just as well. We don't need an escort to the exit. I nod at Adem at the front desk and step into the elevator. We don't speak again until the doors slide open and the cool air of the parking garage seeps into the elevator. "Your place, your transport." I know where Gaeton lives, of course. It pays to keep track of these things, especially since we've both found ourselves in something of a precarious position leaving our old territory, but he's hardly sent out engraved invites to his place.

He nods and leads the way down the ramp to a sleek black SUV. I glance around for a driver, and he catches the look. Gaeton gives a shit-eating grin. "Not all of us are fancy bitches who need to be carted around."

I narrow my eyes. "I prefer to keep my hands free for other purposes."

He snorts. "Whatever you have to tell yourself, asshole."

Isabelle stirs as I open the back door and Gaeton sets her carefully on the seat. She blinks those big brown eyes at us. "Did I fall asleep?" Her hands flutter to her hair, seeming to register how tangled it is, and then to Gaeton's coat. "You ruined my dress."

"Won't be needing it where we're going." I nudge her across the back seat and follow her in, leaving Gaeton to walk around to the driver's door.

Isabelle slaps my hands away when I reach to fasten her seatbelt. "You can't be suggesting I'm not wearing clothes for the next two weeks. Don't be absurd."

Gaeton backs out of the parking spot and heads for the exit. "Depends on how many pieces of clothing you want ruined, Isabelle. Your choice." The easy charm is gone again, leaving a simmering anger I recognize down to my very soul. Another similarity I don't want to share with this man.

I lean back against the seat and look at her. Even out of her depth and looking like she's just been fucked within an inch of her life, Isabelle is a study in perfection. She's always been beautiful, but it's the intelligence in those brown eyes that draws me in again and again despite myself. My position in Carver City would have been a lot more secure if I'd been able to resist that spark. Her father, Orsino, didn't exactly disapprove of our dating her, but that man would have taken the moon right out of the sky for his youngest daughter, though, so he never said a word edgewise. He wasn't exactly thrilled with it, though.

Fuck, but I miss him.

Angry at the loss of another person I cared about, angry at myself, I rake my gaze over her. "What the big man isn't saying is that your pussy is ours for the next two weeks and we won't tolerate anything limiting access."

She jerks back, staring at me as if she's never seen me before. "Have you always talked like this?"

Not to her. Never to her. I bound myself up in love until I couldn't breathe, just so I could be worthy of this woman. All for nothing. *All of it* was for no goddamn reason. I lean forward and give her a cold look. "Only to the people I fuck."

An important distinction, and one she picks up immediately. "I see." She narrows her eyes. "So you're going to fuck me, Beast? Take all that aggression and anger out on me?" She lifts her chin, a clear sign that she's stepping to the line drawn in the sand between us. "Bring it on."

"Isabelle," Gaeton rumbles. "Playing the brat isn't going to make him stick his cock into you out of spite. He's got better control than that."

I'm glad one of us is sure of it. Right now, it's everything I can do not to fall on her and fuck her until she begs for mercy. Until I can get rid of the tight feeling of my skin being too small. No matter what I did for this woman, it wasn't good enough, and when Gaeton finally called it quits and she should have been mine by right, she left me in the dust. And I still don't know *why*.

I turn away from her and stare out the window. We are only a block from Gaeton's, which feels like a block too far at this point. The icy calm I had in the Underworld is unraveling too fast to stop. I don't know what will happen when it's completely gone.

We arrive before I find an answer.

Gaeton's place is like most of the other buildings in the neutral territory ruled by Hades. It's a mishmash of businesses on the lower floors and apartments on the upper two-thirds. We are all silent as we take the elevator up to the twentieth. Not the top, but damn near it.

I raise my eyebrows at Gaeton. He smirks. "Don't tell me —you got some cheap-ass apartment the size of a matchbox."

He's not wrong. We made good money under Orsino Belmonte, known as the Man in Black to everyone else, but with the future so uncertain, I chose not to blow more of it than necessary on rent. Over the years, I've learned the hard way that nothing is for certain and having a financial nest egg can make the difference between surviving and ending up six feet under. If I wasn't so paranoid, I wouldn't have made it out of Sabine Valley alive.

I wish I could have ensured the same survival for Cohen.

I push the thought away. I don't want to think about the past right now. I don't want to think about anything but extracting every bit of pleasure from Isabelle's tight little body in retribution. It's enough. It has to be enough.

Gaeton opens his door—one of only four on the floor— and steps aside to let us precede him. There's no way the apartment was furnished when he moved in. Current trends lean towards the modern look and fragile-as-fuck furniture. The massive couch and chairs dominating the living room look like they could hold three men of Gaeton's size without a problem. He's put down a thick gray rug that softens the marble floors. His dining table isn't particularly huge, but the style wouldn't be out of place in some ancient king's banquet room. A pair of doors leads into what must be a bathroom and a bedroom. The kitchen is small and seems barren as hell, but the appliances are all top of the line. The real perk is the view. The massive windows look out over Carver City painting the night with an array of lights.

Gaeton closes the door and locks it. "Shall we?"

I don't know if he means it's time to talk or time to fuck, but I'm only in the mood for one of those things. I turn to Isabelle, who's looking around with wide eyes, and inject a little snap into my tone. "Lose the jacket. Now."

She hesitates but finally unzips the jacket and shrugs out of it. Good. "Now bend over the arm of that couch and brace yourself on the cushion."

Isabelle flashes me a look. "No."

A dark thrill soars through me. It likely says something unflattering about me that I want her to fight, I want to force her, knowing she's getting off on it as much as I am. "You won't like it if I have to repeat myself."

"Safe word," Gaeton rumbles.

"Candlestick," she shoots back. Isabelle glares at me. "Repeat yourself all you want. I'm not bending over the arm of the couch like some kind of sacrificial lamb."

Interesting that she sees it that way. The dark thrill surges higher. "Now, princess."

She lifts her chin and says the two words destined to toss a lighted match into the gasoline-soaked room that is our current situation. "Make me."

CHAPTER 6

ISABELLE

For the first time in my life, I am acting on pure instinct. No thoughtful consideration of consequences. No playing out scenarios to reach the best solution. I am all animal as I back away from Beast, from the way his expression goes predatory. I brace for him to move, to chase me, to … I'm not sure what comes next. I'm afraid to even guess.

All I know is that I want it more than I want my next breath.

I'm so busy watching Beast, I don't realize Gaeton has moved until he's almost on me. I scramble back, but he eats up the distance in a single stride and grabs my upper arm. I expect him to pull me toward him and immediately dig in my heels, but he keeps moving, knocking me off balance and half dragging me to the pair of doors and into his room. I get a glimpse of his massive bed before he lifts me and tosses me onto it.

I don't have a chance to find my bearings before he snags my ankle and flips me onto my back. Something soft and strong replaces his hand and then he's moved to my free leg and repeated the process. I scramble to sit up and find that he's cuffed my ankles to straps that seem hooked at the bottom corners of his bed. They're long enough that they aren't hurting me, but not long enough for me to be able to close my thighs. I jerk my legs up, but they're too strong. "What the hell, Gaeton?"

He ignores me. "Beast, get in here." He barely waits for the shorter man to walk through the door. "Hold her. I need to loosen the straps."

I tense. "No!"

Beast climbs onto the bed. It's a sturdy four-poster with a square frame connecting the posts that look strong enough to suspend people on. I can't think about that too hard because he's advancing on me. I expect him try to get behind me, but he settles right into the cradle of my thighs, his jeans creating an obscene friction. He props himself over me and studies my face. "Disappointed you didn't get more of a chase?"

"Fuck off."

The strap on my left ankle loosens and Beast uses his thigh to hitch my leg up, keeping me splayed. His grip grinds against my wrists and the ache makes my veins feel like there's pure heat flowing through them. I don't understand. I don't understand any of this. I'm so busy staring up at him in confusion that I barely notice Gaeton loosening my right ankle and Beast shifting me up the bed until the tension is tight again. "What are you doing to me?"

"What we should have done in the first place." Beast looks up and releases one of my wrists. Gaeton clasps another cuff around it, then moves around the bed to repeat the process with my left wrist. I pull on the new bindings, but I am spread out and utterly helpless.

Beast sits back on his heels between my thighs and surveys me. "Nice setup."

"Saves me from having to improvise."

I twist to examine the cuffs on my wrists. They're wide and padded on the inside. Tight enough that I can't slip my hand out, but nowhere near tight enough to cause any kind of damage. It strikes me that he must have used them on others before. He brought others here and tied them up and—

Jealousy spikes, hot and toxic and something I have absolutely no right to.

Beast grips my chin lightly and turns my face back to him. His brows pull together the smallest amount as he considers me. "Is it being tied down that makes you unhappy or something else?"

Safer to say I hate the bondage. Safer to keep the selfish part of me hidden deep, because they will use any and all revealed vulnerabilities against me. I close my eyes. I promised honesty. I can do this. I don't have another choice. "I like the bondage."

"That's a very careful nonanswer, princess."

I swallow past my suddenly dry throat. "I was thinking about Gaeton having other people here. About what happens when he does."

"How very hypocritical of you." Beast looks over, guiding my face to do the same, to find Gaeton leaning against the wall, watching us with shuttered dark eyes. Beast sounds almost amused when he says, "Well, Gaeton? How many people have you fucked on this bed?"

"Answering that question serves no purpose."

Relief twines with something less pleasant. He's definitely had people in this bed. He doesn't want to admit it. Gods, this hurts. It's nothing more than I deserve, but it hurts all the same.

"Tell me something, Isabelle." Beast drags his thumb over my bottom lip.

I'm not going to like what comes next. I already know it. "What?"

His voice is soft in my ear, but designed to carry to Gaeton as well. "How many cocks did you ride in the year since you rode ours?"

The smart choice is to keep my mouth shut, but I'm still dealing with the sting of Gaeton's nonanswer. Beast moves back enough to look me in the eyes, and I have to fight the urge to snarl at him. "Answering that question serves no purpose." I don't know if I thought it would feel good to throw Gaeton's words back in their faces, but all I'm left with is a hollow sense of sorrow. None of those people matter. None of them made up for what I lost.

I expect anger. I expect a mirror of the jealousy sticking its barbs deep into my heart. I don't expect him to laugh in my face. "Sounds like you missed us."

I blink. "How the hell do you make that jump in logic?"

"How many times did you fuck me and go straight to Gaeton because once wasn't enough? Or the other way around?"

My face flames. More times than I care to admit. Because I couldn't get enough, yes, but because they both offered me different things, even while they held back so much. "I'm sure you have a point you're trying to make right now."

"My point is I'm surprised as hell you didn't fuck your way through the entire territory."

"You are such an asshole. Who's to say I *didn't* fuck my way through the entire territory?" I want to spit poison, if only to expel it from my veins. This hurts. It hurts so much and even if I deserve it, I am incapable of taking the pain without lashing out. "Maybe the reason I fucked you both on the same day so often is because neither of you could get the job done."

Gaeton finally moves, drawing our attention back to him. "Seems like Isabelle doesn't need our cocks, Beast."

Beast palms himself through his jeans, expression contemplative. He's so close, I can feel the air displacement from his hand against my pussy. "Seems so," he says slowly. Another stroke. His blue eyes narrow. "I don't know about you, Gaeton, but I'm not inclined to stick my cock where it's not welcome."

"Yeah." Gaeton's voice has gone low. "I'm right there with you."

Beast's blue gaze goes wicked. "There is another option, if you're up for it."

The barest of hesitations. "You're saying the best way to punish Isabelle is to show her exactly what she's missing out on."

I feel like they're reading off a screenplay and I'm left to flounder in the dark. "Wait—"

"What do you say, Gaeton? Just this once."

What? I feel like my eyes are going to pop out of my head. "No way. You aren't saying what I think you're saying. You hate each other. You'll seriously have sex just to spite me?"

Gaeton is watching my face. He finally nods. "Just this once."

Beast finally looks at him. "Be sure it's what you want."

"I don't have to like you to want this. I've seen you fuck." Gaeton gives a lopsided grin. "I'm sure."

"Then strip."

Gaeton is still grinning when he pulls his shirt over his head. My breath stalls in my lungs. Gods, I *missed* him. His body is carved in huge slabs of muscle. Not defined, exactly, but he looks like the men who compete in those Strongman competitions. His pants follow his shirt to the ground and then he's standing there naked before us, his cock hard and ready. He palms it with a big hand and gives himself a rough stroke.

Is he ...

Is Beast ...

I look up, but Beast is watching Gaeton like he's seeing him for the first time. It's still not a friendly look, not really, but there's clear lust in his blue eyes. Whatever his feelings about Gaeton, he's just as affected by this show as I am.

Beast absently runs his hands over my hips. "He looks good, doesn't he, princess?"

No lies. I'm not capable of them in this moment. "Yes." It hurts to look at Gaeton. It hurts so much more than I expected. I loved them both, but Gaeton is the one who left me, the one I harmed with my inability to choose. My voice is hoarse as if I've been screaming for hours. "He looks good."

Gaeton doesn't spare me a glance. "You top."

"I was planning on it." Beast stops touching me and moves off the bed. The men walk together to a large cabinet in the corner and open it. I get a glimpse of a wide array of toys, everything from floggers to things I have no name for, but my gaze snags on Gaeton's round ass and I stop worrying about what they're quietly negotiating over there.

I didn't envision ending up in this position when I went to the Underworld earlier tonight. I'm still reeling from how much these men kept from me in their individual ways. *This* is the kind of sex they got off on all along? The kind of sex I also get off on? Why couldn't we figure that out together? Why did it have to be so ...polite?

I'm partly to blame for that. I let my carefully couched questions fade to silence when I found them resistant. I never pushed for the things I truly fantasized about. I let them put me on a pedestal and I told myself I was lucky to have the two men I wanted most in my life.

The whole situation seems like a clusterfuck in hindsight.

With each passing minute, it becomes clear just how effectively we lied to ourselves and to each other.

Gaeton and Beast finish their conversation and walk back to the bed. Beast has a thick flogger dangling from one hand and Gaeton's lost his grin. They stare down at me, spread and vulnerable. Beast finally says, "You don't get any cock tonight, princess. But be very good and we'll allow you to earn both of ours."

Humiliation burns me even as it stokes something inside me hotter. I am Isabelle Belmonte. I've never begged for anything in my life before tonight, and I'm not about to get in the habit of it. I have to fight to meet his gaze, to not look away. "I make no promises."

"We know." He motions to Gaeton without looking at him. "End of the bed. Hands on the frame over your head."

The big man moves to obey. I have to keep my head lifted to see everything, and my neck already hurts. With his arms overhead, he looks even bigger, and he watches me with those dark eyes that contain too many emotions to name. Anger is there in spades. Desire, too. But that's not all.

Beast moves to the side of the bed and carefully wedges a pillow under my head. I almost thank him, almost forget that they're doing this to punish me. He's gone before I make that slip.

He moves slowly toward the big man, his gaze intense. "How many strikes, Gaeton?"

Gaeton smirks. "How good is your stamina?"

"Good enough." Beast moves out of sight. "Your safe word."

Now Gaeton's gaze drops to me for the briefest of moments. "Rose."

Shock drowns out the sound of the first strike. I barely register the way Gaeton flinches, too busy repeating that word silently to myself. *Rose, Rose, Rose.* A nickname he'd jokingly called me because I love them so much. Roses of every color are my favorite thing. Beautiful and deceptively painful. My father went so far as to create a greenhouse just for roses as a gift for my eighteenth birthday.

I push the memory away. It hurts too much to think about now.

But all I'm left with is the sight of Gaeton stretched at my feet, the sound of the flogger making contact with his back. His eyes have gone a little hazy, and his flushed skin almost hides his freckles. It doesn't take long before even his flinches have disappeared, leaving his body loose and relaxed. *This* is what pain can do to a person?

Beast appears again, holding the flogger with a contemplative look on his face. He transfers his attention to me, and I feel like I have nowhere to hide. This man sees everything. He raises his brows. "The princess wants to try out the flogger."

"She'll have to get in line," Gaeton gives a rough laugh. "Fuck, I needed that."

"I'd wager you need a whole lot more than that." Beast sets the flogger on the nightstand. "But it's a start." He surveys us. "Gaeton, on the bed. Hands and knees."

Gaeton slowly obeys. I can't tell if he's resistant to the position or if he's floating on endorphins from the flogging. It's been a year, but he's a thousand times better at closing himself off to me than he was when we were together. Or maybe he simply never bothered to shut me out before. Neither option makes me happy.

He crawls onto the bed and kneels between my thighs with his hands on either side of my hips. His gaze drops to my breasts and his fingers dig into the comforter as if he has to fight himself not to touch me.

"Gaeton."

We both look over as Beast strips. He does it like he does

53

everything else—efficiently. I can't help drinking him in the same way I drank in Gaeton. Beast is driven by demons he's never named, and it's reflected in his body. A variety of scars cover him from shoulders to ankles, physical marks of things he survived before coming to Carver City. A few of them are bullet wounds, but most are long lines from knives and similar slashing weapons. Each muscle is clearly defined as further evidence of just how hard he drives himself. When we were together, he spent significant time in the gym and gun range, preparing for a war that he wasn't able to win in Sabine Valley, doing what he could to ensure one wasn't on the horizon here.

It's on the horizon now.

A glint of metal catches my eye and I lift my head higher. A gasp escapes my lips at the sight of the metal ring through the head of his penis. "You—You're pierced." That *definitely* wasn't there the last time I saw him naked.

"A lot of things have changed, princess." He gives me a cold look. "You don't know me anymore. You don't know either of us."

Before tonight, I would have said that people don't really change, and certainly not in the timeline of a single year. I still believe it. But there's no escaping the truth that the last few hours have driven home.

I never really knew Beast and Gaeton to begin with.

CHAPTER 7

GAETON

This is a mistake and I can't stop. My shit is all tangled up inside. Anger and need and the one thing guaranteed to still the frantically circling thoughts in my head for a little while. If things were different, I'd have called Hook to do the deed, would have done anything but give my submission to a man who used to be my enemy. Maybe he still is. I don't know anymore. Shit has gotten weird tonight, and it's about to get a whole lot weirder.

Isabelle stares up at me with wide, furious eyes. As if she can will me to fuck her the way I'm aching to. I shake my head. "No."

She blinks. "No, what?"

"No, I'm not going to forget myself tonight." I say it as much to remind myself as to remind her. "A punishment isn't for enjoyment, Isabelle." Isabelle. Not Rose. No matter what comes of this, she'll never be my Rose again.

The mattress gives a little as Beast climbs up behind me. I might imagine the way he catches his breath. Hard to say. He's not my usual type—too mean, too beat-up, too angry—but fuck if seeing him strip didn't send a shiver of anticipation through me. No matter what else is true, Beast won't hold back. He's going to fuck my ass, hard and rough, and I'm practically shaking with anticipation. With need.

He catches my hips, digging his fingers in until it hurts. I moan and have to fight myself not to thrust back against his grip. "That's it," he murmurs. He palms my ass, squeezing and spreading me.

I half expect him to simply go for it. I am not prepared for what sure as fuck feels like appreciation.

Isabelle is looking down my body as if she has a chance in hell at seeing what he's doing. It makes me laugh. "Like I said: punishment."

Beast spreads lube down my ass crack and presses a single finger into me. "You fuck Hook."

"Yeah," I grind out.

"He takes your ass rough."

It's not a question, but I answer it all the same. "Yeah. He pounds my ass."

More lube. "Good." He removes his finger, and then the head of his thick cock is pressing against me. I can feel the cool metal of his piercing and then it's just sheer fullness. I exhale slowly and try to relax into it.

When Beast speaks again, his voice has gone even more gravelly. "Keep your cock away from her pussy. Anything else goes."

"Yes … Sir." The words feel dragged from my throat. It's just for this scene, just to deliver this punishment. It doesn't mean a single damn thing. I don't even like the bastard, even if I want to fuck him.

He grips my hips and shoves the rest of the way into me. Another moan slides free, despite my best efforts. "Fuck, that feels good."

Beast barely lets me adjust to his size before he's moving again. For all his promises of a rough fucking, he takes his time finding the right stroke that has me squirming on his thick length. My body goes hot and my cock is so hard, I have half a thought that I might come without anyone touching it.

Isabelle writhes beneath me, trying to see, to touch, to do something. "I hate you both!"

A small vindictive part of me enjoys how the tables have turned. She's part of this, and yet kept separate. It's nowhere near enough to balance the scales, but it's a start.

Beast presses a hand to my back, urging me down so my ass is in the air and he's sinking deeper yet. "Tease her."

"You bastard, I swear—" She trails off in a whimper as I brace my elbows on either side of her chest so I can palm her breasts and press them together for easier access. Isabelle always did have sensitive nipples, and a year hasn't changed that. I tongue her, but I'm too distracted by Beast's cock in my ass to do a proper job of it.

He's fully fucking me now. Strong, driving thrusts that I'm forced to brace against to avoid being shoved up Isabelle's body. "Fuuuuuck."

"How close?"

Strange that for all I dislike this man intensely, we've worked together for enough years that it's no effort to read between the lines. "I'm close."

He catches my left upper arm and tows me up and off Isabelle, until my back is pressed against his front. I have a good six inches on him, so he has to stretch to sink his teeth into the sensitive spot where my shoulder meets my neck. I curse and shudder and, *fuck*, that's good.

It's even better when his hand closes around my cock and he starts jacking me. I stare hazily down at Isabelle. She's spread out in my bed, her pussy damn near weeping with need. Beast's cock is in my ass and he's fucking me with his hand. I don't know how to comprehend this turn of events, so I stop trying. I give myself over to the pleasure he's dealing out in rough strokes.

His low voice caresses my ear. "Come all over her pussy, Gaeton. Punish her."

Another stroke. Two. On the third I lose control. I come so fucking hard, it feels like the top of my head explodes. My body ceases to be my own. It becomes a thing driven by lust and anger, thrusting into Beast's fist as my come spurts all over Isabelle's pussy and up onto her hips. The sight of it is lewd as shit. I never, ever would have pulled a stunt like this before with her. I never would have dared debase her even the slightest in the way we are systematically doing now.

I love it.

Beast shoves me back down on all fours and resumes his relentless pace. I didn't realize he was holding back, not until the moment he *stops* holding back. Each thrust drives a grunt from my throat, and I have to brace hard against the mattress, my face pressed against Isabelle's sternum, to keep from sliding with the force of them. It feels so fucking good. I never want it to stop.

Against all reason, my cock starts hardening again. I curse and Beast laughs roughly. "Down." He presses me down onto Isabelle, taking the time to line us up so that my cock slides through her pussy lips and up over her clit with each stroke, lubed up with my own come.

"Oh *gods*." She lifts her hips as much as she's able. "Please. Please, Gaeton, please, please, please. I ache for you."

I almost forget myself, almost slide back enough to give me access to where we both want me to be. Beast's hands gripping my hips stop me. "Don't you fucking *dare*, Gaeton." I'll have bruises from his fingertips tomorrow. "You sink into her pussy, and I'm going to put a ring around your cock and play with you for hours before I let you come—*if* I let you come."

Fuck, but that sounds hot as hell. Agonizing, but hot.

Still, I can't let Beast get any funny ideas about what's happening here. I drop my face to Isabelle's neck and groan. "You're not my Dom, asshole. I stop obeying you when this scene ends."

Another savage thrust. "Then *obey*."

I grind down against Isabelle's pussy, on her clit. For just a moment, I allow myself to fantasize about if things were different. If we weren't fighting, weren't punishing Isabelle for a pair of broken hearts that festered instead of healing, if things were simple and I could sink into her as Beast sank into me, if we became something more than a fucked up love triangle.

I orgasm again, and this time Beast follows me over the edge. He yanks out of me and then his come hits my back. I barely manage to catch myself before I collapse onto her, and it's Beast who guides me over to slump next to Isabelle's smaller body. He moves to kneel between her thighs and gives her a cold smile. "You're furious."

"You have no idea," she snarls.

"When's the last time you were denied something you wanted, princess?" He skates his fingers down her stomach, smearing my come across her skin. "You don't need to think so hard. I already know the answer—never. You've never been denied." He pushes two fingers into her. Even over her moan, I hear his breath shudder.

I understand the reaction down to a cellular level. Getting my mouth on her after a year felt like … I don't have the fucking words to describe it. Isabelle might have clawed my heart out of my chest, but I still miss the fuck out of her. Apparently I'm not the only one.

Beast fucks her slowly with his fingers. I don't like the guy, but best I can tell, he's a decent Dom. There are a couple ways to play out the end of this scene depending on what we're trying to accomplish. The cruel thing would be to leave Isabelle hanging on the edge, denied one last orgasm. It's not how I'd handle things, but Beast is leading this time around, so I push back the instinctive desire to make her come screaming again and let him work.

And that's when I realize what he's doing. He's using my come as lube to fuck her. He circles her clit with his thumb again and again until Isabelle digs her heels into the mattress in an attempt to get closer. "Please. Please don't stop."

I don't expect Beast to turn those baby blues on me. "What do you think, Gaeton?"

"Don't leave her on the edge."

"You're so fucking *nice* sometimes." He shakes his head. He's still drawing Isabelle closer and closer to the edge, for all that he's focused on me. This, too, is a dose of humiliation to our woman's pride.

I follow his lead and don't look at her, though I'm clocking her reactions out of the corner of my eye. "Someone has to balance you out. For someone so pretty, you're a real dick."

Amusement flares in those blue eyes, and the warmth it brings would knock me on my ass if I weren't already lying down. "You didn't have a problem with my dick a few minutes ago."

My body sings in response. No point in denying it was good. He's got his fingers coated in the evidence. I shrug. "I like the way you fuck. Doesn't mean I like you."

He drags his gaze over me, lingering on my shoulders, chest, and then down to my hips and where my cock is trying to twitch its way back to life. Fuck, but I don't think I can go again so soon, no matter how motivated this situation makes me. He finally lands on my thighs and calves, before moving back up again, just as slowly, to my face. The warmth isn't gone from his eyes, and I don't know how to deal with it.

He gives a shrug of his own. "On that we can agree." He twists his wrist, and Isabelle's spine bows.

She sobs out each exhale. I finally give into the temptation to look at her, and *fuuuuuuck*. Her whole body is flushed and she's writhing under Beast's touch. She's so wet, I can hear every time he thrusts his fingers deep. He could have taken her over the edge, but he's building her up to one hell of an orgasm, a single stroke at a time.

She turns wide dark eyes on me. Her lipstick got smeared a little somewhere along the way, and the imperfection just makes me want her more. "*Please.*"

I should withdraw, should maintain the distance Beast has established. The better to play this game out. I can't. I never did have a damn bit of sense where this woman was concerned.

I cup her jaw and kiss her. The second my tongue strokes along hers, Beast stops playing around and picks up his pace. I jump when he braces a hand on my thigh and lift my head enough to look at him.

He's leaning over us, his expression intense. "Don't stop."

I don't even pause to consider disobeying. I simply turn back to take Isabelle's mouth again. Kissing her after all this time feels like crashing through a hard shell I spent so long building up from the ruins of my heart. Melodramatic? Fuck yes. But it's the truth.

I never stopped wanting her.

I never stopped loving her, either.

She comes with a cry I drink down, and even as it feels so damn good to be this close to her again, I can't shake the feeling that making this pact is a mistake I'll never recover from.

CHAPTER 8

ISABELLE

*I*t feels like I take one long blink and we're in the shower. It's not a particularly large shower, though it is a walk-in, and with Gaeton's broad shoulders taking up space, it feels small. Even so, neither of the men even brings up the option of us taking turns. I'm not complaining. After the events of the last few hours, I don't think my legs can hold me. That weakness is something that will bother me. Tomorrow. Tonight, I don't have the capacity to do more than lean against Gaeton's chest and watch Beast soaping up.

Gaeton keeps me on my feet with an arm around my waist, and I let myself sink into that touch a little. My whole chest aches from wanting him—from wanting them both—but I know better than to say as much.

If tonight has proven anything, it's that I don't know these men nearly as well as I thought I did.

"You're thinking awfully hard over there, princess." Beast steps beneath the spray of water to rinse off and then moves out of the way. "Give her here."

Gaeton squeezes me a little and then passes me over.

Once again, I feel like a living doll with no will of my own. I frown up at them. "I am more than capable of standing on my own."

"No, you're not." Beast turns me and takes a position identical to the one Gaeton had, his arm around my waist, his chest to my back. He's only a few inches taller than me, so he rests his chin on my shoulder easily. "You're shaking, and if left to your own devices, you'd be a sobbing puddle on the floor."

I try to jerk away, but he easily holds me captive. "I would not."

"Yes, you would." Gaeton ducks under the spray and, when he comes up, he shakes his head like a dog. "The effects of a scene don't end when the scene does."

I cross my arms over my chest, and then feel foolish for doing even that much while we're all standing naked in this enclosed space. "I'm fine."

Gaeton gives me a long look. "The truth, Isabelle."

Damn him. I lift my chin and try not to notice how my body shakes. "I am scared and uncertain and feel entirely unmoored. I'm also pissed as hell that you pulled that stunt in the bedroom with each other to punish me."

"Better," Beast murmurs. He steps back, pulling me with him. "Why don't you go change the sheets and I'll finish up here?"

Gaeton nods and he trails his fingers along my stomach as he passes us out of the shower, leaving sparks in his wake. We listen to him walk out of the bathroom and then Beast moves me a bit away from him. "Let's get you cleaned up."

"I can do it myself."

He shoots me a look that stops me from reaching for the soap. "If I want you to do it yourself, I'll tell you to do it yourself. Now stand still."

I obey. Partly because I promised to. Partly because some-

63

thing in me that's been buried deep responds to the snap in his voice. It wants me to fall to my knees and wait for his next command. I shove it away. This arrangement is required for their agreement to return to the territory. That's it. Yes, I crave rough sex and, yes, I'm weirdly turned on by Beast's harsh words and carelessness with me, but that doesn't mean I want to submit to either of these men outside the bedroom.

Right now, we are outside the bedroom.

"You're doing it again." He doesn't lift his voice as he soaps down my body. "Already contemplating breaking the pact?"

Yes, but I will never say as much. Instead I change the subject. "I don't understand this. Shouldn't you be telling me to sleep at the foot of the bed, covered in come and weeping openly?"

At that, he looks at me and raises his brows. "Someone's been reading some interesting fiction."

Guilty. I flush even as I try to fight down the embarrassment. "That's not an answer."

He moves to my hair, soaping it up with intense thoroughness that has me fighting not to close my eyes. "Yes, it is. There are relationships where that sort of thing might be the norm, and that's those people's business as long as they're both consenting. That is not how I operate, and it's sure as fuck not how Gaeton does, either." He guides me back beneath the water and rinses my hair and body.

I'm still stewing on that by the time he's towed me out of the shower and dried me off. I finally snatch the towel from his hands and glare. "How the hell would I know how you operate, Beast? You didn't *operate* like this when we were together."

He doesn't have the grace to look apologetic. "You're a smart woman, and quick on your feet. Figure it out."

If we didn't need him so much, I might strangle him. I truly might. I start to wrap the towel around my body, but stop when he shakes his head. "What now?"

"While you're in this apartment, you're naked unless one of us explicitly orders otherwise."

I thought my capacity for shock was filled. Unfortunately, that's not the case. "You can't be serious." They implied it in the car, but I thought they were bluffing.

"I am." He tugs the towel out of my hands, and I let it go. As much as I might fantasize about pushing Beast out a window right now, the truth is that I could never dream to overpower either of these men. The thought both thrills me and fills me with dread.

I hate to admit it, but I am in over my head.

It's a fight not to cover myself with my hands. They've already seen every bit of me. Clutching at modesty now would be silly and serve no purpose but to further humiliate me. Part of me wants to do it anyways.

Instead, I follow Beast back into the room to find that Gaeton has changed the sheets as requested. He's tucking them in with a military precision and glances up as we walk through the door. His gaze travels from me to Beast and back again, and he seems to come to some conclusion. "We all sleep here tonight."

The faintest tension works its way through Beast's body. "Making some assumptions, aren't you?"

Gaeton gives an arrogant grin. "By all means, sleep on the couch if you're too precious to share a bed with me. Or, better yet, go home."

If he goes home, I'll be alone with Gaeton, and there's no way we're going to avoid having an uncomfortable conversation if that happens. The thought should make me happy, but it panics me instead. I stride to the bed and climb into it. I can *feel* Beast's attention zero in on my ass, and so I take my time crawling to the headboard. I turn around and slither under the sheets in the middle of the massive mattress. He's still staring, still on the edge of leaving. Damn it.

I prop myself up on my hands, well aware that the position arches my back and offers up my breasts. "Do what you have to do, Beast. I'm sure we'll figure out a way to entertain ourselves while you're gone."

Irritation flickers over his face before he shuts it down. "You two are a pain in the ass."

"That's my line." Gaeton booms out a laugh at the disgruntled look on Beast's face. "Pipe down. I'm not going to maul you in the night." I almost laugh at that, but he turns dark eyes on me. "You, I make no promises about."

Despite my exhaustion, my heartbeat kicks up a notch. "What?"

"Tomorrow you're going to wake up with my tongue in your pussy, Isabelle." He doesn't move toward the bed, for all the lusty threat in his tone. "You ready for that?"

Is this a trick question? As much as they're tormenting me, the truth is that they're tormenting me with *pleasure*. I came harder tonight than I have in longer than I can remember, and neither of them fucked me. I can take whatever they dish out as long as there's orgasms involved. "Do your worst."

"Oh, baby, I fully intend on it." He stalks to the bed and climbs under the covers. Suddenly the massive mattress seems significantly smaller.

I eye the distance between us. Will we maintain it through the night? It seems improbable as hell. My chest gives a sickening lurch. Oh gods, maybe I'm not ready for this after all. Sex is one thing. Sleeping together is something else altogether.

"One last thing."

I turn toward Beast pathetically fast, desperate for a distraction from the direction my thoughts have taken. He holds up the tiny purse I brought with me into the Underworld. I forgot about it, which says something about where my head's been at for the last few hours. He tosses it onto the mattress next to me. "Update your sisters."

My circling thoughts freeze. "Excuse me?"

"You're here at their behest. Update them."

I stare. Surely he can't be serious. "You want me to tell them that I entered into a sex pact with both of you in order to get you back."

The edges of his lips quirk up. "I want what I've always wanted from you, Isabelle. The truth."

That stings. It stings far more than it has the right to. I don't bother to argue. I won't win this one any more than I've won the others. I just dig out my phone and type a quick update to the group text I share with my two older sisters.

Me: I have things handled. They'll both be back in two weeks. I'll see you then.

I've barely hit send when the replies nearly buzz my phone right out of my hand.

Sienna: That is not an explanation.

Cordelia: I'm going to need more details than that, Izzy.

Sienna: What she said.

Sienna: Texting isn't cutting it.

Sienna: Video call incoming.

"Fuck!" I yank up the sheet to cover my breasts and pat at my hair. I don't know if it's a good thing or not that it's wet from a recent shower. My phone trills at me to accept the incoming video call. "Fuck," I repeat.

"Answer it." Beast still hasn't moved from where he stands at the side of the bed. A quick glance confirms that Gaeton has no intention of moving from his spot, either. Currently both of them are out of frame, but I can't guarantee they'll stay that way.

I've run out of time, though. I take a deep breath and answer the call. Immediately the screen splits into two squares, each showing one of my sisters. Sienna has her blond hair twisted up and what appear to be two pencils stuck through to hold it in place, and she's wearing the flannel bunny pajamas that her husband got her for Christmas as a joke. One wouldn't know by looking at her that she's got one of the most brilliant minds in Carver City —and possesses a complete lack of the moral ambiguities that plague most people.

On the other hand, Cordelia looks like she's just come from some kind of event. I rack my brain to remember what was tonight, but I come up blank. Her dark brown hair hangs in waves around her perfectly made up face, and she's got on a dark blue gown. For all that, exhaustion is written on her face.

Exhaustion that disappears as she focuses on me and narrows her eyes. "I thought you were having a meeting with them. Where are you? That isn't your bedroom."

My life would be significantly easier if my sisters weren't so formidable. I draw my knees to my chest to ensure I don't flash them. "I spoke with Beast and Gaeton as planned."

Sienna snorts. "That's not all you did tonight."

Cordelia doesn't blink. "And?"

I can feel the gaze of both men drilling into me from either side. It's a fight not to shiver. "And, like I said in my text, they will both be back in their positions as generals in two weeks."

Cordelia's dark eyes flash. "That's not fast enough. You have to—"

"Cordelia." I cut in before she can pick up momentum. "I am doing what it takes to benefit the family. Trust me when I say that I negotiated the best deal possible, and there is no way to expedite things."

That slows her down a little, but she doesn't look convinced. She's silent for a moment, obviously connecting dots that I'd really rather her not connect. "You made a deal with...both men."

No use trying to lie. "Yes."

"And now you're naked in a bed that's not your own." She frowns. "No, I don't like this. We'll find another way."

"There is no other way."

All amusement flees Sienna's face, and she goes ice cold. "There is always another way, baby sister. Where are you? If those two fuckheads think they can force you to be their sex doll for the next two weeks, I'll castrate them myself." She will, too. Sienna wouldn't win in a fair fight with either of the men in this room, but my middle sister has never fought fair. I highly doubt she intends to start now.

"That's enough." I inject my voice with confidence I don't feel. "I'm safe. I'll bring them both home when this is finished. Please don't try to interfere before then." I keep talking over my sisters' protests. No matter what they think, seeing this through to the end is what I have to do. For them. For the territory. And maybe even for me, too. "I love you both. Be safe." I hang up and switch my phone to silent.

Gaeton rumbles out a laugh. "Was that supposed to reassure them or incite them to come rescue you?"

I close my eyes and press the heels of my hands to them. "You're not helping."

"Wasn't trying to."

"They'll be content enough once we're back to fight against the Sea Witch threat." I open my eyes in time to see Beast move my purse and phone to the heavy wooden nightstand. Part of me expects him to lock them out of reach, but that seems silly now. As they keep reminding me, I'm here because I chose to be here. I could walk out that door right now if I needed to.

I glance down at my bare chest. Well, there are some things impeding that plan, but the fact remains that this is my choice and I'll stand by it.

No matter what tomorrow brings.

CHAPTER 9

BEAST

J don't expect to sleep. Rest and I aren't on good terms, haven't been since I took what little I owned and fled Sabine Valley, leaving the only family I've ever known behind. Leaving the only man I ever loved. Eight years later, and I still have no fucking idea if they're alive or dead, if *he's* alive or dead. I have to assume the latter. We were supposed to meet in Carver City, but if Cohen ever showed up here, I would know about it. He hasn't. He never will now.

I was supposed to protect him and his brothers. I wasn't good enough. Over the years, I've come up with half a dozen things I should have done differently, half a dozen opportunities I alone had to shift the tide. I failed him. His blood is on my hands, and that knowledge still haunts me in both waking and dreaming. Most nights are a slow ticking of seconds marking the path of the moon across the sky interspersed with restless dreams. I expect tonight to be more of the same.

So when I wake in a strange bed to Isabelle's ass rocking against my hard cock, I'm disoriented as fuck. It feels like a dream, though mine are usually soaked in blood and loss. This is something else altogether, more like this moment something too good to be real. I don't trust it, but I also can't help myself.

I don't want it to end.

I keep my eyes shut, unwilling to break the sleepy spell wrapped around me, and coast my hands up her body, tracing the curve of her hips, the dip of her waist, the fullness of her breasts. She grinds her ass more insistently against me. Like she needs my cock, but she's just as caught in the dream as I am. Move too much and it all becomes real. Real motivation. Real consequences.

Another slow stroke down her body and she catches my hand, guiding it between her thighs. If I don't think too hard, this could almost be a memory, rather than something playing out in real time. She didn't sleep over nearly as often as I would have liked, but every time it happened, we woke up just like this. Her body moving restlessly against mine, my cock sliding into her before either of us was fully awake.

I cup her pussy and have to fight back a curse when I find her wet. Slowly, oh so slowly, I trace her opening. Teasing us both.

She goes perfectly still except to spread her thighs to allow me better access. *Good girl.* I drag my mouth over the line of her shoulder and shift down the slightest amount. She rocks her hips again and then my cock is there, pressing against her entrance.

I shouldn't.

I can pretend this is a dream until the end of time, but there's no mistaking the way Gaeton's weight dips the mattress on the other side of Isabelle. We entered into this bargain together, and it feels too close to what we had before to just fuck her now while he sleeps on beside us. Too *separate*.

I circle her clit and open my eyes. And find Gaeton staring directly at me.

Shock freezes me. This is no dream. But then, I knew that the moment Isabelle moved against me. It's been over a year since we woke up like this, except we never woke up *like this*, with Gaeton watching us with a lazy pleasure building in his eyes.

I raise my eyebrows in silent question. Apparently we were putting on a show and I hadn't realized. Maybe it should bother me. This man has been my strongest competition since I accepted a position with the Man in Black. For nearly a decade, we've fought and jockeyed for positions of favor, both with Orsino and with Isabelle.

All that seems so far away right now.

At the end of the day, we want the same things. We always have.

I stop playing with Isabelle's clit and pull the sheets off us, exposing us to Gaeton's sight. There's no mistaking exactly what we were doing, exactly how close to fucking we are. And then I wait, ignoring Isabelle's restless shifting. She obviously hasn't opened her eyes yet.

Gaeton takes his time. He stares at my cock long enough that I can actually feel myself getting harder under his attention. The man looks at my dick like he wants to suck me dry.

Last night was supposed to be a one-time thing, us proving a point, though I'll be the first to admit one has to squint a bit to make that logic work. Truth be told, I don't *want* it to be a one-time thing. All our pent-up aggression is one match strike away from being pure lust. I've always suspected it, but last night more than proved my theory. Having his ass like that was barely enough to whet my appetite. Surely he feels the same way?

Why not take advantage of this opportunity and fuck out some of these conflicting feelings over the next two weeks?

I press one hand to Isabelle's stomach, keeping her pinned to me, and shift down a bit more to grip my cock with my free hand. I hold Gaeton's gaze and stroke it, letting him see the challenge there. Letting him do with it what he will.

He doesn't hesitate. He slides down the mattress and then his mouth is around my cock and I have to press my forehead to the back of Isabelle's neck to keep from making a sound. The man doesn't play coy. He sucks me down like his next breath is on the other side of my length.

In my arms, Isabelle has gone completely still. I feel her lean forward enough to see what Gaeton is doing and she lets loose the most delicious whimper. "Oh fuck."

Gaeton slows his pace, and I don't have to look to know he's holding Isabelle's gaze as he swallows me down. My hands are shaking and I don't know what the fuck I'm doing.

I never, ever, enter a sexual encounter without having a plan. Losing control is inexcusable when engaging in vanilla sex. Losing control when you're in charge of a scene? No fucking way.

I'm not in control now. I didn't have a plan when I started this, and now I'm simply hanging on to Isabelle and riding the waves of pleasure Gaeton's giving me. He moves almost all the way off my cock and gives me several rough strokes while he tongues my slit.

This time, I can't keep my curse inside. "Fuck, Gaeton."

"Mmm." He doesn't loosen his grip on me but his whiskers brush my aching flesh and Isabelle's body jerks.

"Is he licking your pussy, princess?"

I hold her still as she gasps. "Yes."

A movement and he sucks hard on the head of my cock, and then he's gone, obviously giving her clit the same treatment. Over and over again, until my legs are shaking and I can't stand it any longer. "Finish one or both, Gaeton. Now."

"Finish it yourself." He fists my cock, guiding me to

Isabelle's entrance, until I'm buried in her up to the point where he grips me.

Holy shit.

I start to fuck her and she's moaning and whimpering and shaking from his tongue on her clit, but Gaeton's fist keeps us both from what we need. From my cock seated deep inside her. From rough, strong strokes designed to get us both off. Instead, we're poised on the precipice, pleasure tightening further and further.

Then Isabelle cries out and her pussy clamps around me as she comes. It's still not enough. Fuck, but it's nowhere near enough.

Gaeton moves down and then he's licking my cock around where I'm buried in Isabelle, as if trying to clean her orgasm right off me. I reach around her and dig my fingers into his hair. Finally, finally, he releases me and I sink deep into her.

Which is when Gaeton starts on my balls.

I fucking lose it. "Roll over." I don't wait for them to obey. I'm already moving, hooking Isabelle around the waist and going to my knees behind her with Gaeton on his back between our spread thighs. I lean back and press my hand to his chest. "Don't you fucking stop until I'm coming."

"Yes, Sir," he growls, and then his mouth is on my balls again and on the sensitive flesh behind them.

I press a hand to the middle of Isabelle's back and she eagerly lands on her chest, her ass in the air. It doesn't escape my notice that I had Gaeton in damn near this same position last night. It feels so right to do this now, to drive deep into her while his mouth is all over me below.

I feel fucking immortal. I don't ever want to stop.

Gaeton grips one of my thighs with his big hand and then his wet finger is at my ass, pressing deep so that my own thrusts have him fucking my ass even as I fuck Isabelle's pussy.

She fists the sheets, thrusting back to meet my strokes until the sound of flesh hitting flesh fills the room. "Harder, Beast. Fuck me harder."

I comply. I grip her hips and yank her back onto my cock as I surge forward. Again and again and again, fighting against my building pleasure to ensure she comes a second time, to feel her pussy spasm around me again. And then she's orgasming, writhing so intensely, I can barely keep hold of her. It's too much. I can't hold out any longer. I moan as I follow her over the edge, pumping her full of my come. She slumps forward onto the mattress and Gaeton lifts his head to suck my half-hard cock into his mouth. He releases me with a wicked grin. "My turn."

Sweet Jesus, I don't know what the fuck we're doing, but I'm suddenly sure that two weeks is nowhere near enough time.

CHAPTER 10

ISABELLE

J'm still recovering from what we just did when Gaeton crawls up the bed to flop onto his back next to me. "Come here, Isabelle." There's a depth of so many things in his voice, but I focus on the lust because it hurts the least.

I put my hand in his and let him pull me up to straddle his chest. He's so big, I'm spread wide just to maintain my perch. Gaeton drags his thumb over my clit and I shiver in response. "Sore?"

I'm already shaking my head. "No."

"You will be." His grin widens, though it doesn't reach his eyes. He gives my clit another lazy stroke. "We're going to play a game."

Alarm bells peal through my head, but I'm too busy trying not to rock my pussy against his chest like a wanton creature to listen. "Okay."

"You're a dirty little slut who's sharing two men." His voice is warm, devoid of anything but need.

I still jerk back. "Don't."

"A game, Isabelle." This from Beast, who's propped

himself up on the pillows next to us. Close enough to touch if he wanted, but he makes no move to do so. "Your pussy still aches to be filled up, doesn't it?"

Honesty. I promised honesty. I close my eyes, but it somehow makes it worse so I open them again. "Yes."

Beast's lips curve the tiniest bit, though his eyes stay cold and watchful. "Imagine you just left my bed. My come is dripping down your thighs, but it's not enough. You want to feel a little bad, don't you? A little wrong. A little dirty."

How does he do this to me? He keeps drawing for the dark parts of me that I've done my best to hide. Gaeton touches my chin and I'm helpless to do anything but open my eyes. He's not smiling now. "You want to come on my cock while you're still flushed with what he did to you." He pinches my clit between the fingers of his other hand, making me jump. "And then when you're done with me, you want him to bend you over the nearest piece of furniture and fuck you again. Hell, I bet you'd get off on his fucking you right in front of me. Of rubbing it in my face that I wasn't enough for you. And then as soon as he's finished, you come straddle me and do the same to him." He brushes my bottom lip with his thumb. "All day, Isabelle. His cock then mine then his again. And when you ache too much for more, we'll take turns tasting that pussy."

My mind has gone terrifyingly blank. "But—"

"Today we're passing you back and forth just like you deserve." He gives my clit another squeeze. "Do you want to be our little slut today?"

There's only one answer. There was only ever one answer. I don't even have to stop to remind myself to be honest this time. "Yes. I want all that. Everything you said."

Gaeton looks up at me. There was a time when I could read every thought it as it passed through his mind. He never bothered to hide them from me, trusted me enough to be an open book for me to read at my leisure. Or at least that's what I used to think. Now I know better. Gaeton may have been an open book, but he was in a language I only vaguely understood. He traces his hands down my body to land on my hips and gives them a squeeze. "No."

Shock makes me flinch. "What?"

"No. We're not playing that game. We shouldn't be playing any fucking game." He lifts me off him and is already moving before I land on the mattress, climbing to his feet and stalking into the bathroom. The door slams behind him and the shower turns on a few seconds later.

I feel like he turned my world upside and then gave it a shake for good measure. I pull my knees to my chest and wrap my arms around them. "Did he do it on purpose to hurt me?" I don't really expect an answer. Gaeton may have been the touchy-feely type, but Beast never was. It's part of what I loved about him, that he had depths I knew I could spend years swimming through and never reach the bottom. Beast is a mystery in so many ways; a year apart has only increased the mysteries he keeps from me.

He touches my chin exactly where Gaeton did, guiding me to look at him. For once, he's not an icy wall. He's furious and ... hurt? Beast drops his hand. "Time might heal all wounds, but it doesn't mean a damn thing when the specter from your past comes bursting through all the progress you've made. What do you want from him, Isabelle?" He inhales slowly, and I can actually see him tucking away his anger. "He agreed to this, but he doesn't like it. Cut him some fucking slack."

Finally.

Finally, I have something to cling to beyond confusion and what little pride I have left. I embrace the anger that rises within me wholeheartedly. "I didn't set the terms for this, either. *You* did. You both demand honesty and then make me pay for giving it to you. Don't act like I came back into your lives because I wanted to play with your cocks and your hearts at the same time. That was your decision."

"Yes, it was." He moves off the bed and stands. "Which is why I'm taking responsibility for it."

"That's a first." Why can't I stop talking? It's never been a problem before, but I feel like these men have ripped me open and stripped me of everything I thought I knew. Even when I was cursing their names last night, I enjoyed every moment. Even when Beast put me on display for a stranger and humiliated me with his words, I soaked up that feeling like a love-starved creature. And this morning? I still haven't processed what we did this morning.

It didn't feel the same as last night. When Beast began moving at my back, both of us still mostly asleep ... When Gaeton slipped down the bed and started sucking Beast's cock ... When he licked my clit while Beast fucked me ... None of that felt like a carefully directed scene. It just felt like *us*.

I don't know what that means. I'm not sure it means anything at all.

I glare up at Beast, hating how tormented I feel. "Is the purpose of this to punish me for being a dirty little slut or some kind of temptress that entangled you in my web of seduction? That's what you both think, isn't it? That I'm the sole responsible party for how things went so wrong." I *am* responsible for so much of it, but it's not like I tied them up and forced them to agree to anything. *They* pursued me for months before I admitted I couldn't pick one of them over the other, and *they* told me that I didn't have to. My only sin is loving them both and refusing to choose. They are the ones who decided that dating me at the same time was a good idea, but everyone conveniently forgets that when we talk about the past.

Beast looks at me long enough that I have to fight not to squirm. "Are you done throwing your fit?"

"My *fit?* I'm not a child and I'm not throwing a fit, you asshole." I cover my face in my hands and fight down a shriek of frustration. I barely manage it. "Go talk to Gaeton, please. That's what you were going to do. There's nothing left to say here."

"Wrong, Isabelle." Every time he says my name instead of princess, it feels like another nail in the coffin of our past relationship. Another reminder of how lengthy the distance between us is.

I drop my hands and, to my horror, my throat feels tight. "Is it wrong, *Samson*? Is it really?"

He jerks back as if I've struck him with the use of his real name. The one he shared with me the first time he told me he loved me. The one he gave up at the same time that he gave up hope that his past lover was alive. He's been Beast for as long as he's been in Carver City, and his given name was one of the few secrets Beast ever divulged to me.

Maybe I'm a bitch to use it now, but I don't care. I have no power here, and if they're determined to make me pay for every sin of the past, I'll force them to choke on the experience. That hurt goes both ways. It's always gone both ways.

"Yes, Isabelle. Wrong. There is a fuck-ton of things left to say." With one last long look at me, he turns around and walks to the bathroom door. He doesn't slam it, but the quiet click as he closes it behind him feels a thousand times more damning.

Gods, I'm going to cry.

I press my hands hard to my eyes, as if the dull ache it causes will be enough to stem the burning. I knew this would be hard. I knew it down to my very soul and I still agreed. I have no one to blame but myself. My role in this is to let them work out their anger on me until the time is up and they come home. A sacrificial lamb of sorts. That's it.

Only thirteen days left.

The thought has a hysterical laugh bubbling up. Why did I think this would work?

A buzzing cuts through my spiral, and I reluctantly drop my hands and open my eyes. That's my phone. No matter what Beast and Gaeton think, my sisters *are* more than capable of finding this place and busting down the door in an attempt to save me. The only thing up for debate is whether they'll send in a squad of trained killers or my sister-in-law, Muriel. Personally, I'd prefer the team before taking on Muriel. She has a way of making the people who piss off Cordelia disappear. Maybe the men are trusting me to manage Cordelia and Sienna to ensure that doesn't happen.

If that's the case, they have more faith in me than I expect.

There's no time to fix my face. I'm left to scramble for my purse and dig my phone out. Sienna's name flashes over the screen. I shoot a look at the bathroom door and then swipe my thumb to answer. "You have to stop calling."

"Sure." My sister sounds entirely too reasonable. "But the second we stop calling, we're coming to kill those fuckers and save you, so which would you really prefer?" Only Sienna could talk about murder with this kind of ease. She categorizes the world into two bins—people she cares about and people she doesn't—and I can probably count the people in the first bin on one hand.

"Sienna." My voice doesn't sound quite right, but there's not much I can do about it.

"Hold please."

My phone trills as she initiates a video call. I glare at my screen. Sienna is a big proponent of talking face to face, and she's one hell of a human lie detector as a result. But if I ignore her, it's entirely likely she'll follow through on her threats. I sigh and accept the video call.

She's wearing her favorite "working" clothing, which is a graphic T-shirt that appears to depict some kind of cutesy pentagram, her blond hair pulled back into a no-nonsense ponytail. She never wears makeup, and a tiny petty part of me can't help resenting her flawless beauty. No one will look at her face and tell her she's tired or ask if she's been sick because she forgot to put on mascara and lipstick today.

Sienna narrows her eyes at me. "You're still in bed."

I try to stop the heat spreading beneath my skin, but it's no use. Instead, I ignore the question beneath the question. "I have things under control."

I should know better by now. My sister leans in and squints. "Not just in bed. You've been *fucking*." She gives a delighted little laugh. "Which one did you land on? That burly beast of a man or the one actually called Beast?"

My blush gets hotter, and I don't need to look in the little square depicting my face to know that I've gone crimson. "I don't want to talk about it."

"Too bad." She leans back and tilts her head to the side. "Isabelle…"

I already know I'm not going to like whatever she says next, just like I know there's no way to avoid it. "Yes?"

"You fucked both of them, didn't you?"

"Not technically."

Sienna rolls her eyes. "You know damn well that penis-in-vagina isn't the only thing that qualifies as sex, so don't play technicalities with me." She gives me a downright chilling smile. "Unless you would like to see the sex education presentation I put together for when you and Cordelia invariably breed and I need to educate my future niblings."

I blink. "Niblings."

"Gender-neutral term for children of my siblings. One must never make assumptions, don't you agree?"

I love my sister very much, but the fact that she's apparently made a *presentation* to educate any future children that may or may not ever exist? I shake my head and let it go. This is pure Sienna, and asking too many questions is going to result in a headache and no further understanding. "I don't think niblings are something you're going to have to worry about for some time in the future." *If ever.* I want children, in theory, but I don't know if reality can hold up to that desire. Either way, I'm nowhere near ready to take that step.

"I like to be prepared." She waves that away and refocuses on me. "It's rather brilliant of you to use sex to get both of them back in line. For such intelligent men, your pussy makes them into fools."

Is it possible to die from mortification? I have a feeling I'm about to find out. "Sienna, that's not what I'm doing."

"How would I know what you're doing when you won't *tell* me?" She gives me a sly smile. "If you want to insist on playing coy, then I suppose I'll have to keep projecting theories. My next one is—"

"Okay!" I glance at the bathroom door and lower my voice. The shower is still running, but I don't want to tempt fate. "Okay. I'll tell you, but you have to promise to calm Cordelia down and make her wait until this is over."

"I promise nothing."

"*Sienna.*"

She huffs out a sigh. "*Fine.* Tell me. I will calm down Cordelia. Though if I'm not satisfied with the answer, I make no promises about *my* actions."

It's as good a promise as I'm going to get. "I'm in Gaeton's apartment with both of them. I promised them two weeks of submission in exchange for their return. And, uh, I have to pick one of them at the end of it and stick with that decision."

"Two weeks of submission." She says it in a musing kind of way and I can already see the wheels in her impressive brain turning. She brightens. "So, what you're saying is that you agreed to a sex pact."

"No, that is not what I'm saying." *That's exactly what I'm saying.*

She shakes her head. "Oh, Izzy, it might sound like a dream to have them both right now, but it's just going to make the choice harder when it comes down to it. If you couldn't choose before, how are you going to now?"

I don't know. That's one thing I very pointedly haven't thought about. "I'll figure it out when I get there."

"Would you like me to make an algorithm based on their strengths and attributes?" She's speaking faster, her mind already twelve steps ahead of this conversation. "I'll need some key data from you in order to make it accurate. You have your phone on you, good, good, I'll email you the questions. Get them back to me as quickly as possible and I'll have a logical answer by the end of the week."

"Sienna, no."

"You say 'Sienna, no,' but all I'm hearing is 'Sienna, yes.' Trust me, Izzy. The heart might lie, but empirical evidence doesn't."

She's going to do this, and if I don't fill out the damn forms immediately, she's going to pester me until I do. Desperate, I grab onto the only thing I can. "But you married David without any empirical evidence."

She gives me a look like she pities me. "If you think I didn't do a full ancestry DNA history in case I change my mind about procreating, a background check to rival what the FBI can come up with, *and* give him a three-night sex

85

trial to ensure our sexual tastes line up—Izzy, do you even know me?"

There's nothing else to say. I try and fail to paste a smile on my face. "Thank you, Sienna. An algorithm would be extremely helpful."

"You're just humoring me, but wait until you see it. It will help. I promise." She glances over her shoulder. "I have to go. I'll hold Cordelia off, but if you change your mind and need us to ride to the rescue, text or call. We'll be there."

"Thank you." My throat is doing that horrible closing thing again. "I love you."

"Love you, too." She hangs up, leaving me alone once again with all the things that have gone wrong. I wish I could say they started last night, but the truth is that they started a long time ago, maybe back as far as the first time I met Gaeton and Beast.

My father kept his people separate from us, and for good reason. We were always protected in our family home, always had special security whenever we left the grounds, but they were carefully curated individuals. As such, I didn't meet either Gaeton or Beast until they were promoted to generals five years ago. I still remember that ceremony my father insisted on, how *proud* of them he was. He looked at those two like they were the sons he never had. Not better than his daughters; simply different.

They were both on their best behavior, as shiny as new pennies, but there was an element of danger that drew me. And the way they looked at me ... Beast like he wanted to eat me whole. Gaeton like he wanted to fall to his knees and worship me in the most sinful way possible.

I couldn't have known then how that moment would turn into my attempting to date both of them for two agonizingly long years before it all went up in flames. I couldn't have known that smiling at them, that flirting the tiniest amount, would set us on a path that ended with me here, alone in Gaeton's bed while Beast and he do whatever they're doing in his bathroom. Talking? Planning? Fucking?

The thought leaves me both icy cold and agonizingly hot. I have to know. I can't let them lock me out, not if this is really about me making a choice and not simply a form of penance.

I don't allow myself the chance to brace. I simply gather the tattered remains of my courage and pad to the door and place my hand on the knob. That's where my strength and anger fail me.

I can't do it. I don't know why I thought I could do it.

I turn from the door and walk out of the room.

CHAPTER 11

GAETON

a shower isn't enough to clean off the sick sensation coating my skin. I feel like I'm in the middle of a maelstrom, currents whipping me this way and that. I want Isabelle. I never *stopped* wanting Isabelle, even when every moment away from her drove me out of my mind with jealousy because I knew she was with Beast and he was giving her things I never could. That jealousy might be nowhere in evidence now, but it doesn't change the history. There's too much pain there, too many fuck-ups.

And Beast? That shit is *not* as simple as I've let myself believe. I've hated him and yet trusted him at my back for years. And all the questions of *what if?* that I haven't let myself contemplate? I'm no closer to finding answers now than I was before agreeing to this. Last night he fucked me. This morning I sucked his cock. It's one hell of a problem.

Not that I regret it. I don't. But now that I know what he's like in bed, I'm craving more. This was supposed to be us working through our shit with Isabelle. It wasn't supposed to be us working through our shit with *each other*. Another complication I don't want or need.

I never should have agreed to this.

I press my forehead to the cool tile and exhale. The sound almost masks the door opening. "I don't want to talk about it."

"Too fucking bad."

Surprise snaps me out of it long enough to turn to face Beast. "You."

He didn't bother to put on pants before he came in here, and the sight of him naked throws me for another loop. We've participated in scenes together a few times over the last twelve months, but he always, always keeps his clothes on. Last night is the first time I've seen him naked.

I wish I could scrub the sight from my mind.

Scars rope his body from the neck down, as if whoever fucked him up couldn't bear to mar the perfection of his face. Either someone tortured him at some point, or he's been in more knife fights than I can count. Not to mention shot a few times for spice. His enemies left his penis alone, too, which might amuse me if I could dredge up anything but the sick feeling in my chest. The piercing at the head of his cock draws my attention, and it takes everything I have to drag my gaze up to his face. "This was a mistake."

"Last night, I might have agreed with you. Now?" He shrugs. "We need this."

"Which we, Beast? You and Isabelle? Me and you? Sure as fuck not *me* and Isabelle." I've worked so fucking hard to keep my anger locked down. Damn near four hundred days of seeing Isabelle and keeping a polite face like I wasn't dying inside. Of working next to Beast when half the time I want to wring his graceful neck and the other half of the time I'm forgetting myself and fantasizing about sucking his cock. "She was never going to pick me."

There it is. The truth that's eaten me alive since we decided to both date her. I never figured myself for a masochist, but I always am for this woman. I can't do it anymore. I fucking *won't*.

Beast gives me a long look and starts forward. I have six inches on him, but his presence dominates the space, driving me back a step before I catch myself and plant my feet. "What are you doing?"

"You missed a spot." And then he's in the shower with me. Too close, too fucking close. What the hell is he *doing?* He holds my gaze steadily. "Turn around."

"This the part where you bash me over the head and toss me out a window?"

Beast smirks. "If you're not brave enough to give me your back …"

"Reverse psychology doesn't work on me." But he keeps coming. Another step, we're going to be chest to chest, cock to cock. I look at those sinfully curved lips and I may have wanted to kill this man more times than I can count in the past, but right now I really want to kiss him.

I turn around. It's the lesser of two evils.

Beast's hand comes around me to get at the soap and then he's touching me, scrubbing my back in broad strokes. It feels good, far better than it has right to. But then, I'm still hard as a rock. Anything would feel good at this point. Or at least that's what I tell myself as I brace my hands on the tile and his touch turns leisurely.

I should recognize a trap when I see it.

"If her choice was so obvious, it wouldn't have stretched out as long as it did. *You* were the one who left *her.*"

And then she left Beast.

No matter how torn up I feel, I'm not going to rip myself open for this man. I might trust him with my body, I might want to fuck him a truly absurd amount, I might even trust him at my back in a firefight, but Beast is not my friend. He's not one to hold confidences without intending to use the vulnerability against me. "This pact was a mistake."

"No, I don't think so." Beast's hands move to my sides and then around to my chest. He's not *quite* pressed against my back, but I can feel him a bare inch away. I go still, barely daring to breathe. His hands coast down my stomach and stop just short of my cock. He lowers his voice. "Are you furious about the past? Or are you furious because you want my cock in your ass again?"

"I don't want you." The lie doesn't sound the least bit convincing.

"Don't you?" The bastard still doesn't move his hands, doesn't continue the descent I desperately need him to. "You don't want me to jack your cock right now?" I can hear the cruel smile in his voice. "You would say no if I got down on my knees and offered to suck you off?" Each word is a dark temptation brought to light. I stare unseeingly at the tile. I can't breathe. I can't fucking move. I can only stand here while he weaves this spell around me.

The barest brush of his cock against the bottom curve of my ass. "You don't want to sink into Isabelle's sweet little pussy while I pound your ass like I did last night?"

If I turn around, I'm going to kiss him. I'm going to do a whole lot more than kiss him. I try to regulate my breathing, but my body isn't listening. I'm damn near gasping through each inhale and exhale. "What are you suggesting?"

"A pact of our own." His fingertips graze my hipbones. "We close this triangle for the next thirteen days."

I want that, but... "Why offer this?"

"I want to fuck you." He says it like it's the simplest thing in the world. He wants to fuck me, so he will. "You want to fuck me. There's never been a better time to get it out of our system, if you want to call it that."

It sounds reasonable and simple, which means it's

91

anything but. "You know better than most that sex is not that simple. Not with anyone. Especially not with us."

"Gaeton." His mouth brushes the spot between my shoulder blades, there and gone in an instant, and it's everything I can do not to arch back into his touch to invite him to repeat the motion. "Stop thinking so hard about consequences and tell me what you want."

"Fucking *fine*. I want you. I just don't like it."

"Welcome to the club." Another slow drag of his mouth across the sensitive skin of my back and then his hand closes around the base of my cock. Not stroking. Just gripping me like he owns me. "Turn around."

It's a mistake. I know it's a mistake even as I obey his command. He doesn't release my cock as I turn, just uses his hold to urge me back until I'm pressed against the cool tile. "You didn't get yours earlier."

No, I didn't, but that's the least of my issues right now and Beast knows it. He's offering me a gift of sorts, a distraction from the shit all tangled up in my chest. This isn't simple, but compared to dealing with my conflicted feelings about Isabelle, it's a walk in the park. "You offering to get me off?"

"Something like that." His lips curve the smallest amount and that same amusement I glimpsed earlier flickers through his eyes.

Fuck, but he's pretty. It's easy to forget that because he's so hard, but right now, the only hard thing about Beast is his cock. I swallow past my suddenly dry throat. "Be my guest."

Beast doesn't move. "Say yes."

As if I'm in danger of saying anything else. "Hell yes. Suck me off, you bastard. Make it good."

He sinks to his knees as gracefully as any subbie despite the thick scar across his thigh that gives him pain when it rains. Strange that I know so much about a man I used to want dead more than anything else in the world. I didn't realize back then that Beast wasn't the issue with my relationship with Isabelle. He wasn't the fatal flaw. I'm still not sure what was, even after all this time. Maybe it was her independence, her aversion to being tied down in anything resembling a life with a white picket fence or whatever the fuck normal people wanted. As if I'd know where to begin to offer her that life.

Beast taps my thigh sharply. "Eyes on me, Gaeton."

I obey, and just like that, I'm not thinking about Isabelle. I'm held captive by Beast's baby blues as he sucks my cock into his mouth. He has to fight a little to work himself down my length, until his lips meet my base. It feels so fucking good, my thighs quiver and I have to lean harder against the wall.

He growls low in his throat, and I feel it all the way to my balls. The back of my head hits the tile and I have to close my eyes. *"Fuck."*

Beast digs his fingers into my thighs. Hard. It's enough to get me looking down at him again, enough to know I'll be sporting bruises from his fingertips later. That thought should bother me. This man isn't my Dom, even if he wants to come to some sort of agreement for the next two weeks. I'm not even sure I like the asshole.

But, fuck, he can suck a dick.

He works me expertly, using teeth and tongue to bring me right to the brink. All the while, he grips my thighs, giving me that lashing of pain I crave. It's rough and dirty and I wouldn't have it any other way.

I curse. "I'm close."

He releases my thighs long enough to take my hands and place them on either side of his head. A single look and I know exactly what he wants. I rasp out a laugh. "Trust you to top from the bottom, you bastard." His hands go back to my thighs and then I'm fucking his mouth in rough, ragged strokes. So close. I want to make this last and I don't want to make this last.

It's not forever.

It's just an exchange of pleasure. That's all. That's all it can ever be with us. We have too much bullshit between us, but who knows? Maybe this will be the clean slate we could never figure out how to create.

I come with a curse and watch as he drinks me down. Beast keeps sucking me in slow pulls until I gently shove him off my cock. "Enough."

Beast licks his lips. "One last question, and answer it honestly."

I already know I'm not going to like this, just like I recognize that I've gone too far to change my mind now. He fucked my ass last night. We've both given each other blowjobs this morning. This roller coaster has reached its peak and we're half a breath from free fall. "Yeah?"

"Are you furious at Isabelle for wanting to play the part of our dirty little slut? Or are you furious at yourself for wanting it, too?"

I can't take a step back because of the wall, and he's kneeling in my path out of the shower. I know without a shadow of a doubt that he planned things this way. "You are such a bastard."

"Yes." He gives my thighs one last squeeze and draws his middle finger along my cock. "Answer the question."

"Both." I shudder out a breath when he cups my balls. "I'm angry about both." I simultaneously want to slap his hands away and demand that he never stop touching me. "I don't understand why you're *not* pissed about it."

"Life is too short, too uncertain, to deny yourself what you want." He plays his fingers up the underside of my cock and then grips me just behind the head. It's still not enough to do more than tease, not when I just came so hard, but it feels so fucking good. Beast leans forward and bites my thigh just inside of where I can still feel his fingerprints on me, and I can't help thrusting against his grip. His dark chuckle fills the space around us. "Sometimes those wires get crossed, but I know what I want now."

Then he releases me and pushes to his feet.

If I wasn't already bracing against the wall of the shower, I might have fallen. As it is, I'm left blinking and disorientated. Maybe that's why I tell the truth. "It hurts. Even when it feels good, it hurts."

He doesn't ask for clarification, but then out of everyone else in the city, Beast is the one person who might actually understand what I'm saying. "If we don't deal with it, the three of us will rip the entire territory apart."

Leaving is no longer an option. I don't know if it ever was. I finally nod. "Okay. I'm in."

"Trust me to guide you today."

I finally get my balance enough to push off the wall and look at him. He walks out of the shower and grabs two towels. It's weird as shit, but the alternative is standing here out of spite, so I turn off the shower and accept the second towel.

What he's offering ... I shouldn't agree to it. I understand that engaging in what is the equivalent of a prolonged scene is just kink, but I know myself and I'm not certain I can keep up the necessary barriers to walk out the other side of this unharmed when Isabelle invariably chooses Beast. And that's without adding submitting to this man into the mix.

I still find myself nodding. "Today."

Beast gives a little smile, like he finds my qualifying terms cute. That dual urge to punch him and kiss him rises, and I focus on drying off instead. He opens the door and glances out into the room. "Get dressed, Gaeton. Something nice like

95

you'd wear to the old man's house." His brows lower for the barest moment. "I need to have some of my shit brought here." He disappears into my bedroom and I follow more slowly, already bracing for seeing Isabelle.

She's not there.

Guilt pricks me, and no amount of telling myself that I'm balancing the scales makes it disappear. I dress quickly, pulling on a pair of black slacks and a dark red button-down. After the slightest hesitation, I slip on socks and shoes, too. Beast is setting a specific kind of stage, so it pays to be thorough.

For his part, he makes a quick call and then frowns down at his discarded clothes. It would figure that Beast is one of those people who can't stand wearing clothing more than once. I consider him. He'd be swimming in any of my slacks and shirts. "Hold on." I dig through my closet to come up with a pair of lounge pants that I bought on a whim—and promptly shrank in the wash.

He raises his eyebrows when I toss them to him, but pulls them on without a word. They're still a little big, hanging low on his hips despite him tying them tightly. Not quite the look he's going for, but it's a look *I* can appreciate. He glances at the door, but makes no move to open it. "Sit at the head of the table and wait."

I can see where he's going with this, but part of me still wants to dig in my heels. "You know this won't make it right."

"Do I know that?" Another ghost of a smile. "Go sit at the head of the table, Gaeton. Let's restart your day."

In the end, there's nothing to do but obey. I agreed to this —both the original pact and the one that includes Beast's cock at my disposal. Maybe tomorrow I'll be in the mood to fight him, but right now, I'm so fucking tired. Letting him call the shots is exactly what I need, even if I don't want to admit as much to him. Looking into those sharp blue eyes, I realize I don't *have* to admit shit.

He understands.

Fuck, maybe he always has.

I don't know how to grapple with that knowledge, so I put it away and follow Beast out of the room. Isabelle sits on the couch, wrapped in one of the thick blankets I had stashed in the chest coffee table, and staring out the window. She doesn't look over as we approach, which is just as well.

I was a dick earlier. I humiliated her, and then we left her hanging. If it was part of the plan, that'd be one thing, but I can't pretend it was. I wanted to hurt her, and so I did. An asshole move in a normal relationship. Damn near unforgivable when she's entrusting herself to us the way she is.

I make it one step toward her when Beast catches my eye and gives the slightest shake of his head.

Right. Follow his command.

I stalk past the couch and nudge out the chair with my foot. I throw myself into the chair and slouch there.

And wait.

CHAPTER 12

ISABELLE

I hear the men come out of the bedroom, and I can't help tensing as Gaeton walks past me. I don't know what I expect. For him to keep cutting me down the way I probably deserve. For him to pretend like he never delivered that sting. For something else altogether.

I don't expect him to ignore me completely and walk to the table situated just off the kitchen. It's built just as sturdy as everything else in this apartment, a square table that looks like it can easily hold a handful of people dancing on it. He crosses his arms over his chest and looks out the window.

What's going on?

Beast appears on my other side and crouches in front of me. He's wearing what are obviously Gaeton's lounge pants, and the sight of his bare chest has the past slamming into me with the force of a tidal wave. It took six months of dating before he walked around shirtless in front of me the way he's doing now. He'd die before he admitted it aloud, but he's self-conscious about his scars.

He reaches out and runs his hands along the edge of the

blanket I found, his knuckles skating along my skin. "Do you want to use your safe word?"

I flinch back, but his hold on the blanket keeps me from going anywhere. "You can't honestly want to continue after *that.*"

His smile contains the tiniest bit of warmth but it feels like standing in the hot July sun. "Communication has never been our strong suit—*any* of our strong suits. There are going to be hiccups."

"There are going to be hiccups along the way to *where?*" Part of me wants to just let it go, but I can't. I just can't. "Hiccups for the next thirteen days while you punish me for how things fell apart before? Or while you do whatever this is and I have to pick one of you?" The thought of having to make that decision has an invisible strap tightening around my chest. I don't know if I can do it, Sienna's algorithm in play or not. If it was such an easy choice, we wouldn't be here in the first place.

No matter which way I go, I'm going to walk out of this apartment bleeding from a soul wound I might never recover from. No matter what decision I make, I'm going to hurt a man I care about very deeply.

"Trust me, princess." He says it like he has everything figured out, like he has absolutely no doubt we'll reach the destination he can already see in his head. Beast gives the blanket another small tug. "Do you want to use your safe word?"

There's only one answer and everyone within hearing range knows it. I made this choice and I will honor it. A small part of me even *wants* to. This situation isn't playing out at all like I expect, but I can't deny that I feel like a moth to their flame. But no matter what happens, I will *not* be burned up. "No." I lift my chin. "But if either of you ever pull a stunt like that again, I'm out. You want me here and you want me honest, but you don't get to play verbal punching bag with me in response to that honesty." Drawing this line in the sand is a risk, but I can't stop myself.

"Agreed." Beast nods and rises, tugging me along with him.

Beast leads me to the table and stands behind me, his hands on my shoulders. "Gaeton." His voice has lost its warmth and is all snap, which the other man responds to. Gaeton looks over my shoulder at Beast, once again completely ignoring me. Beast squeezes my shoulders, but I can't tell if it's supposed to be a warning or a reassurance. "I brought you something."

Now he finally focuses on me, but there's absolutely nothing in those dark eyes. He looks at me like I'm a stranger, and not necessarily a welcome one.

Gods, that hurts.

Only Beast at my back prevents me from retreating.

Gaeton leans back in his chair, the very picture of an arrogant prince. "Doesn't look like breakfast."

"Doesn't it? Take a closer look." The barest movement behind me and then Beast grabs my hips and lifts me onto the table. I can't help a little squeak of surprise, but I stifle it immediately. I might enjoy submitting, but I'm not going to give either of them the satisfaction of reacting when they haul me around. With a firm grip, he guides my feet to the arms of Gaeton's chair. It's built wide to accommodate his body, so it leaves me spread almost uncomfortably. If not for the blanket, I'd be entirely exposed.

I don't expect they'll let me keep covered for long.

Gaeton doesn't move. "Hard to see this present of yours while she's all wrapped up."

A dark laugh from Beast. "A present isn't a present unless you have to unwrap it. There are rules, my friend."

"I'm not your friend." But he says it in a contemplative

sort of way, as if he's no longer sure it's true. Gaeton brackets my ankles with his big hands and finally, *finally*, meets my gaze. "I'm sorry."

"Gaeton." Beast injects a bit of warning into his tone, but doesn't shift from the spot against the wall at Gaeton's shoulder.

Gaeton ignores him and gives my ankles a small squeeze. "I'm sorry," he says again. "I was a dick."

"Yes, you were a dick." My heart takes a dizzying leap and I press my hands to my chest as if I can keep it from its fatalistic freefall. It takes me two tries to speak. "You've always been arrogant. This morning is the first time you've ever been cruel."

"You sure it's the first time I've ever been cruel?" He skates his hands over my calves and knees, stopping a bare inch below where the blanket covers me. "Sure as fuck seems we don't know each other nearly as well as we thought."

I'm afraid to ask what he means, afraid to dig deeper into the same realization I had last night. We dated for nearly two years and I might know that he likes red, that his favorite food is takeout from the hole-in-the-wall restaurant around the corner from his apartment, that he really enjoys spending his evenings cuddling and watching soapy dramas on the TV, but those are all surface level things. There is so much he kept from me. So much I kept from him. Something like panic takes hold, and I try to shrug out of the blanket. It's a distraction, and not even a good one.

Especially since he pins the fabric to my legs so it gets caught around my upper arms instead of dropping to the table.

Gaeton's expression goes predatory. "You don't want to talk about this."

"No, I don't." Honesty is as heady as it is terrifying. Something has been knocked loose inside me, and it's bubbling closer and closer to the surface; things I can't say, that I need to keep silent. I promised honesty, but I didn't promise that I'd cut myself open for them without prompting.

His thumbs skate over my knees, a contemplative touch that makes me shiver. There's no softness on his face, no warmth to take shelter in. He looks at me like I'm an enemy he will fully enjoy taking apart. "Say what you mean, Isabelle. I can see you fighting it. Stop playing the perfect princess and spit it the fuck out."

I try to clamp my lips together, to keep the truth inside, but it's carried forth on a tsunami of hurt and there's no stopping it. "You *lied* to me."

He flinches. It's a tiny movement, barely perceptible, but there nonetheless. "I never lied to you."

"Really, Gaeton? *Really?*" I look over his shoulder at Beast. "You both lied to me the entire time we were dating. You held yourselves back, you presented me with one side of yourself and nothing more. You *kept* this from me." I try to motion around us, but my hands are mostly trapped by the blanket. "You both decided you knew what I needed and you didn't stop to talk to me about it. Not once." My throat goes hot and tight, but I can't stop now that I've started. "You touched me like I was some breakable precious thing because you knew best. You were *starving* me and neither of you cared, because all that mattered was playing Prince Charming to the princess you put on a pedestal. You can hate me for not being able to choose, but how was I supposed to make a choice when neither of you gave me anything approximating an honest relationship?"

Gaeton leans forward. "Isabelle—"

But it's too late. I can't stop. I'm not even sure I want to anymore. "And what the fuck did you think was going to happen if I *did* choose? That you'd just be happy with sweet, vanilla sex for the rest of your life? That we wouldn't start resenting each other for the parts we weren't allowed to show? That eventually one of us wouldn't set the whole relationship on fire just to *feel* something?"

His brows lower. "I would never cheat on you."

"No one can make promises when they're starving. Maybe you wouldn't. Maybe I would be the one. Did you think about *that?*"

"You're a good girl, Isabelle. Forgive the fuck out of me for wanting to treat you like it."

"No. You don't get to do that. You do *not* get to whore-or-virgin me. I'm a person and people are complicated. You don't get to decide what's best for me." I finally look up at Beast and he's standing there like I just pulled out a gun and shot him in the chest. "Neither of you get to make that call, especially without talking to me."

Gaeton lets go of my legs and sits back. "I'd say we learned that the hard way."

"Did you?" I carefully set my feet on the seat of the chair on either side of his legs. "If these two weeks are about punishing me, then I'll shut up and we can get back to it. But if you really want me to choose and to have a future that won't fall apart inside of a year, then you have to *see* me. Not just the good parts. Not just the parts that hurt you. All of me."

He's frowning at me as if maybe he might be doing exactly that. Gaeton is a smart man. He might play the fool because, more often than not, his size and boisterous attitude make people underestimate him, but there's a big brain and an even bigger heart under all that bluster. It doesn't make him less dangerous, though. If anything, it makes him more so, because once he decides to give his loyalty, there is no horrendous act he won't commit to protect the people he cares about. Once upon a time, he felt that way for me. Now, it's not so simple.

He sets his arms on the arms of the chair, his thumbs brushing the outer edges of my calves. "What do I see, Isabelle?" He says my name like a promise.

I've come this far. I can't shy away now. I let the blanket drop away and carefully move to straddle him on the chair. He makes no move to hamper or help me, just lets me take up this position while he watches me closely. I settle my hips against his and have to bite back a whimper at the feeling of his cock hardening against me. I frame his face with my hands, enjoying the way his whiskers prickle against my skin, enjoying the faint flush beneath his freckles even more. "I am a princess. I'm spoiled and proud and loyal. I value freedom above all else, sometimes to my detriment. I am *not* perfect, and I don't want to be with someone who needs me to be perfect to love me." I rock my hips a little. "I'm also a little slut who loves to be fucked dirty, with a some degradation thrown in for spice." *And I love you. Both of you.* The last I manage to keep in. There's only so much vulnerability I can stand in a single twenty-four hour period and I've long since maxed mine out for this one.

"I see you." Gaeton loosely clasps my hips with his big hands. It brings into focus how much larger than me he is, how different the power dynamic feels with me naked and him fully clothed. He strokes his thumbs over my lower stomach. "You want this cock, Isabelle?"

I don't know if I believe him that he sees me. I don't think a single instance of honesty can combat years' worth of half-truths and lies. It doesn't matter in this moment. Letting myself be swept away by anticipation feels good, like letting go of a weight I've carried for so long. I'll have to pick it up again sooner than I'd like, but for now I'm fully present and holding my breath waiting for what happens next. "Yes."

"Yes, Sir."

I wet my lips. "Yes, Sir. I want your cock."

He releases my hips and drapes himself over the arms of the chair, a king on his throne. "Then take it."

I reach for the front of his pants with a shaking hand. He makes no move to help me, simply sits there and lets me draw down his zipper and pull out his cock. I give him a slow, exploratory stroke, and meet his gaze.

Gaeton gives me absolutely nothing. Instead, it's Beast's voice that comes from behind him in answer to my silent question. "Don't make him repeat himself."

Understanding dawns, bringing with it a delicious burst of pleasure. I brace one hand on his shoulder and shift closer, guiding his cock to my entrance. He's a bit bigger than Beast, so I have to work to take him deep, fighting inch by inch down his length while he holds perfectly still and does nothing to help. The only sign he's affected is a faint flushing of his cheeks. Once he's sheathed completely inside me, I pause, enjoying the feeling of being so full of him.

"Really, little slut? Surely that's not enough for you." I can feel his words in my chest, a rumble that's delicious and oh, so wrong. He cocks an eyebrow at me, as if I'm not impaled on his cock right now, as if we're simply having a conversation he's already grown tired of. "You interrupted my morning with your needy pussy, practically begging me to fill you up. Get yourself off. Now."

There it is, that delicious sting of humiliation. It feels dirty to ride him like this while he sits there and tolerates it. Like I'm just as much a little slut as he calls me. My breasts brush his shirt with every stroke, and the physical reminder of his being clothed while I'm naked only makes this hotter. I want it to last forever, but I also want to come all over him right now. I grind down, working my clit against the exposed bit of skin where his pants have gaped open. "Gaeton," I gasp.

That's when I look over his shoulder and meet Beast's gaze.

The strength of it shocks me so much, my rhythm hitches. I might have expected jealousy if I thought about it at all, but it's nowhere in evidence. He looks at us like he owns us, like we're two players acting out his favorite fantasy, as if he's enjoying this moment even more than I am.

"He's watching, isn't he?"

I glance at Gaeton. "Yes, Sir."

"Mmm. Hold on." He barely gives me a chance to obey before he lifts and rotates the chair a full one hundred and eighty degrees. I can't see Beast any more, but I feel his attention lick down my spine and settle on the spot where Gaeton and I are joined.

I start to look over my shoulder, but Gaeton makes a rumbling growly sound. "No, little slut. You're here for this cock. You don't get to make eyes at him while you're filled up with me." The words almost sound jealous, but Gaeton's eyes are full of heat as he looks over my shoulder at Beast. He refocuses on me. "Finish what you started, greedy girl."

I brace my hands on his shoulders and start fucking him again. I expect him to stay silent, but he keeps spilling out sinful words into the bare space between us. Lower, this time, as if they're just for me. "Lean forward, Isabelle. Give him a good view of the way I fill you up."

I obey, the new position putting my face kissably close to Gaeton. I look at his mouth, but I can't take this step on my own. Maybe it's silly to put so much importance on a kiss when he's had his mouth all over me, when he kissed me last night, when his cock is currently stretching me uncomfortably full, but I can't help it. I shift closer still, my cheek brushing his with every stroke.

"He's watching. Teasing him with the way you ride my cock gets you hotter, doesn't it? Do you think you can tempt him closer?" His lips brush my ear and I whimper. "Maybe you want him to take your ass. He'll hold perfectly still and you'll have to work that tight little body over both our cocks. Using us like toys while you sob and beg us to fuck you properly."

Pleasure spirals tighter and tighter through me. "You're so mean."

"Am I?" His mouth brushes my neck. "Maybe so." His lips trace my jaw. "Maybe mean is exactly what you want, Isabelle. Someone to put you in your place and fuck you dirty just like you need it." He's right there, so close to my mouth that I can taste his exhale. "Maybe one cock will never be enough for you."

"I—"

He grabs my hips and slams me down on his length. I cry out, but Gaeton kisses me, eating down the sound as he works me over his cock, taking exactly the angle I need to get off while he plunders my mouth. He overwhelms my senses. Higher and higher I climb, until I'm sobbing against his lips, a wild thing that can't get enough, will never get enough, so hungry for pleasure that I could eat the whole universe.

And then I'm weightless and everything goes to static as my orgasm takes me. I'm vaguely aware of him following me over the edge, driving up into me until he grinds out an orgasm of his own. I slump against his chest, but I'm still straining to meet his kisses, an addict with my first real hit in twelve long months. Gaeton kisses me like I'm his world. Everything else might have changed, but that hasn't.

I'm still trying to drink down a year's worth of that feeling when an arm bands around my waist and yanks me off Gaeton. I cry out, reaching for him, but Beast hauls me around to the table and bends me over it, his hand in the middle of my back forcing me to down until my cheek presses against the cool wood. "Turn around, Gaeton."

Gaeton moves the chair around to face us. He's tucked away his cock, though there are wet spots from my orgasm all over his lap. He resumes his bored expression as Beast kicks my legs wide. "I suppose she's not satisfied," Gaeton growls.

"Let's see, shall we?" Keeping me pinned to the table, Beast shoves two rough fingers into me. Despite my determination to stay still, I roll my hips, trying to take him deeper. He makes a disappointed sound. "So needy, this one."

"Insatiable."

Beast hooks a hand under my leg closest to Gaeton and lifts it, bracing my knee on the table so that I'm spread obscenely. Gaeton makes a noise, and even without the tableau, I know he can see everything Beast is doing to me. Beast gives me another few strokes. "How many orgasms do you think it would take to satisfy our princess?"

"Only one way to find out."

Beast cups my pussy with a possessive hand, his fingers playing over my clit. "Shall we make things interesting?"

That surprises a laugh out of Gaeton. "Only you would be fingering this woman and offer to make things interesting as if that isn't enough."

Beast spreads me, his fingers tracing my pussy like he wants to memorize every inch. "How about a bet, Gaeton? How many orgasms do you think our Isabelle can stand before she begs for mercy?" He gives my clit a little slap that has me jumping. "I think twelve."

"Give her a little credit. Fifteen, at least."

Fifteen orgasms? I don't know if I can survive it.

"If I'm right, I fuck your ass again tonight." Beast's hand spasms the tiniest bit on my back. "If you're right, you can take mine."

Suddenly Gaeton doesn't sound as amused. "And if she holds out past fifteen?"

Beast leans over me, pressing against my back, his cock

hard against my ass. "Then as a reward, we both fuck her at the same time."

My trepidation turns to anticipation. I arch back against Beast. "I can handle more than fifteen."

His laugh vibrates against my back. "We'll see, princess. We'll see."

CHAPTER 13

BEAST

*C*ontrol is the only god I worship. It's always been that way, because my survival has always depended on it. Sabine Valley makes Carver City's politics look like children playing dress-up, and Cohen was right in the middle of all of it. Watching his back, being *with* him, meant I couldn't fuck around. I learned to set my eyes on a goal and be utterly ruthless in doing whatever it took to achieve it. It wasn't enough back then, but that same drive propelled me up the ranks when I came to the Man in Black's territory.

That control is what allowed me to date Isabelle at the same time as Gaeton. I wanted her. Eventually, I loved her. Competing for her love with him the same way we competed for everything else—power, status, money—felt like a natural extension of our already contentious relationship. Gaeton's only role was as adversary. I wouldn't allow myself to think about him as anything else, couldn't afford to nurture the flicker of heat that sometimes rose when we fought.

With every orgasm we draw from Isabelle, I feel that control slipping. We're playing out a fantasy I never dared allow myself to have, trading her back and forth again and again. Working together in the pursuit of pleasure instead of being at odds. For her part, Isabelle takes it all with a devious glee that I've never seen in her before.

It doesn't line up with what I thought I knew about this woman. When we made this deal yesterday, I wanted her, yes, but I also wanted to punish her. What kind of princess would want to be fucked dirty the way Gaeton and I crave?

Apparently *our* princess does.

I pin her against my chest as Gaeton eats her out, working on her seventh orgasm. He lost his shirt somewhere along the way, but we both have our pants on still. Watching him worship Isabelle's pussy with his mouth…

Fuck.

I'm going to keep them. I don't know how yet, but the vision of a future together is solidifying in my head the same way all my other goals have in the past, so detailed it feels like we're already there. Me, Gaeton, Isabelle. Together. It's the path to reach that destination that's still too murky. We have a lot of shit to unpack.

"You were right before, princess." I pitch my voice so Gaeton can hear, and he slows his movements the tiniest bit.

She arches and whimpers. "I can't … You don't seriously want to have a conversation right now?"

"I do." I cup her breasts with rough hands. "We decided that you were something pure to hold gently in our hands to avoid breaking. We gave you polite sex because we thought that's what you deserved."

She reaches for Gaeton, but I catch her wrists and guide them to the small of her back. I kiss her temple because I can't fucking help it. She looks like a mess, every bit of fucking written across her appearance, from her tangled hair to the sweat glistening on her skin to the faint bruises marking her from our mouths and hands. I love it. Just as much as I love that there are faint nail marks on Gaeton's shoulders from her last orgasm and bruises on his hips and thighs from where I gripped him as I fucked him last night and sucked his cock this morning.

Mine.

Not yet. But soon.

"Make her come, Gaeton. She's not going to focus on shit until you give her that orgasm you've been teasing."

He chuckles, and it must feel good because she moans again. Gaeton zeroes in on her clit, sucking and licking. It doesn't take long before Isabelle bucks and cries out, her body shaking with the force of her orgasm. He softens his touch, giving her one last thorough kiss before he lifts his head and grins at me. He's covered in her orgasm, and from the smug look on his face, he enjoys it as much as I do. "Seven."

"No begging yet." I carefully adjust her position so she's not lying on her arms. She lets me, her breathing harsh and body languid.

His grin widens. "Nope."

I press my lips to her temple. "Good girl."

"I am ... highly motivated."

Gaeton shifts to lay his head on her thigh. Most of his body is on the floor while I'm reclining on the couch with Isabelle on top of me. I reach down and feather my fingers through his hair and he closes his eyes for a brief moment. The feeling in my chest strengthens. *Mine.* Something I never let myself consider possible before last night, and now I can think of nothing else.

Gaeton is nothing like Cohen. He's brash and ruthless, but he's got a heart that's too fucking big. How it hasn't gotten him killed before now is a mystery to me. Taking that on is a risk. If someone Gaeton cares about is in the mix, he will always run toward danger without thinking instead of engaging in a tactful retreat to find a better way.

Cohen was nearly as cold I am these days. The only place he warmed up was in the bedroom, because letting down your guard in Sabine Valley, even during the festivals, is a good way to end up dead. *He* was the one who set our course, the one I was willing to follow to the grave if need be.

Both Gaeton and Isabelle need someone to be that for them.

I stroke her with my other hand, a soft exploratory touch that traces over her hips and stomach and chest. *Mine.* She makes a sound damn close to a purr and relaxes the last little bit into me.

I can be the one to set our course. Fuck, I *want* to be. I am a beast in truth and not only in name, because I don't give a fuck about plans and promises. I want them both, no matter what we agreed on fewer than twenty-four hours ago. I don't care what these two people want right now; this is what *I* want. Both of them for my own. I'm selfish as shit, because I will do whatever it takes—lie, cheat, play dirty—to ensure it happens.

That starts now.

"We're going to play a game, princess."

She tenses the tiniest bit, but it's like her body doesn't have the strength to hold even that position, because she immediately melts back into me. "We're playing a game right now." Her voice is hoarse, but her breathing has mostly returned to normal.

"Consider this a game within a game."

Gaeton is watching me like I'm a snake about to sink my fangs into her. "I'm listening."

"Isabelle hasn't been having her needs met. For every question she answers honestly, she gets that fantasy played out in real life."

Interest flares in Gaeton's dark eyes. "Now I'm really listening."

Isabelle gives a shaky little inhale. "You two are asking a lot of honesty from me and not giving me much in return."

She's not wrong, but I give her nipple a light pinch all the same. "If you have a counter proposal, make it."

"A truth for a truth. I'll answer truthfully, but you will, too."

Instinct demands I say no. Information is more valuable than money, and the power dynamic between the three of us is already precarious at best. Keeping Isabelle off-center long enough to figure out shit with Gaeton is the safest option.

But, fuck, I want some answers, too.

Gaeton gives Isabelle's thigh one last kiss and sits back, disengaging himself from us. "I'm game if you are."

"Yes." I shift to one side of the couch, taking Isabelle with me. "Get up here."

"Sir, yes, Sir." He rolls his eyes but climbs up to take up two-thirds of the overstuffed couch. Isabelle ends up with her legs draped over his thigh and twisted in my lap so her back is against the arm of the couch. No hiding for any of us in this position.

I give him a long look and then focus on Isabelle. "Tell us one fantasy that you want above all others."

She narrows her eyes. "You're really starting off with a softball, aren't you?"

I shrug as if her answer isn't one of the more important pieces of information I'm after. "Answer and we will."

She frowns like she doesn't like it, but finally sighs. "Fine." Isabelle looks out the window across from the couch, and I allow her that space because it means I get the answer I'm looking for. "Gaeton's kind of hit it on the head with the dirty little slut thing. I want to be ... wicked, I guess? The idea of being put on display where anyone could have me, or of walking into a bar and fucking the first person who offers to buy me a drink. I get off to those two fantasies *a lot.*"

Fuck.

If that's the kind of thing that gets her off—and every piece of evidence I've collected for the last twenty-four hours suggests it is—Gaeton and I did her a serious disservice when we were dating. We did ourselves a serious disservice, too.

I touch her chin, the barest pressure to bring her face back to look at us. "Just men?"

She blushes a little. "No, not just men. I said the first person who offers me a drink, and I meant it."

I glance at Gaeton, and the look on his face mirrors the determination filtering through me. Before our time with her is up, we're going to ensure we play out both of these fantasies for her. Safely, because a whole hell of a lot can go wrong with the latter. I twist a lock of her hair around my finger. "It's not enough to fuck a stranger, though, is it? You want to be wicked, you want to be *caught*. Punished. Told what a dirty little slut you are."

She licks her lips. "Yes."

Oh yeah, we can work with this. I give her hair a little tug and release her. "Gaeton, you're up."

This should be easy for us. We both play in the Underworld on the regular, and that place has a way of bringing any fantasy a person can dream up to life. Still, there's nothing simple about this kind of honesty, and I don't blame him for taking his time answering.

Gaeton finally huffs out a breath. "Fuck, fine. You know those parties your father used to throw all the time?"

She tenses, and I can't help doing the same. For a minute there, I'd almost forgotten that he was gone. Another person I care about, dead and buried, a loss in the war with death that none of us will ever win. Isabelle clears her throat. "Yes, though Cordelia was the one organizing them."

"I want you to wear one of those short little numbers, the

ones that are just shy of being proper, with no panties under it." He holds her gaze as he speaks, his expression so intense, it steals *my* breath. "And halfway through, I want to fuck you in that side room off the ballroom, the one where everyone hangs out at the end of the night. I want to fuck you until I have to cover your mouth to keep you quiet so no one hears you coming only a few feet from the party, and then I want you to walk back out there and make small talk while filled up with my come." He barely waits a beat. "And then I want to do it again, and again, until we're caught for real, until someone walks in to find me fucking the pure princess the rough and dirty way you crave."

"Oh."

It's not exactly a mundane fantasy, not with the implications of what enacting it would mean, but the answer still surprises me a little. "How long have you been holding on to that one?"

He transfers his gaze to me. "Since the first time I saw her."

I stroke my hand over her hip, aware of the way his fingers play over her legs. "The entire time you were having polite missionary sex with her, you were thinking about defiling her where everyone could see."

"Yeah." He gives a rough laugh. "No one could say she's anything but mine if they caught us like that."

Mine, not ours.

It's fine. I have time to bring Gaeton over to my way of thinking. I sit back and give myself five seconds to imagine telling them exactly what I want.

Once, about a year into us dating, I had shown up unexpectedly to Isabelle's room to see her. Halfway through opening the door, I realized she wasn't alone. If I was a better person, I would have left then, but I opened the door a little more so I could see her bed. Where she was riding Gaeton's cock. I was jealous as fuck, yeah, but it wasn't nearly as cut and dried as I expected it to be. I wanted to be the one under her, but I also wanted ... Him. Fuck, I wanted both of them.

Playing out my fantasy would be walking into that room. Interrupting them. Punishing them. And then making them continue fucking while I join in.

I won't say it. Not now. No matter what I told them, now isn't the time for honesty from me. Too much truth can harm, and we're sitting too precariously for me to do something to spin us out of balance.

So I lie.

"I always wanted to fuck you in your father's office."

Gaeton shoots me a sharp look, but Isabelle is frowning at both of us. "You two can't be serious. Both of your fantasies are around me?"

"You make quite the impression." Gaeton picks up her foot and starts massaging, digging his thumbs into her arch.

She gives a sweet little moan. "That feels good."

"I know." He waits for her eyes to slide shut to give me another long look. He knows I'm lying, but apparently he's content to let it happen. It's something I'll no doubt pay for later, so I'll need to have my story straight by that point and a legitimate reason for breaking the rules of the game I constructed. Gaeton runs his hand up her leg and spreads her wide. "That's enough of a break, don't you think, Beast?"

"But—"

I nod slowly. "We'll play another round later." I cup Isabelle's breasts. "I'm feeling generous, princess, so I'll even let you pick how you want to come this time. My hands, mouth, or cock?"

She shivers. "Your mouth. I want your mouth on me."

I shift her to Gaeton's arms, and he picks her up with no effort, spreading her thighs over his large ones, holding her open for me. It's not exactly natural to go to my knees before them, but looking up at the tableau they create makes the effort more than worth it. Gaeton guides Isabelle's hand to his neck, stretching her body out for me, and then he runs those big hands over her. She rolls her hips, instinctively seeking the hard cock he has pressed against her ass. Her pussy is pink and wet from everything we've done to it, but she's nowhere near begging for mercy. Not yet.

I allow myself a tight smile as I dip down to drag my tongue over her.

Before we're through with her, she will be.

CHAPTER 14

ISABELLE

J make it to thirteen before my body gives out and my sanity breaks. I'm stretched out on Gaeton's chest while Beast fucks me from behind, the friction from Gaeton's cock in his slacks sending me over the edge. It no longer feels like pleasure, though. I'm so oversensitized, it's almost pain.

I bury my face in his chest and sob out the words that will end this. "Stop. Please stop. I can't take any more."

Beast slows, but doesn't pull out. "You know how to tell us you've had enough."

I have an instant of resistance to using my safe word, but Beast's strokes have me rubbing against Gaeton's cock again and it's too much. "Candlestick!"

Just like that, it's over.

Beast pulls carefully out of me and Gaeton lifts me and cuddles me in his lap. My body still smarts from all the sensations, and I can't stop shaking. Against all reason, my eyes burn and the first tear slides out. Gods, I feel so weak right now. "I wanted to last."

Beast tucks a blanket around me and Gaeton and then

kneels between Gaeton's thighs to hold me from the other side, so that I'm completely encompassed between the two of them. "You'll have both our cocks at the same time when you're ready, Isabelle."

The thought makes me shake harder, but I can't tell if it's anticipation or trepidation. "Not tonight."

Gaeton huffs out a laugh. "No, not tonight."

Beast brushes a soft kiss to my lips. It's the first time he's kissed me since we started this and I'm too frazzled to enjoy it. "You did well." He doesn't move back as he looks at Gaeton, and I have the strangest feeling that he wants to kiss the big man, too. The moment stretches out like taffy, sticky and fraught, until he finally sits back. "I'll get a bath started. You're going to be sore."

"I already am."

He chuckles and gives me one last squeeze. Then he's gone, his footsteps soundless as he heads into the bedroom.

Gaeton's arms tighten around me, the contact tethering me to this world when I feel like I might float away. I make myself as small as possible and cuddle into his chest. "I'm sorry."

He rests his chin on the top of my head. "What are you sorry for?"

Some part of me is clamoring for me to shut my mouth, but the loose feeling has invaded my body and my brain, and I can't seem to stop. "I never wanted to break anyone's heart. I was selfish, but I didn't realize I could hurt you the way I did. You and Beast are larger than life, and you always have been." My eyes are trying to close, ignoring my mind's command to stay open. "I was selfish and I couldn't choose. I wanted it all."

He strokes a hand down my back. "After today, it's pretty fucking clear that we all made mistakes."

That should make me feel better. I don't want to be the

only one who got things wrong before. Except it doesn't. Time peels back and we're in my room again, Gaeton angrily pacing with a ring box in his hand and me perched on the edge of my bed, my heart in my throat. I loved him so much, but I could only see that ring as a cage I'd never escape from. I couldn't give him the answer he needed then, and he walked away from me because of it.

I'm not sure I can give him the answer he needs this time, either.

"I don't know what to do," I whisper.

"You don't have to know what to do for twelve more days." His hold tightens and he lifts me as he stands. "You have time."

Time. I might laugh if I didn't think I'd start sobbing. "We dated for two years and all that time didn't make things clearer."

"We weren't operating with all the information then. We are now." He carries me through his bedroom and to the bathroom where Beast has the massive tub halfway filled already. The thing is obscenely large, more hot tub than actual bathing tub. Gaeton pauses. "Straight into the tub?"

"Yes." Beast walks to us and I'm still trying to figure out what he's doing when Gaeton's pants hit the ground and he steps naked into the tub.

The first hit of hot water makes me whimper but as he settles in behind me and coaxes me to stretch out my legs, the warmth starts to ease my shakes. I let loose a shuddering sigh and relax against Gaeton's chest. The tub is easily large enough for him to stretch out fully and leave room left over. "Orgy-sized bed. Orgy-sized tub."

His chuckle warms me as much as the water. "Gaeton-sized bed. Gaeton-sized tub." He hooks an arm around my waist and shifts sideways a little. "Get in here, Beast. We all could use it."

I half expect Beast to say no. He's been right there with us all day, but something remains held apart. I don't know what it is. Beast has always been a mystery to me. Even when he's fucking me, he's holding back. It's part of what attracted me to him in the first place, but mysteries were meant to be discovered, a trail of answers through the years until you get to the very heart of them. With Beast, I never made it past the first layer.

He doesn't say no. He simply steps out of the lounge pants and into the tub, settling opposite us so that all our legs end up tangled together. It feels weirdly right, but even in my blissed out state, I know better than to say as much. The rift between these men didn't start with me, but my presence made it worse.

Another sin to lay at my feet, another form of penance to make. Another apology presses against the inside of my lips. Beast's gaze lands on me and he shakes his head. "Stop that."

"Stop what?"

"If you want to be flogged, one of us will be the one to do it. You don't need to mentally flog yourself over the past."

Irritation rises, but it doesn't quite drown out the guilt. "If I hadn't made mistakes, you two wouldn't have basically strong-armed me into a sex pact to punish me."

Beast gives that infuriating small smile and stretches his arms over the side of the tub. "Fuck yes, you made mistakes, Isabelle. You weren't the only one, though." His gaze flicks to Gaeton and then back to me. "Did you ever think that we offered the sex pact because we wanted to?"

He's simplifying things and ignoring the anger that's laced so many of our interactions since I showed up in the Underworld. I narrow my eyes. "Am I the only one required to be honest in this scenario?"

"Yes." His gives a dry laugh at my outraged expression. "Tell her, Gaeton."

The big man shifts against my back. "Speak for yourself. I was angry."

"Was?" Beast lifts his brows.

"Stop twisting my words, asshole. I still am." His touch is gentle on me. "But you're right. It took three people making mistakes to get us to that point."

Relief courses through me. At least we're all on the same page there. It's the tiniest of steps, but one we've taken together. I don't know what it means for the future. There's still the deadline bearing down on us, the choice I'll be forced to make. Even if we move past the sins of the past, at the end of these two weeks, half my heart will be walking away from me. It's just a matter of which half.

I don't realize I've started to shake again until Gaeton gathers me close. "Stop thinking so hard. Enjoy the aftermath, let the hot water soak out some of the soreness, and then we'll feed you."

My stomach chooses that moment to growl uncomfortably loud. We took a small break for food earlier today, but I was too out of my head to eat a proper meal. Still ... "I don't understand how you can just focus on the here and now and worry about everything later."

"Who said we're doing anything of the sort?" Beast shakes his head. "We have a lot of shit to wade through, Isabelle. A lot. We treated you like spun gold, but you weren't exactly honest, either. Did you ever actually tell either of us what you wanted, in the bedroom or out of it?"

My flushed skin has nothing to do with the heat of the water and everything to do with embarrassment. "Not exactly." When he just watches me, I feel compelled to elaborate. "At first, I liked the pedestal you both put me on. But the longer it went on, the more I felt constrained by it. Every time I even tried to suggest something, I was shot down." Could I have been more explicit? Probably, but my pride wouldn't allow it. Even as I was starving for the things I needed, I'd somehow decided it was a better option than begging one or both of them to fuck me dirty. "Do you remember the dressing room when you were escorting me to pick out the gown for Sienna's birthday party?" I had opened the door wearing only a pair of thigh highs and pulled him in with me for a quickie, except Beast just pressed a soft kiss to my lips and told me to get dressed before we were late.

That makes him look away. "Like I said; mistakes on all sides."

We sit together until the water starts to cool and then Gaeton passes me to Beast and stands. I start to argue that I'm more than capable of moving my body around, but the sight of him rising out of the water like some kind of barbarian god stills my protests. Why waste energy arguing when I can enjoy the view?

He steps out of the tub and snags a couple of towels. I'm distantly aware of Beast going perfectly still behind me, but I'm too caught up in my voyeuristic tendencies to think about it too hard until his lips brush my ear. "He's beautiful, isn't he?"

I don't know if beautiful is the right word for Gaeton. *Beast* is beautiful with his perfect cheekbones and model good looks. Gaeton is ... "Powerful." He looks like he'd be at home on an ancient battlefield, swinging an oversized ax and soaked in the blood of his enemies.

"Yes, powerful." Beast's rough voice goes the slightest bit deeper. "Thick thighs, thick torso, thick neck, thick fucking everything."

Gaeton catches us watching him and frowns. "What are you two up to?"

"Nothing right now." Beast answers for both of us. He gives me a nudge and I rise up on wobbling legs to allow Gaeton to wrap me in a surprisingly fluffy towel. He ignores my attempts to take it from him and dries me off while I stand there, feeling silly and cosseted.

And loved.

I swallow hard. "You know I'm not a doll you need to cart around and move yourself, right? I'm more than capable of taking care of myself."

He looks up from where he's gone to one knee before me to dry my legs. The position is another echo of the past, of the moment when our carefully balanced act went spinning into ruin.

Marry me, Isabelle.

No. I can't. I won't.

The stark pain that flashes through his dark eyes lets me know he's remembering the same thing. He stands slowly and tucks the towel around me. "I like taking care of you." He speaks so low, I have no idea if it carries to Beast where he's drying off a few feet away. "I want to do it, so I do. It has nothing to do with what you're capable of." Layers upon layers within those words. I'm afraid to dig past the surface for fear of what I might find.

I don't know what I'm supposed to say to that, so I just nod. It's enough for now. He disappears into his closet and returns wearing sweatpants and holding a T-shirt. This, at least, he allows me to pull on myself. It hits my knees, and the feeling of being wrapped up in Gaeton's clothes is so bittersweet, tears prick the backs of my eyes. I clutch the fabric to me. "I missed this."

"Me, too." He passes a second pair of pants to Beast. "I'll get food started."

It's only when he walks out of the bathroom that I realize he's intentionally left us alone. My stomach does an uncomfortable flip as I look at Beast. He's swimming in Gaeton's pants, but it doesn't seem to bother him in the least. Then again, nothing bothers Beast. He's unflappable.

I force myself to stop clutching Gaeton's T-shirt. "I'm afraid."

"I know." He crosses the distance between us and takes my face in his hands. Even as his thumbs coast over cheekbones, part of me is all too aware of the violence he's done with them. Violence that he's never once turned on me. That knowledge feels strangely like power, and I drink it up. It's something I've always loved about both men, but with Beast, the difference is so stark. He leans forward and presses a kiss to my forehead. "Trust me, princess. I have this all under control."

I'm not sure I believe him, but I'm exhausted. Handing off worrying about the future feels good right now. Maybe I'll regret it tomorrow. Maybe I'll wake up ready to draw my own personal line in the sand and refuse to budge. Tonight, I just want him to take care of everything.

To take care of me.

I nod against his hold. "Okay. I trust you."

"Good girl." There it is again, that flicker of true warmth in his blue eyes. "Let's get you fed."

We find Gaeton in the kitchen, lining up stuff for sandwiches. He catches me looking and shrugs almost self-consciously. "I'll put together a real meal tomorrow."

I try for a smile. "This looks perfect." Things feel so fragile right now, like one wrong word will splinter our tentative peace into a thousand shards.

We are silent as we put together our respective sandwiches. One for me. Two each for them. Silent as we eat. Silent as we clean up what little dishes there are. Just when I think I might scream from the glaring lack of communication we're capable of without someone being naked, the door's buzzer goes off.

Instantly, both men are on high alert. I barely register the sound when Gaeton steps in front of me, like someone is going to announce themselves before they blow a hole in the fortified doorframe. I peek around him to see Beast stalk to the buzzer like he expects it to explode, too. He presses the button. "Yes?"

A tinny male voice answers. "I have the delivery you requested this morning."

That sounds suspicious as hell, but Beast nods. "Bring it up."

Two tense minutes later, there's a knock on the door. Gaeton shifts slightly and I catch sight of metal in his hand. Where the hell did he pull the gun from? He must have it hidden somewhere in the kitchen because there's no way he was hiding it in his sweatpants. Without looking, he snags my hip and pushes me back behind him, using his body to shield me. As a result, I only hear the door open and low voices as Beast confers with whoever is handling the delivery. Three slow exhales later and the door closes.

Gaeton still doesn't relax. "Check it."

"Already on it." Rustling. Beast curses. "No nasty surprises, but a little birdie left a message."

Gaeton does some creative cursing of his own. "Bring it here." He finally steps to the side, allowing me a full view of the room. There are two small suitcases laying open on the ground, plain black and utterly indistinguishable from thousands of others like them. I recognize some of Beast's clothing, but that's not where my attention lands. It's on the pretty blue card in his hands. As he crosses to the kitchen peninsula, I recognize the stylized blue seashell on the front of it. "Ursa."

"Yes." Beast sets it on the counter and spins it to face us. "The Sea Witch sends her regards, apparently."

I read the flowing script and then reread a second and third time.

Congratulations on your reconciliation with the little princess.

It would be a shame for such an epic love story to end in anything other than a happily ever after.

On the surface, it looks like a friendly overture, but I know better.

It's a flat-out threat.

CHAPTER 15

GAETON

*W*e manage to distract Isabelle until exhaustion takes hold and she passes out between us in bed. She looks younger and more relaxed in sleep, her chest rising and falling in an even rhythm. Less formidable somehow. We worked her hard today, hard enough that I should be passed out right next to her. I'm tired right down to my bones, but it has barely taken the edge off my need for her. I've always liked to fuck, but it's on a different level with this woman.

With both of them.

I can admit that to myself even if I'd walk through fire before I admit it to Beast. It feels natural to trade dominance back and forth between the two of us. And what happened this morning? It's still got me twisted up. Having my mouth all over Beast was something I've wanted for longer than I'll ever admit. He's not for me. He never was.

That's not what we need to talk about right now, though.

I pull the sheet up more firmly around Isabelle and lean back. "Ursa knows where we are."

"It would seem so." He sits against the headboard, his

muscles shifting beneath his scarred skin. There's a wealth of information in those scars, if one knows how to look. Shit he's survived left people around him six feet under. He doesn't need to tell me the stories, to put names and faces to the loss, for me to understand. I really don't *want* to understand Beast, but that resistance gets weaker and weaker the more time we spend together. There was a point where I would have happily put a bullet between his eyes just to get him the fuck out of my way, but it's been a long time since I felt that level of anger. It slipped away while I wasn't paying attention, swept out to sea on a wave of grief and loss.

I push the thoughts away. There's no time to drown in that grief right now, not the grief of losing Isabelle the first time and sure as fuck not the loss of Orsino Belmonte. "Is she warning us off or is she going to strike at us directly?"

"The latter is what I would do." Beast isn't looking at me, his eyes focused on something a thousand miles away. "We're both damn good generals, but we represent more than that. Cordelia already has a handful of damn good generals who could ensure she didn't feel our loss too strongly. The Man in Black—" His voice hitches the tiniest amount. "Orsino left a strong and stable territory when he died. Strong enough to survive the changeover to his daughter and give her time to settle in." He finally looks at me. "Or it would have been if we hadn't left."

He's right. There are other generals, but we're different. We're symbols of a sort. Two men with reputations that stretch the distance of the city and give pause to anyone who considers crossing us. If we hadn't walked out … But we did, and now we have to deal with the consequences.

I drag a hand through my hair. "Did you know how little time he had left?" I knew he was sick. *Everyone* knew he was sick. But up until three days before he died, he was sitting in a meeting with the two of us just like he had a thousand times before. He'd looked frailer than normal, but he hadn't breathed a single fucking word to let me know that he was that close to the end.

"No. He didn't tell me, either." His voice is perfectly devoid of emotion. Once, I thought that meant Beast didn't feel a damn thing. Now I know better. He feels just as deeply as I do. He just hides it better.

"I thought we had months left, years even. The last treatment seemed like it was working." My chest feels like someone dug a hole in it and forgot to toss me into my grave. That man was not perfect, and there were days when I hated him, but he was as close to a father figure as I've ever had. "I couldn't stay there. I just needed some fucking time to work shit out."

"It felt like the walls were closing in." He speaks so softly, I can't tell if the words are meant for me or himself. Beast tilts his head back against the headboard and looks at the ceiling. "It was like losing Cohen all over again; different, but the same, too."

There was a time not that long ago when I would have ignored this new piece of information. Where I didn't want to know more about Beast, because it's easier to hate a near-stranger, even if they're a brother-in-arms. I'm not there right now. I crave getting inside his head in a way I'm not prepared to examine too closely. "Cohen is from your time before Carver City."

"Yeah." He's still not looking at me, still speaking softly. "He was someone very important to me. He and his six brothers were set to take over their part of Sabine Valley when they were driven out. His enemies were hunting him, and we ended up separated." He exhales slowly. "He was supposed to meet me here in Carver City, but he never made it."

I was rising up the ranks when Beast arrived in the city

and landed in our territory. He's cold now, but he could damn near freeze a room back then. He scared the shit out of people, which only led to a whole lot of confusion when Isabelle took up with him. It didn't make him less scary, but it sure as fuck made people more cautious about dealing with her.

Comfort has never been my thing, but I can't just leave this new information hanging out there awkwardly. "I'm sorry."

"Yeah, me too." He gives himself a shake and looks down at Isabelle. "She's not safe here."

"Safer here than in her sister's house, at least until we figure our shit out."

Beast shakes his head. "It's our fault she's sniffing around. And pulling the stunt we did in the Underworld won't have helped. Hades's people might not gossip, but everyone else does. If they think we're using Orsino's death and the resulting imbalance of power to punish Isabelle—"

"Fuck." I close my eyes. I hadn't been thinking about any of that when she showed up. I'm an exposed nerve for this woman. The highest pleasure for the last twenty-four hours still comes with a slice of pain because this entire situation is temporary. It's always been temporary, even if I was too shortsighted to see it before. Isabelle won't marry me. She was never going to. Even if she somehow chooses me and we end up exclusive, she loves her freedom too much to put my ring on her finger. Not when she sees marriage as a trap ready to close around her leg and keep her in place.

I don't know if I have the control necessary to hold her with a loose grip. The control required to keep her happy. No matter how many different scenarios I play out, they all end in heartbreak. Maybe in twelve days. Maybe in a few months or even years.

Why the hell did I agree to this?

"Gaeton."

I open my eyes to find Beast watching me, a strange expression on his face. He doesn't exactly shut it down when I look at him, but I can't divine out what the fuck it means. He gives a small smile. "We can buy ourselves some time with a little show."

No need for him to spell it out. When people in Carver City want to make a statement to the other territories in a way that won't start a war, they do it at the Underworld. Relationships announced. Peace pacts made. Even the occasional spat. All of it happens under the protection of Hades's neutral territory.

"If we go in there and tell everyone that we're hers, there's no taking it back. We can't change our minds later." Not if we want to stay in the city. It doesn't matter how much power we have individually, or how great out reputations; if we cross someone we promised allegiance to, no territory leader in Carver City will touch us.

Beast snorts. "You've made your decision already, same as me."

"Yeah, I guess I have." I smooth the sheet over Isabelle, tucking it a bit higher so she's covered from the neck down. She shifts under my touch, moving closer to me in her sleep. My heart gives a sickening lurch. We're on an out-of-control train that's sure to jump the tracks at the next turn, but I can't bring myself to give a fuck. I don't want to get off this ride, no matter how devastating the end result.

I look up to find Beast watching me, watching us. It's not the first time he's done it today, and I can't define the expression on his pretty face. All I know is that it's dangerous as fuck. "Do I want to know what's going through your head right now?"

"No." Just that. Nothing more. Nothing to clarify or shed some light.

I give him a long look. "Pretty sure you won the bet we had earlier."

Beast laughs, a low rasping sound. "Gaeton, you're sexy as shit, but when I fuck you next, I want it to be when we're not both exhausted and about to pass out."

"I want to argue, but you make a good point." Best not to think too hard about Beast calling me sexy as shit. I shake my head and lie down. Gravity seems to increase the second my head hits the pillow and my eyes close despite my best intentions. "She's not going to be handle another day like today so soon. I don't think any of us can."

"I know." I can't quite tell without seeing his face, but Beast sounds amused. Almost indulgent. "I have something else in mind."

I should demand to know what his plans are, should remind him that we're equals in this and so I should be involved in any big decisions and plans. I should do a lot of things. "Whatever you want, then."

Exhaustion weighs me down, but I swear I feel the faintest brush of fingertips against my forehead, smoothing my hair back and his low voice saying, "I want it all."

CHAPTER 16

BEAST

*A*nother night of rest, another night unbroken with the nightmarish memories riding me hard. Both Gaeton and Isabelle relax in sleep, and both of them are cuddlers. It amuses me to no end to wake up with Isabelle's nose pressed to the middle of my back and Gaeton's heavy arm over both of us. It's so fucking tempting to just stay in bed and soak up the closeness of these two people who are so determined to keep everyone at a distance.

Instead, I carefully extract myself and head to the bathroom. A quick shower later and I'm once again dressed in my own clothes. It feels a little strange after damn near twenty-four hours of wearing Gaeton's pants, but I need my head on straight for what comes next.

We have Ursa to deal with.

I don't think for a second that making a public show of solidarity will make her back off for good. She's hungry and ambitious, a shark scenting blood in the water after Orsino's death. If we hadn't tipped the balance, she might have contented herself with poking at our borders. No use worrying about what *might* have happened. We have to deal in facts.

That means contingency plans.

I'm on my third call of the morning when Isabelle wanders out of the bedroom. I'd heard her rustling around fifteen minutes ago and put on a pot of coffee, and she makes a beeline for it. I watch her pad around wearing Gaeton's shirt, and the sheer domesticity of this moment nearly knocks me off my feet. I want this. I'm determined to have it.

Nothing will stand in my way.

Not our history. Sure as fuck not the Sea Witch's ambitions.

Isabelle pours a cup of coffee and brings it to her lips. I don't know how she has any taste buds left when she drinks scalding hot coffee like that, but she's managed to get by for years just fine. How many mornings did we have like this when we were together? More than I want to count. The woman is a force to be reckoned with, but she's like the walking dead before her first hit of caffeine. I found that unbearably charming before, and I find it unbearably charming this morning, too.

She makes a little humming noise that goes straight to my cock and opens her eyes fully for the first time since she walked out. "Hi."

"Hi." I hang up, slip my phone into my pocket, and cross to her. She watches me, some wariness flickering into her dark eyes as she seems to remember all the history and bullshit. I carefully take the mug from her and set it on the counter and then catch her hips. "Morning."

"Morning," she echoes, still watching me as if she's trying to draw my thoughts right out of my head. "You seem different."

"Do I?" I snake a hand up her spine, pulling her flush to

my chest, and cup the back of her head. "It strikes me that I haven't kissed you properly in more than a year."

She licks her lips. "I noticed that, too."

How many times have I tugged her into my arms and kissed her? A hundred? A thousand? I can't begin to count. Never once did it feel as fraught as this moment, as if one wrong move will cave in the ground beneath our feet. "I'd like to."

A small furrow appears between her brows. "You've been commanding me to do all sorts of filthy things and now you're asking for a kiss?"

"It's different." Maybe it's sentimental as shit, but I want her to choose this in a moment when I'm not railroading her. Sex and kink can be the glue that holds the three of us together long enough for us to figure out something more permanent, but it *can't* be the only part of the foundation I fully intend to build. Not if I want it to last.

I massage the tight muscles at the base of her skull and she weaves a little on her feet. "Can I kiss you, Isabelle Belmonte?"

She hooks her arms around my neck and lets her mouth answer for her. I have to concentrate on keeping my feet at the first taste of her. This woman always kisses like she might never get the chance again. No hesitance. No shyness. She gives it her everything, every single time. It's different than I remember it. Better. Neither one of us are holding back now.

Lips and tongue and the barest tease of teeth.

Her kiss is a challenge I'm only too happy to meet. I dig my hands into her hair, tilting her face up for a better angle, and she makes a happy little noise. I could kiss this woman until my dying breath, but I force myself to gentle the contact, to finally break it and lift my head. Her eyes have gone a little hazy and she's leaning on me like she might not be able to hold herself up if I let go.

Isabelle licks her lips. "Good morning, indeed."

There are so many things I could say, so many options that will push us toward my endgame or leave us in disaster. Instead, I kiss her forehead and gently set her away from me. "Take a shower and get ready. We're having guests in an hour."

She blinks at me, something dangerous flickering into her dark eyes. "Beast, I have *none* of the things I need to get 'guest ready.' Gaeton doesn't even have a hairbrush in his bathroom."

That's what I suspected. "Trust me."

"Is this a kink thing?"

If I tell her yes, she'll stop arguing, but while I might lie to get my way when it suits me, honesty is the best bet right now. "No."

Isabelle picks up her coffee and stares at me over the rim. Her expression goes downright dangerous, every inch the powerful princess. "You know better than most that I have a public image to uphold. That's not vanity; it's fact. You bring anyone in here that aren't my sisters, and it's a territory issue. You *know* this. You can degrade me all you want for the next twelve days in private, but you don't get to do it in public."

That's about enough of that. I give her a long look that has her shifting her stance like a bratty submissive that just realized they've crossed over their Dom's line. "I know what's at stake, and I'm not going to do anything to jeopardize your standing or reputation. But I *will* degrade the fuck out of you in public when the situation calls for it." I step closer, caging her in with an arm braced on either side of her body. "Because that's what you get off on, princess. You want me to put you over my knee and flip up your skirt so everyone in the room can see how wet your cunt gets when I spank that pert little ass of yours. You'll get off harder knowing you have an audience."

She's breathing hard enough that I take the coffee back again to prevent her from spilling it on herself. Isabelle narrows her eyes. "That's not fair. You just said this wasn't a kink thing and now you're throwing a kink thing in my face. You don't get to have it both ways, Beast. You just don't."

She's not wrong. "I'm telling you to trust me, Isabelle. No more. No less." I state it blandly, as if I'm not asking for the stars when we both know I am. She might trust me with her body, with her safety, but she's never quite trusted me with her heart and future. Not yet.

She considers me for a long moment and finally nods, but not like she likes it. "Okay. But if you're only giving me an hour, I have to start now."

I step back. "By all means."

She picks up her coffee, as prim as the princess we call her, and strides back toward the bedroom. Gaeton walks through the doorway right as she gets there, and she goes up on her toes to give him a quick kiss. No telling if Isabelle notices the tension that thrums through his body at the contact, because she's gone before I get another look at her face.

Gaeton, though. He's not awake enough to hide from me. His expression reflects the growing determination not to let this go. Or, rather, not to let *her* go. I still have to seduce him into agreeing to a new set of terms.

Time. It all takes so much damn time.

I pour him a cup of coffee and hand it over as he reaches me. He eyes it like I might have tossed some poison in, too, but ultimately takes a sip. "I'm sore as fuck."

That surprises a snort out of me. "If you came out of yesterday *not* sore, you wouldn't be human."

He leans a hip against the counter next to me. A little too

close to be strictly professional, but not close enough to see it as an invitation. He's wearing those gray sweatpants again, and his big cock is a clear imprint against the front. Fuck, those things should be illegal.

"Beast." He says my name slowly, amusement flickering to life in his tone. "Are you checking out my dick?"

No point in denying it. If I want him to come to terms with us wanting each other, playing coy is the wrong call. "Yeah."

"Funny fuck, aren't you?" He takes another sip of coffee, watching me over the rim of his cup.

I lean back against the counter. "Don't think I'm going to forget the raincheck from last night."

"Hmmm." He doesn't look away, though a faint blush darkens his cheeks. Finally, Gaeton says, "Why is Isabelle in a huff?"

Part of me wants to ignore his changing the subject, but I've learned to be a patient hunter over the years. I don't have weeks to play this out, but I *do* have a little time. It'd be foolish not to utilize it. "She needs clothes. If we send for ones she already owns, Cordelia will figure out where we are and retrieve her."

Gaeton grins. "You called Tink."

"I called Tink."

He stretches, his fingertips brushing the ceiling. The move puts his entire body on display, and I allow myself to enjoy the show. Gaeton snorts. "Guess I'll get dressed, too. Tink and Hook might appreciate the sweatpants, but it hardly sends the right message."

I nod. "They'll be here in an hour."

Gaeton rumbles out a laugh. "You only gave Isabelle an hour's notice? No wonder she's pissed." He fills his coffee cup back to the brim. "We doing this tonight?"

"I don't think it's wise to wait. It's a Band-Aid, but it

might make Ursa back off long enough for us to figure things out and return to the territory." Even that might not be enough to divert her at this point, but I don't think she's hungry enough to try for a full-scale war. I could be wrong. I've been wrong before, and people I cared about paid the cost.

I won't let it happen again.

Gaeton stares at his bedroom door. "Think it's a mistake to plan this without talking to Isabelle first?"

My first instinct is to say no. We're the generals, we're the ones trained in what is essentially urban warfare. Orsino got his hands dirty right there with us until he was too sick to do so. He always kept his younger two daughters out of it, but Cordelia and her wife were there the last couple years, working on earning the trust of the people they command without Orsino overlooking everything. Sienna is dangerous in her own way. But Isabelle has always, always been kept away from the darker parts of what it means to be the Man in Black's daughter. I want to keep her shielded from it now.

But he's right. Trying to protect Isabelle Belmonte is what got us into this situation to begin with. If we'd both been honest when we started dating her, if one of us had slowed down long enough to realize that our hatred for each other felt a whole lot like stifled lust... The list goes on.

I finally nod. "We should talk to her."

"Ha." Gaeton slaps my shoulder. "So you *can* see reason."

He has no fucking idea.

CHAPTER 17

ISABELLE

I'm a disaster. A shower helps clear my head, but Gaeton's not set up for anyone but him. And Gaeton does not use makeup, hair products, or own so much as a hairbrush. I'm left to finger comb my wet hair and braid it back from my face. I don't know that I'll be able to get it *out* of this braid without a vat of conditioner, but it'll do for now.

It's not until I'm finally finished that I realize my next hurdle. "I have no clothes."

Beast looks up from his phone, frowning at me like I've just said something obvious. "That's the point."

Gods save me from dominant men. I speak slowly because the urge to yell is almost overpowering. "I have *no clothes*, Beast. People are showing up in fewer than ten minutes and I'm naked."

Gaeton walks out of the bedroom dressed to the nines in a black suit and a button-down shirt in a deep blue that's almost the same color as Beast's eyes. I wonder if that was on purpose. Beast is wearing his normal uniform of dark jeans and a plain T-shirt; today it's black. I wish I'd grabbed the shirt of Gaeton's that I wore to sleep in. Standing here naked is not an option, no matter how cavalier these two are acting.

"Isabelle." There's a strange soberness to Gaeton's voice that brings me around to face him again. "If we choose to have you naked, that's how you'll be." Before I can argue, he raises a hand, dangling a length of fabric from it. "Come here."

Even as I cross to him, recognition slams in to me. I know this fabric. It's a black silk robe that I bought him years ago, because I wanted to see his big, rough body clothed in a decadent fabric that I could open like the best kind of present. I still remember how hard we laughed when he put it on, and how much I enjoyed the sex that came after.

I reach out a shaking hand and touch it. "You kept it." I would have thought he took everything connected with me, dumped it in the nearest trash can, and doused it in gasoline for good measure. I certainly hadn't left the things that reminded me of him lying around.

But I hadn't had the heart to destroy them, either.

Every one of the little rose trinkets he bought me over the two years we dated currently occupies a carefully packed box in the back of my massive closet back home. I look up into his dark eyes, trying to find answers to questions I can't begin to voice. "You kept it," I repeat.

"I kept it." Nothing more, but what more answer do I need? He could have a thousand reasons for hanging onto it, and none of them might mean what I hope they mean.

That he still loves me. That maybe he never stopped.

He holds it open so I can step into it. The robe dwarfs me, pooling at my feet and gaping at my chest despite my attempts to tie it firmly. It's hardly a good option for meeting strangers, but they would have to pry it off me to make me change at this point. I can't stop stroking the fabric, can't stop remembering all the times I lay sprawled across his chest and did the same.

There are so many things to say, and I can't find the words to even begin. Before I have a chance to, the buzzer announces the arrival of Beast's guests. I take a seat on the chair facing the door and don't miss the way Gaeton leans against the wall at my back while Beast goes to answer the door despite it being Gaeton's apartment. Do they even notice how they've shifted their relationship since my father's death?

I rub my hand against my chest. Maybe there will come a time when the reality of my father being gone forever doesn't hit me with an almost-physical blow. When the loss of him doesn't rise like a rogue wave to drown me when I least expect it. Maybe.

I tense as the door opens, but the woman who walks through isn't the stranger I expect. I blink. "Tink?"

Tink stops short and narrows her eyes. She's a pretty, plus-sized white woman with a mass of blond hair and the personality of a honey badger. She's also a brilliant designer and responsible for most of the formal clothing in my closet right now. The man at her back is tall with medium-brown skin, a close-cropped beard and black hair that falls to his shoulders. Hook, the leader of one of the smaller territories in Carver City.

Tink looks at me for a long moment and then turns and levels a glare at both Beast and Gaeton. "What. The. Fuck." She points at me. "What the *fuck* is going on here?"

"Um," I say.

"No, they get to speak for themselves." She talks over me like I'm not even here and turns to point that accusing finger at Hook. "Did you know about this?"

He raises his hands. "I know as much as you."

"Good, because we would be having *words*." She spins

back to Gaeton and Beast. "We're friends. I consider us friends."

I have to twist to see Gaeton and he looks like he's facing down the honey badger I compared Tink to. "We are friends, Tink."

"That's good. Then you won't mind explaining why Isabelle Belmonte is sitting here in your robe, looking like she's been run over by a truck." She spares me the briefest glance. "No offense."

"None taken," I say faintly.

"There's a simple explanation," Beast interjects. *He* doesn't look ruffled, but Beast always shuts down his reactions in stressful moments.

"That's good. Because from what people are saying, it sure as fuck sounds like you hauled Isabelle out of the Underworld by her hair and have kept her locked up here as some kind of sex slave and, friends or not, I will castrate you right fucking now if that's the case." She's wearing a pair of jeans that look painted on and a cute flouncy crop top, so I don't *think* she has a weapon hidden anywhere, but both men tense up as if she just pulled out a gun and pointed it at them.

Beast takes half a step in front of my chair. "It's none of your business."

Hook whistles under his breath. "Good luck with that."

"You made it my business when you sent out an invite to bring me here—an invite, I might add, that sounded a *whole lot* like a command." Tink crosses her arms under her breasts. "I talk to Isabelle alone or I walk—and I will be walking right to Meg and letting her know that this fuckery is taking place in her and Hades's territory. Your choice."

I fully expect the men to fight her on this. Neither of them takes orders well from anyone other than my father, and Tink's married to the leader of an entirely different territory. But Beast finally steps back and Gaeton brushes a light hand across my hair. "Tell her whatever she wants to know, Isabelle."

I twist to look at him. I truly do not understand the power dynamics in the room right now. "What? Why?"

"Because she's a friend." He gives a smile that's almost a grimace. "And she doesn't bluff."

Their friend.

Maybe it's true, but there's a lot more in the way of undertones here that I don't understand. Or maybe I simply never stopped to think about what Gaeton and Beast would look like as friends with other people. They socialized with the people that work under them, but that always felt almost like an obligation. Both men keep others at a distance as a matter of course. The fact that this woman is here, is close enough to demand answers without them seeing it as a threat or digging in their heels …

Every new revelation about these two drives home the truth; I really don't know them as well as I thought I did.

Tink looks around and nods at the door to the bedroom. "In there. Now." Another cross look at the rest of the room. "Keep an eye on these two, Hook."

I follow slowly, clutching the robe to keep from flashing her. I've been alone with this woman many times in the past, but it feels a little like locking myself in with a tiger as I shut the door behind me.

She frowns at me and lowers her voice. "Look, I know better than anyone how the rumor mill churns in this city, but if you need me to get you out, I will."

I blink. "Why would you do that? You're their friend."

"No shit I'm their friend, and sometimes that means taking a hard line when they're fucking up." She hesitates, but finally props her hands on her hips. "I would like to believe that neither of those guys would keep you here if you didn't want to be, but Beast and Gaeton are fucked in the head when it comes to you, and the Man in Black dying has fucked them up worse. So as much as I'd like to say that they'd never do something so unforgivable, I can't guarantee it, which is why we're having this conversation." She crosses to me and flicks open the robe a little. "So I'll ask you again and I want an honest answer; are those bruises consensual or do I need to get you out?"

I look down. My body aches from everything we did yesterday, and I barely noticed the bruises. I flush with something like shame, though there's a level of possessive pride in there. I *earned* these marks. I meet and hold her green eyes. "It's none of your business, but I'm willing to give you an answer because I appreciate your offer, unnecessary as it is. The marks are consensual. I'm here because I want to be. If I wanted to walk out that door, they wouldn't be able to stop me."

She searches my face for a long time and finally exhales in a rush. "Thank fuck. I hoped they wouldn't drop into the deep end like that, but grief does weird shit to people and I couldn't be sure." She starts to sit on the bed and changes her mind halfway through. "I don't need any details you're not comfortable sharing, but I'd like some."

Most of it is common enough knowledge at this point. Beyond that, it's not a bad idea to have this woman in my corner. "They left after my father died." I wrestle down the grief pushing at the inside of my skin, just waiting to spill messily over everything. "Ursa is testing our boundaries, and we need them back."

"Uh-huh." Tink is still studying me. "And none of you three got over that mess from a year ago."

"And none of the three of us got over that, either," I confirm. It's difficult to keep my expression locked down. "We agreed on two weeks. It'll all be figured out by then."

Tink raises her brows. "Sure it will." She presses perfect

red-painted lips together. "Okay, fine, I won't hustle you out of here. You know why they called me?"

They haven't explicitly stated their plan, but I can hazard a few guesses. "I need clothes." They want to make a statement and Tink's designs are sure to do that, though I don't know what she can accomplish on this timeline. None of us have thought through things as much as we need to.

"You need a whole lot more than that." She shakes her head. "Damn men. We'll take care of this. Trust me."

Strangely enough, I do. Tink and I have never been friends. She's snarly and brilliant and all of our interactions have surrounded her measuring me, making suggestions, and then delivering stunning clothing items when she says she will. That said, I know plenty about her reputation. Anyone who can go toe-to-toe with the power players in Carver City, both in and out of the bedroom, is not someone to be taken lightly. "Okay."

She leads the way back into the main room of the apartment. The men are more or less exactly where we left them. Hook lights up like Tink has been gone a week instead of a few short minutes. Gaeton and Beast just look guarded.

Tink props her hands on her generous hips. "You two are acting like fools."

"Jeez, Tink, tell us how you really feel." Gaeton smiles, but it doesn't quite reach his eyes. Somehow, I know that if this situation wasn't about me, he'd be fully enjoying her attitude.

"Don't worry, I have an itemized list." I can't see her expression from here, but she sounds fearsome. "I'm going to text it to you, and then you and Beast are going to retrieve every single thing on the list for me. I don't want you back before then."

Beast is already shaking his head. "No. We're more than happy to pay your steep fees to get something put together now, but we're not leaving."

"Wrong again." She pulls her phone out and types quickly. Seconds later, both Gaeton and Beast's phones chime.

Gaeton's brows rise as he reads. "This list has twenty things on it. Some of this shit, I've never heard of."

"Get familiar. You want to seduce someone who invests as much into their appearance as Isabelle does—that wasn't a dig, by the way—you need to figure out the products that they need to accomplish it, and you need to figure it out fast." A sugary sweet edge filters into her voice, one that doesn't do a single thing to cover the poison beneath. "Get the fuck out, or I'll leave all three of you high and dry. And don't think for a second that I'm not charging you hazard pay for this entire day."

Beast and Gaeton exchanged one of those silent speaking glances. Finally, Beast shrugs. "You get a few hours on the condition that Hook stays." He looks at the other man. "I'm assuming you have a team in the building."

"You assume correctly."

"It'll be enough." Beast crosses to me and tips my chin up with a finger. "What do you want, Isabelle?"

That's a question I still don't have an answer to. I'm starting to fear I never will. I try for a smile, but the expression doesn't feel right on my face. "Tink appears to have things well in hand."

He searches my expression and nods once. "We won't be long."

Not a single person mentions that it'd be simple to order the items and have them couriered here. There's a bit of shuffling around as Hook's people bring up a sewing machine and a rack filled with wardrobe bags. Then Gaeton and Beast are gone, Hook's team are sent to secure the perimeter, and I'm left with these two people I barely know.

Hook brushes a soft kiss to Tink's lips. "I'd tell you to be gentle, but I know better."

"That's right. You *do* know better."

He drops into the chair Gaeton occupied and pulls out his phone. Seconds later, he seems entirely consumed with whatever he's reading. Tink turns to give me a long look. "You shy?"

"Not particularly."

"If you want Hook in another room or facing away, it's fine, but I need you to try on a few things. We don't have a time to put together a dress from scratch, so we'll adjust some of the stuff I have on hand."

I glance at Hook, but he doesn't seem to pay us the least bit of attention. I know it's a lie. If he thinks for a second that I'm a threat, he'll neutralize me immediately. But I appreciate how respectful he's being. He has a good reputation, both as a man and as a territory leader, and so far he's living up to it. "It's fine."

"I'll take you at your word. Lose the robe."

I shrug out of it and drape it over the arm of the couch. Tink circles me and whistles. "They did a number on you."

Impossible not to blush. "I enjoyed it."

"Yeah, I'm getting that." She stops in front of me and narrows her eyes. "You've lost weight. I can see that even without measuring you again. You're not taking care of yourself."

"It's been a rough couple of months." The understatement of the century.

Tink winces. "Right. I'm sorry. My condolences on the loss of your father."

I never know what to say to people who offer their condolences or apologies. No amount of words in any combination will bring him back or lessen the pain of losing him. *Nothing* can combat the gaping hole in my chest, though being with Beast and Gaeton helps distract me. Without their presence in the apartment, the darkness nips at my edges, tearing away bits of my armor and what little peace I found in the arms of the two men I love.

I clear my throat. "Thanks."

If Tink sees the way I blink too often to avoid the wetness in my eyes overflowing, she chooses to ignore it. Instead, she turns to the garment bags and unzips them one by one. "I grabbed everything I have ready. We'll get you a few options to work with, and when I'm done, you'll look amazing enough that no one will wonder how you're feeling."

She gets it. Somehow, she understands. I manage to smile past the burning in my throat. "Thank you." This time, I truly mean it.

CHAPTER 18

GAETON

We hunt down every single item on Tink's list. Like she said, it takes longer than I expect. The woman was mighty specific when it comes to cosmetics and all the products that apparently go into the upkeep of hair and body and, fuck, I'm exhausted just thinking about it. It's also pricey as hell.

Through it all, Beast and I don't talk much. His head is obviously a million miles away, and I'm still wrapped up in a whole lot of conflict. It's not until we're on our way back to the apartment that I finally put the feeling into words. "Are we doing the right thing?"

"There is no such thing as 'right.' Not in our world." Beast shifts the bags around on his wrist. "We're not the heroes. Pretending otherwise is enough to get people killed."

I shoot him the look that statement deserves. "Someone's feeling melodramatic."

"Sorry, am I stepping on your toes? I know you're the drama queen of the trio."

I bristle, ready to snap back, but stop when I catch a faint smile curving his lips. I frown. "You're fucking with me."

"I'm fucking with you," he says. He gives that rasping chuckle that I'm starting to like so much. "There will be plenty of time for serious shit and overthinking. Try to relax. We got this."

"Do we? Do we really?" I narrow my eyes. "You didn't answer my question. Are we doing the right thing?"

Beast slows and stops in front of my apartment building, finally turning to give me his full attention. "I don't know if we're doing the right thing. I don't think there *is* a 'right thing' in this scenario. There's only what we want." He stands there, steady and oh so serious. "I don't give a fuck about *right*. I don't want to stop. Do you?"

"No, I don't want to stop." As much as the last two days have hurt, it's a sweet sort of pain. It almost feels like this experience might actually lance the festering wound of losing Isabelle the first time. Something I never thought possible.

Then again, I can't see how losing her a second time won't make everything worse. It almost killed me to walk away from her before. Doing it again…

Not to mention my feelings for Beast are hardly cut and dried. The more we smudge the lines, the more I see that maybe they never were. Rage and lust can be two sides to the same coin, just like hate and love. Maybe I was never able to admit that before, but I can now.

It's funny, though I don't feel much like laughing, but the one thing I couldn't have anticipated when I agreed to this was that I might miss *Beast.* No matter what else happens, when this is all over, I'll never be able to look at him again without thinking about how good he tastes, about how good he made me feel when we were together.

It might feel good now, but that's just setting us all up for a bigger fall at the end. "There is no happy ending when this is over."

"Are you so sure?" He starts walking before I can divine what the fuck he means, moving fast enough that I have to hustle to make it to the elevator despite his shorter legs.

I glare at him in the mirrored doors as they slide shut. "What the hell is that supposed to mean?" The question doesn't come out as sharp as I intend it. No, I sound like I'm asking him to reassure me.

"It means, Gaeton, that you're thinking too hard and your emotions are getting the best of you. Enjoy this time we have."

As if it's that simple. I turn to face him. He looks just like he always does, cool and calm and collected and far too beautiful to be real. I'll never tell him as much, but his scars make him more human, more grounded in reality with the rest of us. They aren't flaws. They're proof that he's not some otherworldly being with perfect control who is above making mistakes.

"How did you get your scars?" I blurt out the question before I can think better of it.

He doesn't seem to breathe for a second. "Some of them are from the reality of a life like ours. You have scars too."

"Not like yours."

"No, not like mine." He holds my gaze. "I made a mistake and paid the price."

It means everything and nothing. For all his reputation, Beast is human and humans make mistakes. I've just never heard him admit as much. "So you can make mistakes." I knew that. Of course I knew that. But, aside from my personal feelings, the man has been above reproach when it comes how he operates as a general. He's fearless and bold and his mind makes jumps that I don't always understand but that always, always seem to be the right calls.

He's even saved my life a time or two, though neither of us have ever spoken about it.

"Yeah, I can make mistakes." His eyes go icy. "I lost the person I cared about once, Gaeton. I'll do anything to ensure it doesn't happen again. Fucking *anything*."

I can understand that, even if it makes some part of me heavier in response. I should have known that Beast wouldn't let something as mundane as lust get him twisted. He wants me. He wouldn't have proposed we muddy the waters by fucking if he didn't. But it's obvious that's all it is for him. Fucking.

No reason for that to disappoint me. The last thing this situation needs is further complications. It's smart as shit to lock my heart away until I know how things will fall out.

Too bad I was never as good at protecting myself as I am at protecting others.

I turn back to face the doors. My voice sounds rougher than I intend it when I finally manage to speak. "I get it. We both want her. That's why we're doing this." It's what we agreed on to begin with, so I don't know why it stings to say it aloud. "Don't think I'll make it easy on you, Beast. She'll get both our A-games right up until she makes a choice."

"Mmm." The noise he makes means absolutely nothing to me. Apparently he's not in the mood to elaborate, because the second the doors open, he steps out and leaves me to follow in his wake.

The first thing I notice upon entering my apartment is the faint scent of garlic and marinara that permeates the space. Someone's been cooking. Then my attention lands on where Tink has set up shop at the table. She's packing up her sewing machine and doesn't bother to look over as we walk in. She's pissed, and part of me feels bad about it, but not enough to change our plans. Beast's right. We have to see it through to the end.

Hook pulls something out of the oven and sets it on the

stove. He glances at me and gives a faint smile. "Figured you three could do with the calories."

Tink finishes fastening the sewing case and marches over to me. I brace for anything from a sharp word to a punch, but she just pulls me into a hug. She's so short, she barely reaches my chest, but I let myself enjoy the comfort for a few seconds before she lets go. Tink looks up at me, her expression fierce. "You are fucking up. I don't care what you decide when it comes to her and Beast, but don't you dare hurt yourself to make them happy." She glances at Beast. "The same goes for you, asshole."

He gives that shrug that means everything and nothing and starts unloading the bags on the coffee table. "We've got it covered."

"No, you don't." She shakes her head. "But you aren't going to listen to me."

"We have it covered," I say softly.

Tink gives me one last squeeze and steps back. "You are my friend, and I care about you, but if you don't figure this out, it's going to rip you to pieces."

"Tink," Hook sinks enough warning in her name that her eyes flash in response. He moves to secure her stuff on the wardrobe rack and pushes it toward the elevator. Hook pauses in front of me. "Be careful."

I don't know what to say to that. I appreciate their concern, but I've gone too far to turn back now. One way or another, we're seeing this through to the end. "Thanks for the help."

"We're friends." He shrugs, and then gives me a bright grin. "And don't thank me until you've seen my wife's bill." The way he says *wife* speaks volumes, and I have to stifle a surge of jealousy. Even when he and Tink were dancing around each other, there was only the two of them figuring things out. Hook never had to compete for her heart, and he sure as fuck didn't have to compete with someone as perfect as Beast.

We wait until they leave to go looking for Isabelle. I'm not at all surprised to find her curled up in my bed, but the sight still rocks me back on my heels. It feels so fucking fleeting, a dream I'm afraid to sink into for fear that I'll wake up alone.

"You're up," Beast murmurs and shifts past me to haul the bags into the bathroom.

I don't know if I should appreciate his bowing out of this moment or be suspicious because he's so confident that he's not greedy for every second of experience with her. In the end, it doesn't matter. I kick off my shoes and climb onto the bed to settle next to her. She's not under the comforter; instead, she's wrapped up in one of the throw blankets from the living room. I trace my finger down her temple and over her jaw. "Isabelle."

Her eyes flutter open, and the happiness I find there takes my breath away. She smiles and stretches like a cat. "Hi."

"Hey."

Isabelle wiggles closer, tucking herself against me, and my heart gives a dull thud as I pull her into my arms. This isn't forever, but my goddamn fucking chest isn't listening. It feels so *right* to hold her like this while she surfaces from her nap.

She nuzzles my chest. "Tink is scary."

That surprises a chuckle out of me. "Yeah, she's definitely that." She's also become one of my closest friends over the last year. She caught me in the midst of my spiral after losing Isabelle, and kicked my ass until I figured my shit out.

"You know she would have gotten me out if I asked? I thought she was your friend."

"She is." It should piss me off that Tink would go around me like that, but it feels strangely good. There was a time when she wouldn't have even considered making that offer.

"But just because she's my friend, doesn't mean she's giving me carte blanche to act like a monster."

"You're not a monster." She wraps her arms around me and hitches a leg over my hip. It's not sexual, exactly; more like she wants to be as close as she possibly can be. "You do monstrous things sometimes, but you're not a monster. Neither of you are."

There it is again. The reminder that I'll never be her one and only. I tense, waiting for the slap of pain that knowledge always brings, but there's only a settling deep inside me. I don't know what it means. Maybe I'm just resigned to the truth now.

She leans back enough to meet my gaze. "Gaeton, I—"

Something akin to panic shorts out my brain at the possibilities of what she might say next. "We got all the shit on Tink's list, and Hook made dinner. Figure we should eat and then get ready. Glad you got a nap, since tonight's going to be a long one. Let's eat and get moving."

A small furrow appears between her brows, but she finally nods. "Okay."

When I agreed to this, I didn't think for a second that I would win. Even with all the truths coming out to play, my opinion hasn't changed. Why would she choose me when she can have *him?* Beast might make me want to punch a hole in a wall half the time, but he's a brilliant general and an even better Dom. Now that he's off his leash, I can't imagine a scenario where Isabelle chooses me over him. I just don't see it.

Fuck, I'm not sure *I* would choose me over him.

I climb out of bed before that knowledge sinks beneath my skin and tears me down. We have this time. It has to be enough. I have to be okay with watching them fall back in love, with knowing that there's no way Beast will let her go again, with living the rest of my life almost within touching distance of the future I want more than anything.

I don't know what Beast sees on my face when we walk into the main room, but he frowns. "We'll talk after dinner, while Isabelle gets ready."

It should be as simple as planning out the kink for the night, but one of the downsides of working with an excellent Dom is that they're equally excellent at reading people. We have to be during a scene. Communication is vital to everyone having a good time, but it's also vital to be able to course correct if a submissive isn't one hundred percent there with you and isn't able or willing to spell it out.

I really don't like being the submissive in this scenario.

Dinner is a subdued event. The food is amazing, but then Hook always had a knack for putting together a meal. I still circle around to his and Tink's place once every couple of weeks for dinner and some friendly fucking. If Isabelle chooses me, that's out of the question for obvious reasons.

If she doesn't choose me, I'm going to need Hook and Tink more than ever.

I'm a morose fucker tonight, but I can't shake the feeling adding weight to my skin. Even with all the emotional bull-shit to wade through, it's *too good* with Isabelle and Beast. It doesn't feel like getting her out of my system. In fact, it's the exact opposite. It feels like I've invited him in, too, like both these people are digging deep enough to rip me to shreds when this pact reaches its inevitable conclusion.

I start in on dishes because I need to keep my hands busy. It doesn't do a damn thing to help my spiraling thoughts, but it's still better than sitting still. No matter how intently I try to distract myself, I'm still aware of Isabelle padding into my bedroom and the shower turning on. I'm equally aware of Beast taking up a position at my back, leaning against the counter across from the sink.

I brace, but he doesn't start in on me the way I expect. Instead, he lets loose a nearly soundless sigh and grabs a towel from the drawer. "You wash, I'll dry."

No point in arguing. It's not one I'll win, and while there are times when the act of fighting is enough, tonight isn't one of them. We wash and dry the dishes, and with his help, it takes far less time than I'd like. Then there's nothing to do but turn to face him.

I study his expression, but there's no evidence that he's feeling anywhere near as conflicted as I am. "This was a mistake."

"Was it?"

"Don't do that."

He raises his brows. "Don't do what?"

"Don't act like this is such a simple situation." I haven't had the urge to punch that perfect face in longer than I care to admit, but I kind of want to punch him right now. "She didn't reject *you* before. Fuck, she's so wrapped up in you, she can't see straight. So forgive me if I'm not exactly elated to know that at the end of this, I'll be the one left hanging in the wind."

I expect him to gloat a little. To confirm what I've seen with my own two eyes. Fuck, maybe even to laugh a little in that dry way of his.

Instead he stares at me like he wants to shake some sense into me. "You think she didn't reject me? We didn't last a month after you walked away. Even when we weren't a true triad, we didn't work without you there to balance us."

"We *aren't* a true triad, Beast. That's the whole fucking point."

He opens his mouth, but seems to change his mind at last minute. "You're borrowing trouble and it's going to drag down the rest of our time together if you're determined to be so focused on the end."

Why is he being so intentionally naive? It's not a word I would have dreamed to apply to this man, but there's no other way to describe it. He's too smart to believe the shit he's spewing. "It's not like it's a year-long pact, Beast. It's fewer than two weeks. The end is already in sight. It was the second we agreed to this."

His jaw goes hard. "Will you or will not you not honor it?"

I draw myself up, ready to fight if only to expel this poisonous feeling worming through my chest and stomach. "Maybe I should make it easy and walk right now. Clear the way for you."

Beast steps to me, getting right in my face despite the difference in our heights. "I thought you loved Isabelle."

"I do. I did."

His eyes freeze over and his voice gains a cruel edge. "Some marriage you would have given her if you're ready to run scared at the first sign of trouble. Did you really want forever, or did you just want the prize?"

"Fuck you."

He lowers his voice. "Get your head in the game, Gaeton. This isn't about just us anymore, and you being all up in your feelings is going to get someone killed. It's going to get Isabelle killed."

Low blow to throw that in my face, but he's not wrong. I drag my hand through my hair. "How is this not fucking you up, too?"

"How is *what* not fucking me up?"

"Don't play coy, Beast. You know what is. The pact. Us. All of it."

"Us ..." He carefully places his hands on the counter on either side of me, his expression going predatory in a way that makes my stomach leap. "Did you ever think about it before?"

That pulls me up short. "What are you talking about?" I should know better at this point. Beast never comes at a confrontation head-on. He prefers to flank his opponent, to catch them flat-footed. The reminder that *I'm* the opponent feels like a slap in the face.

"*Us.*" He doesn't wait for me to catch up, just keeps talking in that measured way of his. "I lied when I told you what my fantasy was."

"Yeah, I know." I'd wondered about it at the time, but was too tired to press the issue. "Why bring it up now?"

Beast closes the last bit of distance between us, bringing us chest to chest. My instincts get all tangled up. I can't tell if we're about to fight or fuck, and I freeze. He leans up and his teeth graze my jaw in a nip. "You're not being honest with either of us, Gaeton."

"Obviously neither of us are," I grind out. "What are you talking about, specifically?"

"Do you remember that afternoon?" He keeps going even as my mind tries to flicker away what I *know* he's talking about. "You were in Isabelle's bed, and she was riding your cock. The sunlight bathed your skin golden and she was so wet, I could hear it from the door."

Just like that, I'm back in that memory I've shoved down deep. Isabelle's pussy clamped tight around my cock, her tits bouncing a little with each thrust, her eyes closed as she rides me. A movement behind her as the door slides soundlessly open. My gaze snagging Beast's across the distance and, for the first time, not seeing loathing reflected there. Only desire.

It wasn't aimed solely at Isabelle, either.

I draw in a ragged breath. "Yeah, I remember."

"We pretended it never happened. Never spoke of it." He presses his hips to mine, demonstrating that he's just as turned on by the memory as I am. "In my fantasy, I walked

162

in. Stripped. Joined you both in that bed. I punished you for getting started without me, and then we all fucked until we exhausted ourselves."

The air in the room has gone hot and sticky. I can't seem to inhale fully. "You never said anything."

"Neither did you." He leans back just enough to hold my gaze. "Do you trust me, Gaeton?"

A few days ago, I would have shot back a negative answer. It wouldn't have been the full truth, not when I trusted this man over and over again through the years to watch my back and keep our people safe. Even when we were at each other's throats, he never hesitated to ensure I came home every night, no matter how dangerous a mission or task we were sent out on.

My heart wasn't on the line then. It is now.

It's possible that this is all part of some deeper plan to fuck me over, that Beast wants me off my game so he can walk with Isabelle at the end of this. But... I don't think so. We're in unmarked territory, but for the first time since I agreed to this pact, I don't feel like I'm walking this strange path alone. "Yes."

"Good." He gives me a faint smile. "One last question. Do you want to walk through our plans for tonight together or do you want me to handle it?"

"Together." I exhale slowly. "Let's figure it out together."

CHAPTER 19

ISABELLE

*I*t feels so good to get ready with a full array of hair products and makeup; like I'm reclaiming part of myself that I haven't been on speaking terms with for the last forty-eight hours. I'm not delusional enough to think it will affect the power balance, but it makes me feel steadier all the same. The woman looking back at me in the mirror is still in over her head, but at least she looks good while she drowns.

My phone pings as I finish touching up my lipstick. I almost don't want to look at it. Undoubtedly, it's one of my sisters, and neither option sounds appealing right now. Cordelia will demand to know where I am so she can retrieve me. She's got the makings of being as good a leader as our father, but she's not rational when it comes to the people she loves. It doesn't matter that we need Beast and Gaeton back; she thinks I've sold myself for their loyalty and my being hurt by that choice is something she can't abide by.

Father never would have let it get this far.

I close my eyes and concentrate on breathing slowly until the burning behind my eyelids passes. It doesn't matter what Father would or would not have done. He's gone, and the responsibility that he seemed to shoulder with such ease has fallen to us. Cordelia needs her head in the game, and I cannot fail in bringing these men back into the fold. Lives depend on it.

Easier to focus on that purpose than the conflicted feelings inside me. If the last two days have taught me anything, it's that I never stopped loving Gaeton and Beast. Worse in some ways, now that we've forcibly torn down the film of *niceness* that coated our past relationships, I love them more. Something I didn't think was possible. Suffice to say it's an inconvenient truth. There is no walking away from this unbloodied. I check my phone before I can procrastinate further.

Sienna: Check your email and get the answers back to me ASAP.

Me: You know, algorithms aren't the answer to everything.

Sienna: Do you have a better option?

Me: ...

Sienna: I didn't think so. Answer the questions and I'll get the program put together.

I don't exactly have a high horse to stand on for this situation. Her algorithm sounds like a terrible idea, but so does a two-week sex pact. I open my email and find the shared document she wants me to fill out. I hold my breath and click through. The questions are both what I expect, and not what I expect. Everything from the ability to give a dual orgasm to cuddling to whether or not they leave their laundry in a pile on the floor or put it away immediately. I'm a little impressed at her thoroughness despite myself.

I glance at the time and perch on the edge of the tub to fill out the answers. It's weirdly nostalgic to type them out, a reminder of a time when things weren't exactly simpler, but there wasn't a deadline hanging over my head. Answering these questions brings up memories I haven't allowed myself to think of since my respective relationships ended.

Like how Beast had a knack for showing up when I least expected it with a sweet treat or a cup of coffee. Or the one time I came back to my room after a long day dealing with my sisters and found that he'd cleaned it so every surface practically shone. He didn't always use words to tell me how he felt about me, but he spoke through his actions time and time again.

And Gaeton? He was always, always willing to try anything I was into, whether it was to listen to a book I was reading on audio or to marathon a show I wanted to try out. We could laugh and giggle and sing in the car like goofs and I never felt like I had to be cool and collected in order for him to want me.

Even when we weren't communicating our deeper needs, it was so good being with them in other ways. I swallow hard. *Just answer the questions and move on.* I finish quickly enough and send a text letting her know. I still don't think an algorithm will help me decide things, but Sienna won't leave it alone and, honestly, it can't hurt.

Then there's nothing to do but get dressed. Tink left me three dresses to choose from and I run my hands over one after the other. Black and a deep purple and a cheery yellow. I touch the yellow. Another time. The black is a better option, though it's something more in-your-face sexy than I've ever worn in public.

I carefully pull it on. The fabric fits like a second skin, making it impossible to wear anything under it, an asymmetrical cut that is long sleeved on one side and sleeveless on the other. It featured two cut-outs, one a deep diamond between my breasts, the other a circle right at the curve of my waist that leaves half my hip exposed. It's not exactly indecent, but it's the kind of dress that makes one think of easy access and fucking. The fact that it hits the top of my knees does nothing to combat how naked I feel; more naked than when I actually *was* naked.

I take another deep breath and shake out my hair, giving it a little extra toss for volume. I look like a sex kitten, like the dirty little slut I play for these men.

I … like it.

Beast is waiting for me in the bedroom, dangling a pair of strappy black heels from his finger. He drinks me in, his gaze going hot and intense. "You look good, princess."

"Thank you." I clear my suddenly dry throat. Strange to feel so affected when I've literally been naked with him for two days, but nothing makes sense when it comes to this situation any more. I reach for the shoes, but he shakes his head. "Sit."

"I can do it myself."

"I know. But I want to."

Impossible to argue with that. I sit on the edge of the bed. My heart leaps into my throat as he goes down to one knee before me. "Beast—"

"I have a question, and I want you to answer it honestly." He lifts my foot and slips it into the first heel. His hands have committed more acts of violence than I can begin to guess, but he touches me like I'm something priceless, due the utmost care. It should irritate me, should be a reminder to how he never let me see the truth of him before. It's different this time. I don't know why.

He doesn't speak again until he has my second shoe on, and then he pins me with a look. "Why didn't you choose one or the other to begin with?"

A lump forms in my throat. It's a question I've been asked dozens of times, from my father to people who are barely more than strangers. The only two who never actually asked me are Gaeton and Beast. They're the only ones I owe an answer to. "Because I'm selfish." When he just waits, obviously wanting more, I press my lips together. I can do this. I can be honest. "You are both so different. I wanted you because you're this mystery wrapped up in the prettiest package I've ever seen. I wanted Gaeton because he's giant and brutal and yet has the biggest heart of anyone I've ever met. Being with you brings out different things in me." My voice wobbles a little bit, but I power through. "And I *liked* that you were both mine, that I was both of yours. The things Gaeton accused me of are the truth of it. Part of me got off on bouncing back and forth between you."

His expression gives me nothing. No condemnation. Certainly not forgiveness. "There are people who aren't meant for monogamy, Isabelle."

I'm not sure if he's trying to absolve or condemn me. "If you really believed that, you wouldn't be having me choose at the end of this." I hold up a shaking hand when he starts to speak. "I'm not trying to get out of the choice. I'm just saying that what we had before didn't work. We can't go back to that."

"No, what we had before didn't work." He rises smoothly to his feet and tugs me off the bed. "Do you trust us to take care of you tonight?"

I try for a smile, but it doesn't feel natural on my face. "I thought you wanted to punish me."

"Those two things aren't mutually exclusive." He brushes strokes a finger down my jaw. "You're going to be on display, princess. Are you ready for that?"

I don't know. I truly don't. Part me wants to curl up in a ball at being the center of a scene in front of an audience. But the rest of me? My skin goes hot and my pussy gives a pulse of desire. If it was just me, maybe it would feel different, but it's *not* just me. I have Beast and I have Gaeton and, if things are beyond complicated between us, I still trust them to guide me through. "Yes."

"Good." He leads me out into the main room where Gaeton is waiting for us. "We have something for you."

Gaeton's the one who opens the large square box before me. The smile he had for Tink is nowhere in evidence now. I want to apologize, but words aren't enough anymore. Maybe they never were.

To distract myself, I look down and go still. The solid black collar is plain enough, but the carefully crafted rose in the center needs no other ornamentation. I reach out tentatively and brush my finger against the red petals. They're all jewels, cut into a perfect rendition of my favorite flower.

"This tells everyone in the Underworld that you're ours." Gaeton holds perfectly still. "Will you take it?"

"Yes." I don't have a choice, but that's not why anticipation thrills through my blood. This marks them as mine as much as it marks me as theirs. I want that marking. I want the world to know that I am connected to these two men. That I am owned by them. A primitive, uncomfortable feeling, but I refuse to shy away from it. The last couple days haven't been easy by any means, but the harshness of our words and actions have been a strange sort of balm for my soul.

This is that nebulous thing I always craved but could never define. The element missing from both my relationships with them.

Beast takes the box from Gaeton. "Put it on her."

Seeing the delicate collar in his big hands does something for me. I press my lips together and hold perfectly still has he lifts my hair off my neck and fastens the collar around my neck. His fingers linger against my nape for the barest second. "Too tight?"

"No."

He steps back, depriving me of his solidness at my back. I close my eyes for a long moment to try to get control of my emotions. I feel like an exposed nerve right now. No matter how close we get, Gaeton keeps holding himself at a distance.

I don't know if he can ever truly forgive me.

I don't know if I can pick him if forgiveness isn't on the table, even if it's a forgiveness I don't deserve.

When I open my eyes, it's to find Beast watching me. I catch him completely unfiltered for an entire breath, the longing on his face potent enough to rock me back on my heels. I don't know if he's looking at me or at Gaeton at my back. Before I can figure it out, he locks himself down again, his expression carved in ice just like it always is. "Let's go."

The trip to the Underworld is no less strange this time around, albeit in a different way. Beast leads us past the beautiful front desk guy, with Gaeton half a step behind me. Through the towering door and into the carefully dim lounge. I start to look around, but Gaeton's quiet "eyes forward, Isabelle" jerks my gaze to the center of Beast's back. I promised I'd follow their lead, and this is the barest of an order. It'd be foolish to disobey over something so mundane.

We end up in a booth in the middle of the section, with me between the two men. Beast and Gaeton exchange a look, and Beast slips away before Gaeton has a chance to say anything. The big man glares, but remains at my side. I smooth my hands down the slick fabric of my dress. "Have I done something to piss you off in the last twelve hours?"

"What?" He finally looks at me, *really* looks at me. "Why would you say that?"

I lift my brows. "Really, Gaeton? Can you think of anything you've done that might lead me to this conclusion?"

He flushes a little and leans back, some of the tension bleeding out of his body. "I suppose since we demand honesty from you, offering anything less in return is a shitty thing to do."

"I suppose so." I find myself holding my breath. If we were good at communicating before, maybe we wouldn't have left a trail of trauma behind us to get to this place. If we have any hope at a future, we have to be able to *talk*. "Can you just tell me this—is there any chance of you forgiving me?"

Shock widens his eyes a little. "I've already forgiven you."

"No, you haven't." I shake my head. "It's okay that you haven't. I hurt you terribly. But what I need to know is if there's a possibility I can earn your forgiveness."

He inhales like he's going to argue with me, but further tension bleeds from his body with his exhale. "I don't know. I ..."

I fight for a tentative smile even though his answer feels like a punch in the solar plexus. "Thank you for being honest."

Gaeton reaches to smooth my hair back from my face, his hand moving as if he can't help himself. "I never stopped loving you. I don't think either of us did. It's just all tangled up in the other shit."

"There's a lot of other shit." That's the crux of the matter. Maybe if we'd all been this honest the first time around, we'd have a chance. Two weeks is not enough time to fight for both the future and to be free of the sins of the past. Choosing one of them might very well be a moot point, just prolonging the inevitable crash and burn. "I don't know if we can find a way through."

His gaze trails to where Beast is leaning against the bar, wearing his customary dark jeans and plain T-shirt. "Beast has a plan. I just can't decide if it's a good one or downright disastrous."

I cautiously lean my head against his broad shoulder

and nearly whimper with relief when he wraps his arm around me and tucks me against his side. "I missed you," I whisper.

He tenses, but it's almost like he can't hold it. Gaeton pulls me closer and brushes a kiss to my temple. "I missed you, too."

I half expect Beast to be irritated that we're cuddling while he's retrieving drinks, but he looks inordinately pleased as he walks back to the booth to find me nearly in Gaeton's lap. He carefully sets the drinks on the table in front of us. Whiskey for him and Gaeton. A gin and tonic for me. He slides into the booth on my other side and then I'm sandwiched between them. Beast starts to speak, but a new group of people walk into the lounge and he leans back, words unsaid.

I see why when the pair of men peel off, leaving two women striding toward the bar. One is white and slight, with short white-blond hair. She's wearing pleated gray trousers that stop at her ankles and show off red-bottomed heels. Suspenders cling to her narrow shoulders and frame her pristine white blouse.

The other woman is tall and Black. Her long hair is styled in thin dreadlocks that start black and shift to a rich red at the ends, and she's wearing a wrap dress that shows off her generous curves to maximum effect.

The women are stunning.

They're also two of the most dangerous people in Carver City.

Malone and Ursa.

Ursa's attention lands on us and she gives a satisfied smile as if we're right where she expected us to be. She motions for Malone to keep heading to the bar and strides to our booth, her brightly printed dress swishing with each step. She glances at the men and then narrows her attention on me.

"My condolences on the loss of your father." She almost sounds like she means it.

"Thank you." The reply is automatic.

Ursa's gaze flicks to the collar around my neck. "I didn't realize you were a patron of the Underworld."

Neither Beast nor Gaeton seem that inclined to jump in, but it's just as well. At the end of the day, they are generals and I'm the sister of the new territory leader. I have to be able to stand on my own, or run the risk of telegraphing a weakness that will have sharks circling, scenting blood in the water. Ursa's already at our doorstep. We can't afford to have anyone else sniffing around. "It's a recent development, brought along by a mutual interest." I lean back a little, letting Beast and Gaeton's strength cushion me on either side. "I'm sure you understand."

"With those two delicious specimens, no one can blame you." She finally gives the men her full attention. "It is *both* of you, isn't it? I would hate to see another situation like before, where you're hauling these boys around by their heartstrings. It's an entertaining spectacle, but hardly sends the message of strength."

"Ursa." I draw on every bit of training I've had growing up, knowing how to wield words as effectively as my men wield weapons. "I would think our current situation speaks for itself."

Her smile widens as if I've delighted her by daring to push back. "I suppose we'll see, won't we? Have a good night, Isabelle. The Underworld has a number of delights to offer. It'd be a shame if you left without partaking."

I match her smile, feeling more than a little vicious. "I wouldn't dream of it."

"Wonderful." She nods at Beast and Gaeton and then strides to the bar where Malone waits, having watched the whole thing.

I don't let myself relax. "No going back now."

"There never was, princess." Beast laces his fingers through mine and lifts our joined hands to press a kiss to my knuckles. "Don't worry about performing. Just trust us to take you through it."

As if it's that easy. Maybe it *is* that easy for them.

I glance up at Gaeton, but he's back to shielding his thoughts from me. It's just as well. This isn't the time or place for the conversation we need to have. I don't know *when* the time and place is, though. I don't have the answers he obviously needs. He doesn't know if he has the forgiveness I crave. We are an unmitigated mess.

Beast squeezes my hand. "Ready?"

No. Not in the least. And yet a part of me is more than happy to nod, to do anything to muffle the thoughts crowding in, threatening to suffocate me. "I'm ready."

"Then let's go."

CHAPTER 20

*B*east moves to let me out of the booth as a familiar-looking Black woman walks up. I frown. I know I've seen her before, but it's fuzzy. She's slim with blue hair and is wearing a short white dress that leaves her mile-long legs bare. Her toes are painted a bright blue to match her hair and she gives me a sunny smile. "You probably don't remember me, but I'm Aurora."

"Hello." I glance at the men, but they both have their expressions locked down. "Was your hair pink before?"

"Yep." She shoots them a look that's both friendly and one of warning. This, I recognize. She's another friend who isn't pleased with recent events but cares for them nonetheless. "The room's ready for you, gentleman."

At this, Gaeton cracks a lazy arrogant smile. "Aw, Aurora, don't ice us out. You know you can't stay mad at us long."

"That remains to be seen," she says primly, but she looks like she's fighting a smile. "This way, please."

One last look at my men and then I follow her to the door leading deeper into the club. She leads the way through the main room, moving quickly enough that I don't

175

have a chance to see more than a flash of skin, hear the heavy thud of a paddle hitting flesh. Then we're in the hallway interspersed with many doors. Deeper and deeper into the hallway, until she finally opens a normal-looking door.

I step inside and look around. It's ... "A locker room?"

"Hmm? Yes." She grins. "Who hasn't fantasized about fucking the quarterback after the football game?"

I manage a smile of my own. "Guilty."

"We also use it to store some of the extra stuff. These lockers aren't just for show." She makes a face. "Though they smell better than the real thing."

I like her. I have no doubt in my mind that she's fucked both the men I love—I suspect Tink has, too—but I like her. "You aren't happy with Beast and Gaeton."

Aurora looks like she considers whether to play naïve, but finally shrugs. "I know enough of the details to know that they haven't gotten over you. Just like I know that revenge fucking you, or whatever it is they think they're doing, is only going to complicate things further. They should know better than to scene when they're angry, but they're ignoring the rules they don't want to deal with."

I don't know why I'm compelled to defend them, but I can't help it. "They haven't done anything I didn't want them to do."

"That's because they're not monsters." Another shrug. "But it doesn't change the fact that all the strings you three have aren't going to become untangled by fucking alone." She spins the lock until it clicks and opens the locker. "They want you to wear this. Keep your heels and the collar."

I stare at the scrap of fabric dangling from the hanger. "Okay."

Aurora hands it to me. "You can store your dress here and someone will retrieve it when you're finished." She turns around. "Go ahead and change and then I'll show you where they want you."

On display.

I don't know what that entails when it comes to their plans tonight. Not knowing has both anticipation and trepidation singing through my body. No matter what happens, they'll take care of me.

The dress turns out to be even more indecent than the one I wore into the club. It also hugs me like a second skin, barely covering my ass and stretching up to tie around my neck. The halter top has my breasts in danger of spilling out with each inhale. It's a black that looks almost like an oil spill against my skin. "Okay."

Aurora turns around and whistles. "Damn, girl, you look good." She smiles, and there is a whole lot of heat in her dark eyes. "If you three ever decide you want to play wider, I'm totally interested."

My skin goes hot and I know even without a mirror that I'm blushing. "I—Um, maybe." She's beautiful in the way priceless paintings are beautiful. I lick my lips. "I'd like that."

Aurora takes a step toward me and then gives herself a little shake. "You're going to get me into trouble." She grins as if delighted by the prospect. "I'm becoming quite the little brat. Oh! I almost forgot." She leans back into the locker, giving me a glimpse of the lower curve of her ass, and just like that, I can fantasize exactly how it would play out if we decided to be wicked.

How she'd go to her knees before me and shove up my skirt. How my back would hit the lockers with a rattle at the first swipe of her tongue. How I'd dig my fingers into her hair and drag her up my body and—

Aurora turns to hand me a single white card. "This is for you."

I take it with a shaking hand. I never would have considered myself a sex addict, but I'm standing here fantasizing about a woman I don't even know while the two men I love are waiting for me. What is *wrong* with me? Beast might have made that comment about monogamy in passing, but surely juggling two men is enough for me? I shouldn't want to be passed around like a party favor and licked and stroked and fucked until I'm limp with spent pleasure.

It takes me two tries to focus on the bold scrawl inside the card. And another two tries to comprehend.

Fuck the first person who offers to buy you a drink.

I blink and lift my gaze to Aurora. "He's not serious."

Aurora leans closer, her breasts pressing against my arm, and reads the card. She whistles. "I feel like I just got an unfair advantage in this game."

"He's not serious," I repeat.

"Honey, you know better. Beast probably came out of the womb serious. He's sure as hell not joking around about a scene." She gives me a concerned look. "Unless you don't want to play? You don't have to. Consent is really important."

I start to say that I don't want to play, but I can't force the lie past my lips. The truth is that I *do* want to play. I really, really do. "Can you show me to the room?"

Her dark eyes flash with glee. "I like you, Isabelle. I was prepared to hate you just out of solidarity, but I should have known that wouldn't stick."

I find myself grinning back at her. "To be honest, I'm pretty sure you've hooked up with both of them, so I was prepared to hate you on principle, too."

"Hating past flings out of principle is so overrated." She loops her arm through mine and tugs me toward the door. "It's a good thing we're enlightened ladies, huh?"

"I suppose it is."

She guides me around a corner and then another, to a door that looks identical to the one we just left. Aurora pauses with her hand on the doorknob. "This may be a little too honest, but …"

My blush is back. "Tell me."

"I'm not going to cheat at the game, but I hope if I'm very, very good, I'll have you coming all over my face later tonight." She gives me a fleeting grin and then pushes the door open.

I make it one step into the room before the scene fully registers. It looks like a hipster bar, one of those hole-in-the-wall places that make up for the lack of square footage with a whole lot of carefully curated decor. There are a handful of tall tables with people I don't recognize standing around them. I do a quick count. There are seven, but the small space makes it seem like more.

Aurora walks behind the bar and immediately leans in to speak to the two men sitting there with a careful space between them, watching me in the mirror situated so they can see the entire room. Beast and Gaeton.

I hesitate. The command was clear. Fuck the first person to offer me a drink. I might laugh if I could find the breath. Trust them to orchestrate the acting out of one of my fantasies in a way that's entirely within their control.

Are they really going to have me fuck someone else?

I don't know, and because I don't know, my next step is cautious. I can't decide if I'm relieved or not that I don't recognize anyone else in the room. It lends a certain kind of freedom that gives me a little more confidence. I can do this. I *asked* for this, though I couldn't have dreamed at the time that they'd bring it to life.

"I haven't seen you in here before."

It takes everything I have not to startle. A lean white man turns and gives me a long look from my feet up to my face. He's attractive in that roguishly handsome sort of way—dark hair a little too long, square jaw, the kind of face that will tempt a partner to a night free of inhibitions, only to find themselves waking alone the next morning. He grins, the effect dazzling. "I'd definitely remember you."

I tuck a strand of hair behind my ear and then curse myself for the nervous gesture. Then I stop. Why *shouldn't* I be a little nervous. This is playing a different kind of role. Even if Beast and Gaeton have this planned down to the tiniest detail, if we were in a real bar, I'd be just as nervous and turned on as I am right now. I could fuck *anyone*. I have to because they ordered me to. Because I have no interest in using my safe word. I want this. I'm allowed to have it. The thought makes me a little lightheaded. "I'm Isabelle."

"Isabelle." He says my name like he's sifting through it the way a person does with fine wine, detecting the notes beneath the surface flavor. He offers his hand. "I'm Alaric."

"Nice to meet you."

He gives my hand a little tug, pulling me a step closer. Even with my heels, he has a few inches on me, putting him just over six foot. "I think those guys at the bar were looking for you, but when you're done with them, you should come chat with me." He winks.

How does this man walk down the street without people throwing their panties at him? "I don't know if they'd like that."

Alaric raises his eyebrows. "Sounds like you might enjoy how much they wouldn't like that."

There it is again, the compulsion rising beneath my skin. I want to be *wicked*. I give myself a moment to imagine if Beast and Gaeton's command was different. If they ordered me to seduce every single person in this room. Would I start by taking Alaric's hand and slipping it beneath my dress?

His grin goes white-hot. "You're nothing but trouble, huh?"

"You have no idea." I run my finger down the center of his

chest. He's wearing a pair of slacks and a graphic T-shirt with a superhero on it. The combination is strangely charming to me. What if I asked him to buy me a drink?

Follow the rules.

I give me a small smile. "Maybe I'll see you later."

"You can count on it, beauty."

I feel his eyes on me as I pick my way through the remaining tables and sidle up to the bar between Beast and Gaeton. I catch Aurora's eye and lean down enough that my breasts are in danger of popping out of my dress. "What's good here?"

Aurora licks her lips, her gaze glued to my chest. "We have a whole list."

"Mmm." I glance at Gaeton. "What do you recommend?"

He turns to me. There isn't much space, not with Beast at my back, so I end up nearly pressed against his chest. He leers at my breasts. "Nice dress."

"Thanks." I tug at the hem, arching my back a little. My nipples are stiff points against the thin fabric. "You don't think it's too much for a place like this?"

"Nah." He leans down a little, backing me up closer to Beast. "You wearing it to send your men a message?"

"Maybe a little." Just like that, I settle into this almost-me role I'm playing. I look up into his eyes and smile sweetly. "Can I be perfectly honest?"

"Always."

I press my hands to his big chest and go up on my toes. It makes me wobble a little, and he catches my hips, his pinkie fingers dipping down to the bare skin of my thighs. I tug his shirt until he lowers his head so I can whisper in his ear. "I want to be wicked."

"That so?" His voice lowers. "Is your pussy needy, little slut?"

181

There's a deeper game, a deeper role playing going on here, and it thrills me that I'm so out of my element. "Yes."

Gaeton shifts my hips back, putting a little distance between us. I'm about to protest when I feel Beast's hand on the lower curve of my ass, delving forward to cup my pussy. Shock steals my breath and I look up at Gaeton. He uses his hold on my hips to rock me against Beast's hand. "Just an appetizer."

"For what?" I spread my legs a little and Beast pushes three fingers into me and then spreads my wetness up around my clit. I'm soaked and they've barely touched me. It's the situation, the fantasy, that has me shaking with need. Beast firms up his hand again and Gaeton resumes moving me against his palm.

It feels dirty. Like they own me. I love it. I have no idea if anyone is watching them get me off right here at the bar, but I don't care. I *want* people to watch. I want Beast to yank up my dress so they can all see how wet I am, how aching. Pleasure sparks, gathering in my lower belly. "Gaeton, please."

"Please, what?" He's speaking low, the words meant just for me.

"What is *wrong* with me?" I grip the front of his shirt, hanging on even as he uses me to grind in that agonizingly slow rhythm that's about fifteen seconds from sending me to the moon. "Why do I feel like you've doused me in gasoline and I might die if someone doesn't light a match?"

"Because we're the ones who will give it to you." Gaeton doesn't touch me except where he holds my hips, but he surrounds me despite that. "Because the next time you orgasm, it will be when you're fucking whoever offers to buy you a drink because *we* will it." His lips brush my temple. "Come all over Beast's hand, Isabelle. Try to be quiet so no one knows that you're a little slut who couldn't wait to get somewhere private before riding her man's hand to orgasm."

I cling to him as I come, clamping my lips together to keep my moans silent. Beast carefully removes his hand and then Gaeton lifts me to sit on Beast's lap and nudges my legs together. Just like that, Gaeton's got his cocky grin in place. "Did you see who she was talking to, Beast?"

Beast bands an arm across my hips, holding me to him so tightly, it's almost uncomfortable. "Do you often flirt with other people when your men are right here?"

Confusion flares, quickly followed by a delicious curl of shame that makes my pussy pulse. "I'm sorry. I didn't mean anything by it."

"Didn't you, princess?" His lips brush my ear. When I glance at the mirror angled above the bar, his eyes are cold and calculated. "Your pussy was practically dripping before you made it to the bar. Were you fantasizing about fucking Alaric?"

"I—"

Gaeton runs his hand up my thigh and pushes two blunt fingers into me. "Answer honestly."

"Yes."

Beast nips my neck, making me jump. "That's not all, though, is it. You were flushed when you walked through the door." He winds his free hand through my hair, tilting my head back. "You were thinking about Aurora, too, weren't you?"

"I—"

Gaeton gives me several rough pumps of his fingers. "*Honesty,* Isabelle." His skin has gone flushed and I can't tell if he looks angry or turned on. "Were you thinking about her pretty mouth all over your pussy? Fantasizing about walking in here for our date while your knees are shaking from how hard she made you come?"

"*Yes,* okay? I was thinking about it."

He smoothly withdraws his fingers and nudges my knees together. "Thought so."

"Two cocks aren't good enough for you." Beast releases me and sets me carefully on my feet. "You wound us, princess."

I tug my hem down a little. I can't tell what's pretend and what's real. "You told me—"

Beast's eyes flash. "Mind the card. That's the presiding command tonight." He leans in and brushes a kiss across my lips. "But that doesn't mean you won't be punished for playing the little slut."

Understanding dawns. A new layer they've offered me. To be wicked, yes, to be *caught* and *punished*. I smile up at him. "I love you." I turn that smile on Gaeton. "I love you both."

Gaeton looks away as if gathering himself. "Then prove it by being good tonight."

Be good by being bad. Obey by disobeying. The conflicting feelings crash through me, sending my desire to new heights. "I promise."

Aurora chooses that moment to walk up on the other side of the bar. "Want to learn to make the special?" She smiles at me, a hint of sin in those pink-painted lips. "First drink's on me."

CHAPTER 21

I glance at Beast and Gaeton for permission. "Can I? Pretty please?"

Beast lowers his brows, but I know him well enough to see the heat lurking in the blue depths of his eyes. "Be good, princess."

"I will. I promise." I'm both lying and not lying and my body buzzes with anticipation as I round the bar to take up position next to Aurora. There isn't much room back here. This bar is more for show than for practice, and it certainly wasn't created with more than one bartender in mind. We can't take a step without touching each other. "Show me."

Her smile is saucy and dazzling at the same time. "First up, you need the glass." She points at the shelves of glasses, her arm brushing my breasts. "Oops." She backs me against the wall and reaches past me for several bottles, her chest brushing mine with each movement. I'm struck by the overwhelming desire to tug down her dress and suck on her nipples that I can see faint outlines of against the fabric.

She clears her throat. "Can you grab that top one? It's a little out of my reach."

We switch positions, her back to the wall and mine to the bar. I lift my arms to grab the bottle in question. She tugs my dress a little to the side and looks up. "No, not that one." Her mouth closes around my nipple and I jerk. Beast and Gaeton are *right there* and if we move the slightest bit, they'll see exactly what she's doing to me. She lifts her head a little. "Sorry, wrong again. The first one was right." Her tongue darts out to flick my nipple and she hurriedly pulls my dress back into place as I lower the bottle down.

Holy shit, it feels like I'm in a fever dream.

Aurora turns me around, the space forcing us to be plastered together, her front to my back. She reaches around me to line up the ingredients. "Now, start at this end and pour until I say stop. Then we work down the line. A little of this, a little of that."

"Okay." My voice hardly sounds like my own. I look up and meet Beast's gaze as Aurora's hand drops to my thigh and curves inward until she's stroking my pussy. There's no way Beast can see exactly what she's doing from his position, not with the bar in the way, but he's looking at me like he owns me, like he owns every second of this.

Because he does.

"Pour," Aurora murmurs in my ear. "We don't want them to get suspicious." She circles my clit with soft strokes and barely-there touches, which somehow makes this a thousand times hotter.

I pour the first liquid, something I can barely focus on, until she says stop. As I lean forward for the next bottle, she pushes two fingers into me. I fight down a moan and look up to find Gaeton watching me. He leans forward on the bar, still not close enough to see Aurora finger-fucking me, but close enough that I'm fighting not to gasp. "Is there a problem, Isabelle?"

"No."

His gaze drops to the bar and even though I *know* he can't see her hand beneath my dress, he licks his lips. He looks ... Gaeton looks like he doesn't want to be enjoying this as much as he is. "Your hands are shaking."

"Are they?" They definitely are. Aurora is leisurely stroking the tips of her fingers against my G-spot. I manage to pour the second bottle until she tells me to stop but I don't know if I'm going to make it through the next one.

"Mmm." He sits back and half turns to Beast. They speak in low voices, and I'm too distracted by what she's doing to me to focus on them.

Aurora's lips are at my ear again as she moves back to my clit. "You're so wet, baby. I'm dying for a taste." She takes the last bottle with her free hand and expertly finishes the drink. "Do you think they're distracted enough that we can slip away for a minute?"

I turn my head enough to see the mischief sparking in her dark eyes. This is all pretend and Aurora is enjoying the hell out of it. I lick my lips, clinging to my role even as I grip the counter and fight not to ride her fingers. "I shouldn't. I'm supposed to be good."

"I'll make you *feel* good." She gives my clit another stroke. "What they don't know won't hurt them, right?"

I turn in her arms and she has to stop playing with my pussy to allow it. I'm *drenched*, drugged on lust and need and the knowledge that I'm doing exactly as I was told. "That drink is on you?"

She grins. "Consider it me buying it for you." Aurora shoots a look to where Beast and Gaeton have their heads close together. They seem entirely wrapped up in each other and for a moment that distracts me enough that I pause. If Gaeton turned his head a little, they'd be kissing. My body gives another pulse at the thought.

Still, I hesitate even though I want what happens next more than anything. "I don't know."

Aurora leans up until she's pressed against me, her thigh sliding between mine and rubbing against me. "Baby, I *need* your pussy. I feel how wet I made you and it makes me crazy. I need to worship your perfect breasts and I need you to come all over my face." She shifts a little, grinding me down against her thigh. "I'm good. I can make it quick." She nips my earlobe. "No one has to know."

"No one has to know," I repeat, nodding.

"This way." She takes my hand and leads me to a narrow door tucked back behind the shelves. I might laugh if I could draw enough breath. Apparently I'm not the only one who fantasizes about getting fucked by the bartender. The door Aurora drags me through leads to a tiny supply closet. I barely get a chance to marvel that it's legitimately filled with cleaning supplies before Aurora shuts the door and pushes me against the wall.

She kisses me like she needs this as much as I do. As if maybe this is real and I'm hooking up with the pretty bartender while my boyfriends drink a few feet away. She tastes of something sweet and I sink into the kiss. I cup her breasts, but it's not good enough, so I tug down her dress to get to bare skin. She's so soft and the way she sighs against my mouth makes me crazy. So wrong. So right. God, I can't stop.

I don't want to stop.

I kiss her harder and run my hands down to her ass, to dip beneath her dress even as she's undoing the top of mine, to squeeze her ass, and then I reach farther and stroke her pussy from behind. She's so wet. Holy shit, she's so wet.

Aurora yanks down my dress, wasting no time sucking on my nipples and leaving little love bites on the curves. I have to let go of her ass, but I instantly reach between her thighs to touch her. She pauses for a second as I slide a finger into her and I moan. "You feel so good. You're so fucking sexy."

"You are a goddamn delight." She cups my breasts together as I work her, and it doesn't matter that I'm fumbling and not an expert at this because she's riding my hand. "That feels so good." She shoves my dress up around my waist. "It feels better because we're not supposed to."

"I know." I can feel her pussy clenching around me and I push a second finger in. Now it's my time to whisper in her ear. "When I walked in here and saw you behind the bar—I wanted this from the second I saw you."

She's stroking my pussy again as she exhales against my nipples. "You wanted what, baby? Tell me." We should be going fast, should be hurrying, but we've both slowed down. It's as if we can't get enough of each other, even knowing the clock is ticking until we're caught, as if we don't care because the pleasure we can give each other is our only aim.

"I want your mouth on my pussy. I want you to make me come."

"I will."

"Hurry." The word sounds strangled. "Hurry before they miss me."

She doesn't hurry. She drags her tongue over one nipple and then the other. Teasing me. "What will they do if they catch us?" Aurora hits her knees and urges me back to a box that's the perfect height for what we're about to do. I sit on it and spread my legs wide. She runs her soft hands up my thighs and pushes them wider yet. "What will they do if they come in here and my tongue is in your pussy? When you look up and keep riding my face even though they're watching because you're so close, you can't stop."

"I don't care. I need you to make me come."

"Baby, I'm going to take care of you. Don't you worry."

She dips her head and then her mouth is on me and, holy fuck, it feels good. In the low light of the storage room, I can see that she's left pink lipstick all over me, a clear mark of what we've been up to even if we walked out of here without getting caught.

That's when I realize that this box is facing the door. If someone opens it, there's no chance at hiding. No time to do anything but have them witness everything.

I reach down behind me and brace myself. "Don't stop. Please don't stop."

"I'm not going to stop." She gives my clit a playful lick. "You taste too good."

The door's ripped open and suddenly Beast and Gaeton are there. I startle, but Aurora has me held too tightly to jump up. She doesn't stop, doesn't move, just keeps licking me as Beast and Gaeton glare. If anything, she slows down further, drawing this out, sending my pleasure spiraling with shame. "I can't stop," she whispers, her brown eyes on mine.

I glance at the men and then down at her. "Don't stop," I whisper back.

Beast makes a tsking sound. "We asked one thing of her, Gaeton. One simple thing."

Gaeton glowers at us from the doorway, but there's no mistaking the cockstand pressing against his slacks. His gaze rests on Aurora's face between my thighs, touching on my bare breasts, skating down Aurora's back to her ass. There's no mistaking exactly how much of a willing participant I am —her dress is wadded up around her waist, the same as mine. "Is this what you call being good, Isabelle?"

"I'm sorry," I say again, but I'm lifting my hips to meet Aurora's tongue.

Beast slides into the small spot between the box and the wall and grabs my hands and pins them to the box. "We caught you and you're still riding her mouth. You're close to coming, aren't you? Knowing that we asked you to be good and you didn't last ten minutes before you were in here with Aurora's tongue all over you." He glances at Aurora, who can't quite hide her glee. "Don't think we've missed *your* role in all this."

She sits back on her heels a tiny amount. "You mean my role where I was about to make your girlfriend come harder than either of you ever could?"

Beast blinks, actual surprise on his face before he locks it down. "You're just asking for a hard fuck, aren't you, Aurora?"

She holds his gaze and drags the flat of her tongue over my pussy. "Are you offering?"

He sifts his fingers through her hair and shakes his head slowly. "There's only one woman for us, even if she's determined to fuck everyone who will have her." He tightens his grip and guides her face back to my pussy. "Finish what you started. You think you can make her come harder than either of us? Prove it."

"Happily." She murmurs against my skin. And then she starts licking me again, this time with Beast holding me down and Gaeton watching.

It was hot before, knowing we'd be caught, knowing it was the exact purpose for this scene. It's a thousand times hotter now, while they watch with stony disapproval while she eats me out. The shame of it curls my toes and arches my back. I try to hold out, to make this moment last as long as possible, but it's too good.

Beast's hand covers my mouth as I orgasm, his rough voice in my ear. "So it's like that? You want everyone to know that she's got her tongue all over you in here?"

"You want to make a scene, Isabelle?" Gaeton sounds downright ominous. "Then we're going to make a fucking scene."

Aurora lets loose a little shriek as he hooks her around the waist and drags her off me. Then he's gone, disappearing through the door. I blink. "I'm sorry."

"No, you're not. This is what you wanted." He hesitates and leans back a little, some of the coldness leeching out of his expression. "You good?"

Did I think I couldn't love him more? His checking in only boosts the feeling higher. I draw a breath so he knows I'm actually thinking about it instead of just responding and nod. "I'm good."

"Remember your safe word." His grin is quicksilver, there and gone in an instant, replaced by the coldness I'm coming to associate with his kink play. He hauls me off the box by my arm, not giving me a chance to fix my dress. It's bunched around my middle, exposing me from the waist down and ribs up. There is *no* mistaking what I've been up to.

Beast drags me out into the bar. I half expected everyone to be gone, but no, they're all there. Watching with varying degrees of delight as Gaeton strips off Aurora's dress and plants her on the bar. He points at me. "Get over here."

As if I have any choice. Beast half carries me to stand next to the bar and strips off my dress, too. I have half a second to feel self-conscious, but then desire takes hold. I watch Gaeton cage Aurora's throat casually, as if he's done it a thousand times before, and guide her down onto her back on the bar. Just like that, I can imagine them fucking, her smaller body riding his cock and ...

I don't hate it. I don't hate it at all.

I blink.

"What are you thinking, princess?" Beast murmurs in my ear.

It doesn't even occur for me to lie. "That the thought of her fucking either of you—both of you—is hot as hell."

He pulls back and gives me a long look. "Are you sure?"

"Yes." Again, no hesitation. No lies. Just a truth that I've discovered and feels strange and new and a little wonderful.

He nods once. "We'll discuss it another time." Then he lifts me onto the bar and sets me right between Aurora's spread thighs. He grabs the back of my neck and forces me down to where her pussy is wet and pink and pretty enough that my mouth waters. "Lick her pussy, princess. Make her come sweetly and we might lighten the punishment you so richly deserve."

I lick my lips. "Yes, Sir."

CHAPTER 22

BEAST

Isabelle delights me to no end. I knew I loved the woman, but even when I spun out the terms of this pact, I didn't expect *this*. Amazed, I lift my gaze to find Gaeton looking the same kind of shell-shocked as he watches Isabelle eat Aurora's pussy. I find lust and surprise and the tiniest bit of anger in his dark eyes. But then, Gaeton is always angry these days. He just covers it better than some.

I keep my hand on the back of Isabelle's neck, though she's not fighting me in the least. His big hand cages Aurora's throat in a similar way, preventing her from sitting up, but not putting any pressure on her. "Did you know Aurora was such a little brat?"

He shrugs massive shoulders. "She worked with Tink too long."

Aurora cries out and her back bows, Isabelle wrenching an orgasm from her. I lift my brows, but our woman doesn't seem interested in stopping. Despite myself, I chuckle as I haul her off the Aurora. "Greedy. So endlessly greedy."

She tries to look repentant, an impossible feat with the

happy grin on her face. "I'm sorry, Sir." She looks at Gaeton. "I'm sorry, Sir."

Gaeton shakes his head slowly. "No, you're not." He pulls Aurora up into a sitting position and narrows his eyes on her. "And *you*, little troublemaker. I ought to put you in time-out for pulling that shit."

She gives him a radiant smile. "If you think it would help."

Gaeton snorts. "Nah. You'll just get off again and then next time I turn around, you'll be buried between our woman's thighs." He considers her. "We'll have to think of something better."

I turn to the rest of the room watching avidly. If I had my preference, the rest of the night would play out in private, but we've started this, so we'll have to see it through to the end. "Show continues in the public playroom."

Someone whoops and a few people clap and they all file out quickly enough. It's only when the four of us are alone in the room that I turn back to the other three. "Isabelle, I'm disappointed in you. Go kneel by the door and wait for us."

She opens her mouth like she might argue, but finally gives a jerky nod and hops off the bar. I keep a close eye on her as she pads to the door and sinks into a kneeling position, but she's not wobbly at all. Good.

I narrow my eyes at Aurora. "Get dressed. We'll deal with you presently."

She scrambles off the bar and snatches up her dress. I point at Gaeton. "With me."

"Not on your life." But he follows me into the cramped storage closet and allows me to shut the door. Gaeton huffs out a breath. "I'm fine."

"You aren't even close to fine." I cross my arms over my chest. "This scene was your idea. Are you regretting it?"

"No. Nothing like that." He drags a hand over his face. "Shit is just complicated, you know? I get caught up in it."

I catch his wrist and pull it from his face. "Talk to me."

"You're not my fucking therapist, man. I don't have to walk you through it."

I give him the look that comment deserves. "I'm not your therapist, no, but I'm someone who cares about you."

"Sure." Gaeton snorts, but his derisive expression fades as he studies my face. "You're not shitting me."

I could shake this man for being so intentionally dense at times. "No, I'm not shitting you. You think I'd commit to two weeks' worth of scenes with someone I still hated? Do you think I would have brought up my fantasy earlier if I didn't mean it?"

He shifts his wrist until his fingers play along my forearm. "You're a vault, Beast. Not exactly an open book when it comes to literally anything."

"Pretty fucking open when I tell you I care about you." I want him to reciprocate, but it's still too soon for that. He can barely comprehend that I might want him for more than fucking right now. Pushing too hard will damage what little progress we've made. I squeeze his wrist a little. "Let's go put on a show, and then finish the night out right."

"Okay." He finally nods. Gaeton glances at the door. "Isabelle's shame kink is a trip."

"Gaeton." I wait for him to look at me and then pull him closer, inch by inch. "It's not *her* kink that's tripping you up. It's how much you enjoy playing it out with her. You like it, her being a little slut, and you like punishing her for it."

"Yeah. I do." His breath ghosts against my lips. "I'm taking lead for the next part."

"I wouldn't have it any other way."

The moment stretches out between us, and I'm almost convinced I can feel the earth getting soft and sticky beneath our feet, ready to suck us down. I'm about to take a step back when Gaeton curses and grabs the back of my neck with his free hand. He bends down and tows me that last little distance to his mouth.

He tastes like whiskey, and he doesn't dick around with teasing. He tilts my head back and claims my mouth. I allow it for half a second, reveling in the fact that we're kissing, that *he* made the first move, and then I grab his shirt and kiss the fuck out of him back.

I almost forget myself when he presses his hips against me and I feel his big cock against my stomach. Almost.

I wrench away. My breath comes out as raggedly as his does. "Later."

Gaeton blinks down at me and gives himself a little shake. "Right. Later." He suddenly grins. "Figures that you couldn't resist all of this." He motions to himself.

"Good to know that this situation hasn't damaged your arrogance any."

"Not even a little bit." He gives the door an assessing look. "Bets on if they managed to obey this time or if Isabelle's riding Aurora's face again?"

I shake my head and start move past him, enjoying the way he holds still as our bodies drag against each other. "We good?"

"Yeah." He nods. "We're good. This whole situation has been one hell of a head trip, but you're right. I was fucking up earlier."

"Nothing you can't make right if you want to."

His eyes gleam with arrogant amusement. "I know." Gaeton grabs my arm, holding me in place. "After we're done here…"

"Yeah?"

He strokes his hand down my chest and grips my cock through my jeans. Gaeton curses softly. "After we're done with Isabelle's fantasy, why don't we try yours on for size?"

The storage room suddenly seems significantly smaller. I

look up at him, my heart beating harder than it has right to. "We don't have to do that."

"It has nothing to do with *having* to do something, and everything with wanting to do it." He leans down and licks my bottom lip. "Maybe Isabelle isn't the only one with a little bit of a shame kink. Maybe I don't want to wait for later, at least for this." He exhales slowly and reaches for the button of my jeans. I hold perfectly still as he unzips me and draws my cock out. "And maybe you weren't the only one that day who thought about what it would be like with three of us in bed together."

I have to fight not to hold my breath as he strokes me with his rough hand. I thought I'd have to slow play things more to bring Gaeton around, but it feels like we've all tipped over the edge and are barreling to the only conclusion that makes sense. I let Gaeton guide my back to the wall and watch him sink to his knees. The truth bursts out of me without my having any intention of speaking. "It pissed me off so fucking much to watch you suck Hook's cock. To know that he had your ass whenever he wanted it."

Gaeton grins in the near-darkness. "Jealous."

"Fuck yeah. And furious about it." I sift my fingers through his hair. "We do this, and there's no going back. Your mouth is mine. Your ass is mine. *You* are mine, just like she is."

"Or maybe that's not what it means. Maybe it means I just want to suck you off right now." Gaeton licks the head of my cock.

Frustration nips at me, but I shove it down deep. We'll get there. He's already made his decision, for all that he's playing the denial game right now. I tug on his hair just hard enough to hurt. "Then stop fucking around and suck my cock, Gaeton. We have two pretty subs waiting for their punishment out there."

"They can wait."

He sucks me down and I can't stop myself from cursing at how good it feels. It's more than his mouth around my cock. It's what this portends. Gaeton *is* mine. And I'm his, which he'll acknowledge when he finally comes to terms with this. I give him a full fifteen seconds of playing with me before I take control, tightening my grip and choosing my rhythm. His big hands shift to my hips, holding me lightly as I fuck his mouth. The look on his face. *Fuck.* He's blissed out, in heaven as I shove my cock down his throat.

I love this big-hearted asshole. I'm never fucking letting him go. Not now. Not ever.

I don't try to hold out. I simply take what I need and let my orgasm roll through me. Gaeton drinks me down with a happy growl and gives my cock a few extra pulls before he moves back. "That was one hell of an appetizer."

I huff out a laugh. "You're as much of a brat as she is."

"Guilty." He tucks my cock away and does up my jeans. "You like it."

"Yeah, I do." I pull him to his feet and kiss him again. It's tempting to stay here a little longer, to keep overriding his fears about what the future brings. We have the rest of the night, and several fantasies to play out, though. I slowly pull away. "Think Isabelle is coming all over Aurora again?"

"Suppose we'll see."

I give another laugh and slide past him to open the door. I'm honestly a little surprised to find the women kneeling in identical positions in front of the door, the very picture of obedient submissives. "I should have taken that bet," I murmur.

"Yep." He strides around the bar to stand over them. "Up, little sluts. We still have your punishment to deliver."

I hang back a little as he leads them out of the door and down the hall toward the public playroom. It's quite the sight, Gaeton striding strong and tall in front, a naked Isabelle walking next to Aurora in that tease of a white dress of hers.

The public playroom is about as crowded as I expect. People love a show, and we're about to provide them one. The knowledge sits uncomfortably in my stomach as I catch sight of Ursa and Malone perched on a couch next to each other, their heads bowed together in low conversation. We should be fighting Ursa, not participating in a scene for her entertainment.

If there's a way to avoid the fight, though, we have to try.

For Isabelle's sake.

Gaeton stops at the scene we had requested set up. There's a spanking bench and a low couch positioned right in its line of sight. He points at the couch. "Kneel, Aurora."

We hadn't exactly planned on Aurora ending up in this scene, but it worked out beautifully when she requested permission the second she showed up in the bar room. She flounces a little, but sinks gracefully to her knees in front of the couch.

"And you." Gaeton turns to Isabelle. "On the bench. Beast, assist."

I follow her to the bench and help her position herself. Spanking benches come in a wide variety, but the one we picked for tonight has spots for her forearms and shins with a higher section in the middle to lift her ass into the air. She squirms a little as I fasten the straps across her calves, holding her into place. I move around to her front and go to one knee to give her arms the same treatment. "Too tight?"

"No. They're perfect." She lifts her head and bites her bottom lip. "Everyone can see my pussy."

"Yes, they can." I press a quick kiss to her mouth. "Safe word, princess."

"Candlestick."

"Good girl." I tilt her chin to where Gaeton has sprawled on the couch. "Aurora gets her punishment first. Try not to be too jealous."

Gaeton crooks his fingers at me. "Come sit here, Beast."

It's not domination, not exactly, but I can't deny the draw of this man. I cross to sink down next to him. From this position, it's clear that the scene was set up to maximize everyone's view. We can see them all. Just like they can see us.

Gaeton snaps his fingers. "Up, Aurora. Over my knee."

She has that sweet smile on her face again, as if she wasn't just playing the part of the siren tempting our girlfriend away from us. This is the Aurora I'm most familiar with, the one I've scened with in the past, but the bratty version of herself is just as real. Gaeton grabs her hand and yanks her forward until she's sprawled over his broad lap, her face against my thigh. He turns her face to look at Isabelle. "Watch her. She's knows this is coming for her next, that her punishment will be much more prolonged."

"Worth it." Aurora squirms a little and laughs. "She tastes too sweet."

Gaeton and I exchange a look, and I have to muscle down the urge to laugh. Aurora is fucking fearless right now, and I'm enjoying it far more than I should. I lift my brows. "Sounds like you need to double whatever number you had in mind for her."

"Sounds like I do." He shakes his head slowly. "You were always so nice and sweet, Aurora. Look at you now." He hooks the hem of her dress and pulls it up, baring her from the waist down. Isabelle makes a strangled noise, but neither of us look at her. This lack of attention is just as much a punishment as what comes next.

Gaeton doesn't give Aurora any warning. He simply starts spanking her, one punishing strike after another, alternating cheeks and spacing. She squirms and whimpers, and I stroke her hair absentmindedly as I watch Isabelle watch what's happening. Even with her comment about watching Gaeton fuck Aurora, I'm still unprepared for the sheer lust in her eyes every time his hand lands with a meaty *thwack* on Aurora's pert little ass. Knowing Aurora, she's practically dripping from this treatment, and Isabelle's angle will give her a glimpse of that desire.

She looks like she wants to lick Aurora clean.

I shift, my cock hardening again to press against the front of my jeans. The desire to skip right over the punishment and get to the fucking is tempting, but it would cheat all four of us to do it.

"There." Gaeton's rough word brings me back to the present. He hauls Aurora up and frames her face in his big hands. "I suppose it's too much to ask that you never do it again?"

She smiles beatifically and dips down to press a quick kiss to his mouth. "Yep."

"Scamp." He lifts her and deposits her in my lap. Without another word, he rises, his giant cock straining the front of his slacks, and stalks toward Isabelle.

I dig a blanket out from the basket beneath the couch and tuck it around Aurora. "You good?"

"I'm good." She shivers and presses her face to my neck. "Damn, Beast. If you three ever, *ever* want to play again, promise I'm the first on your list."

My gaze tracks to where Gaeton now stands between Isabelle's forcibly spread knees, staring down at her ass as if he wants to jump past the punishment as much as I do. "I think we can arrange that."

"Yay." She wiggles excitedly, and then moans a little.

I lean back. "Aurora." I inject a bit of bite into my tone.

"Stop rubbing your ass all over my cock or I'm going to start spanking you again. You'll have bruises upon bruises."

"Promise?"

"Beast." Gaeton's command brings my head up. He's watching us closely. "Aurora hasn't learned her lesson."

"It appears not."

"Mmm." He leaves Isabelle and walks over to us. Before I can figure out what he intends, he grabs the bottom edge of the couch and hauls us forward to within touching distance of the spanking bench. "Better."

His strength sends a surge of desire through me and I let him see it, just for a moment. "Much better."

Gaeton gives me a quick grin that's full of the promise of *later*, and then he moves to Isabelle's other side. "We're going to start with my hand. One stroke for each of you until I'm satisfied that you won't be sneaking off to play with her pussy every chance you get." He waits for me to take the blanket back from Aurora and, after a moment, to take her dress, too. Gaeton narrows his eyes at her. "Don't be rubbing your pussy all over Beast's leg, either. You're fucking shameless, Aurora. Take your punishment."

"Yes, Sir!" she says it so primly, there's no way a soul in this room believes her.

He shakes his head slowly. "Such a little brat."

I pull her over my lap and shift her up until her ass is higher than the rest of her, her cheek against the couch cushion as she looks up at Isabelle. Gaeton and I time our strikes perfectly, and both women cry out. Aurora's ass is a deep red, but I've played with her enough to know she can take more.

Again and again and again.

I know exactly what Gaeton's strength can do when he puts his mind to it. He's being careful with Isabelle. No matter how much she cries out and how pretty her tears, he's holding back. Ideally, we wouldn't be experimenting with pain without knowing her threshold in a public scene like this. The concentration on Gaeton's face every time he lifts his hand to spank her ass is so fucking hot, I can't stand it.

Aurora squirms in my lap and I put a little extra snap behind my next strike. She moans and I shake my head. "Shameless."

"You know it," she gasps out, but her voice has gone a little hazy and lost some of the bratty bite. Just as well. Isabelle can't take much more.

As if I beamed that thought right into Gaeton's head, he runs his hands over Isabelle's ass, earning a sexy little whimper from her. "Are you feeling repentant, little slut?"

"Yes, Sir." A single tear escapes the corner of her eye. "I'm sorry," she whispers.

I know what comes next in Gaeton's head. He has no problem fucking in front of people. It's not my preference any more than scening publicly is, but once again, I have little choice in this moment.

We have to finish it.

"Are you ready to show everyone just how sorry you are?" He's talking to her, but he's looking at me.

I nod. Let's finish this.

CHAPTER 23

GAETON

*B*y all rights, I should hate every single moment of this scene. Having Isabelle "cheat" so we could catch her. Seeing her completely undone by someone who isn't one of us. Watching how much she enjoyed licking Aurora's pussy. It all should be triggering the fuck out of me.

That was the problem before. I wasn't enough for her. She had to have *him*, too. I didn't really get that Beast wasn't enough for her, either. It's only now, as I stroke her ass, red from the spanking, and watch Beast tuck a blanket back around Aurora in preparation of us fucking Isabelle at the same time that I feel settled.

Yeah, I should hate this scene, but instead it's been the hottest one I've ever participated in.

Aurora tucks her legs up underneath the blanket and snuggles back into the cushions with a happy smile. She catches me watching her and winks. It's an effort not to give her my normal grin, to maintain the stern boyfriend persona. It's not how I usually like to play but I'm enjoying the hell out of it.

Beast moves to stand near Isabelle's head, waiting for my

direction. It might be the first time in his fucking life where he's answering to *me*, and it's not submission, but it feels just as good as everything else we've done tonight. This was supposed to be about putting on a show for Ursa to prove that we're united beneath Cordelia and too strong to fuck with. Somewhere along the way, it became solely about *us*.

I squeeze Isabelle's ass again, making her jump and moan. She's ready. I nod at Beast and he moves to undo one of her arms and shift the bench around to drop the section beneath her head and give him room to work. I pitch my voice low, just for the three of us. "If you need to safe out, slap his hip with the hand he just freed. Do you understand?"

"Yes, Sir."

Beast wraps her hair around one fist and undoes his jeans with the other. I'm tall enough that I get a good look at his cock and, *fuck*, the guy is freakishly perfect everywhere. He looks up, his blue eyes full of the memory of what we did in the storage closest, full of the promise of what comes later. The metal of his piercing glints and then Isabelle is sucking him deep.

I give her a few seconds let her adjust to him. There will be no mercy once we get going, but I can afford a little now. I undo my slacks slowly and take my cock out. Isabelle is so wet, the evidence is all over her thighs. Our woman likes spankings as much as she likes Aurora.

I drag my cock over her pussy, teasing her. "You ready to take this cock, Rose?" The endearment slips out, and I don't try to take it back. I never stopped loving this infuriating woman. The feeling should have soured long before now, turned brittle and poisonous. Instead, it's only gotten stronger. I don't know what the future holds, but we have right now.

It's enough.

It has to be enough.

I slam into her hard enough to rock her forward the tiniest bit despite the restraints. She cries out around Beast's cock, and it's the prettiest sound I've ever heard. "Don't hold back," I command.

Beast nods. "I won't."

We fuck her. There's no other word for it. I don't want one. I drive into her tight pussy again and again, searching for the salvation I know is just out of reach. Beast is doing the same thing with her mouth, though he's being slightly more careful. The goal isn't to hurt her, even if we're technically mid-punishment.

We make a good show of it. There's no other way around it. We fuck Isabelle until she's sobbing around Beast's cock and her pussy is clenched tight enough that I'm having to fight against coming. From past experience, I know the angle of the bench is *almost* enough friction on her clit to get her off, but this part of the scene isn't about her. Or, rather, it is and it isn't.

She'll come plenty later tonight.

Beast holds my gaze and, for the first time since I've known him, he's not wearing a mask. He's looking at me like he did in the storage closet. Like he wants me. Like he ... owns me. Maybe that's why I throw caution to the wind. I've never been that good at restraint. Not when it comes to the things I want, not when it comes to a single damn thing in life. It's gotten me into trouble more than once, and it will again. Probably right fucking now, because I want to kiss him and I can't think of a single reason not to.

So I do.

I lean across Isabelle's body and snag the back of his neck. I'm tall enough to make the position work, and he doesn't resist as I take his mouth. I come deep inside Isabelle with the taste of Beast on my tongue and it feels like the something clicks into place in my chest, a ragged edge smoothed.

This feels *right*, so right that it scares the breath right out of my lungs.

The last time I wanted someone as desperately as I do these two people, I was left kneeling with a ring box in my hand while the woman I held above all others backed away from me. I don't know if I can survive another rejection like that.

Beast carefully pulls out of Isabelle's mouth and gives me that look again, the one that promises things to come. I want to believe it. I want to so desperately, I forget to hold myself back. I ease out of Isabelle and press a kiss to the back of her neck. "You've pleased us."

We get to work unfastening her and I carry her to the couch where Aurora's pulled out another of the blankets they keep for aftercare. Beast helps me tuck it around Isabelle in my lap and then drops onto the other side of Aurora, who looks so happy she's practically purring. Satisfied that she's good, I focus entirely on Isabelle.

She smiles up at me, a little dazed and loopy. "That was something else."

I hold her close, letting my body steady her as she swivels a little to look at Aurora upside-down. "*You* are something else. All of you." She laughs a little as if amazed. "Is it always like this?"

"It can be." It's a lie. It's never like this. I have scened with near-strangers and scened with friends, have fucked both. None of those experiences come close to what we just shared. The emotional intensity drove everything to new heights. Beast catches my eye and he looks like a cat who got into the cream. Satisfied and a little lazy with it. Fuck, but that's just as sexy as Isabelle's buzzed joy.

Aurora stretches and climbs carefully to her feet. "Thank you for including me." She presses quick kisses to each of our mouths in turn, and then returns to grab

Isabelle's hand and squeeze it. "I like you, Isabelle Belmonte."

"I like you, too." Isabelle's laugh edges into a giggle. "Not just the sex stuff."

"Not just the sex stuff." Aurora smiles. "See you three around." She lets the blanket drop next to where Beast tossed her dress on the floor earlier, and waltzes naked in the direction of the hallway leading to the private rooms. The employee areas are back there, too, which is no doubt where she's headed. I'm not the only one who notices the little swing in her step, either. I catch Malone staring at Aurora, but she turns away before I can tell if it's loathing or lust in her eyes.

Isabelle wiggles a little in my lap, and Beast moves closer until he's pressed against my side and she's in both our laps more than just mine. She gives a happy sigh as if this is exactly what she wants. "I—" She licks her lips. "I didn't know shame could be so sexy, something to play with and enjoy instead of trying to shove down deep."

She's killing me. I touch her chin with the tip of my finger. This is where I need to establish some kind of boundary, to remind her—both of them—that this is just for show, not for us. I can't do it. It's not the truth, and I don't know where that leaves us, but if they're both being honest, I can give it a try, too. "Consent is the only rule, Isabelle. Everything else is up for negotiation. Even shame. *Especially* shame."

She leans up and kisses my jaw. "Thank you."

I don't ask what she's thanking me for. I just hold her and lean against Beast as he does the same, his hand brushing mine as we stroke Isabelle's back. It feels right. So fucking right.

I'm still not so wrapped up in them that I'm ignoring our surroundings.

People began dispersing when we started aftercare, moving on to their own entertainments or heading for the lounge to resume drinking. Not Ursa. Malone left quickly after Aurora did, but Ursa remains on her fainting couch, a queen in waiting. Alaric kneels near her feet, but she ignores him, her entire attention seeming to be on us.

I hold her gaze over the distance of the room. Talking to her now would just undermine what we've done. If we're powerful enough not to be fucked with, we're powerful enough that we can't walk around issuing threats. That kind of bravado reeks of weakness, and Ursa's too smart not to see through it.

We can take her if it comes to a territory war; even with Cordelia being relatively untried, the combined experience of the people under her is more than enough to hold us. Plus, we aren't looking to expand. Defending territory is a whole hell of a lot easier than claiming it.

But there will be lives lost if we go to war. People I might have been willing to walk away from a month ago, but that doesn't mean I won't fight to prevent their deaths. I couldn't save Orsino. It didn't matter how strong I am, how smart, how ruthless. Cancer doesn't give a fuck about any of that.

I miss that old fucker. I don't think I'll ever *not* miss him. Going back to the territory, to spend time in his home ... It's going to be uncomfortable as hell to be faced with the ever-present reminder of him, but maybe it won't be all bad. Maybe it's good to remember.

Maybe someday I'll get to the point where I appreciate it.

Either way, I won't allow Ursa to fuck with the territory or the people in it. I've never been that great at silent communication, but I can threaten like a motherfucker, and I put every bit of threat I can into the look I send her.

She raises her brows and smiles widely as if I've amused her. Before I decide if that's a good thing or a bad thing, she rises gracefully from the fainting couch, smooths down her dress, and says something to Alaric that has him climbing to his feet and following her toward the private rooms.

I let out a long exhale and refocus on the two people that matter. "Let's stay here tonight."

Beast raises his brows at that, but I give a slight shake of my head. He finally shrugs. "Works for me."

Isabelle stretches out across our laps, still buzzed out of her mind from subspace. "I think I've been bad enough for one night. I'm okay with whatever you two decide."

"Bad enough for one night." I snort and stand, lifting her easily in my arms. "Don't try to play the innocent now. You come down off this high and you're going to be begging for your next filthy fix." Beast and I are planning on it by agreeing to play out his fantasy.

"Probably." She laughs, and for the first time in longer than I can remember, it sounds completely uninhibited. Unencumbered.

Beast shakes his head and moves toward the lounge. He'll touch base with Meg or Hercules and get us booked in one of the overnight rooms. Normally, I'd prefer to head directly back to my apartment to finish this night, but Ursa has already proven she knows its location and can get to us there. I don't *think* she'll try it tonight, but I *know* she won't fuck with Hades's hospitality. There might be some leniency outside of the Underworld, but only a fool would cross Hades beneath this roof.

Fifteen minutes later, Beast is opening the door so I can walk through with Isabelle still in my arms. I haven't spent any time in these rooms—I prefer my own bed and the idea of sleeping next to someone was too much of a reminder of sleeping next to Isabelle, which was no longer an option. It's decorated with the same understated opulence that the rest of the club is. This room is all shades of soothing blue and stark white, its bed large enough to fit me and the other two without issues. Three narrow windows stretch from the floor the ceiling on the other side of the room, giving us a glimpse of Carver City through the sheer curtains. In the corner is a dry bar and a small fridge.

It'll do.

Isabelle shifts in my arms. She's coming down, sleepy and cuddly and too fucking cute, and it's harder than it should be to set her on the bed. She blinks up at us both. "We should talk."

For the first time since we started this thing, the idea of actually talking it out doesn't make me want to get the fuck out of the room. "Yeah, I guess we should."

Beast goes to the mini fridge in the corner and comes back with bottled water. He passes one to each of us and climbs onto the bed next to Isabelle. He barely waits for me to get settled on her other side to drop a verbal bomb on us. "I want both of you."

Even though I'm expecting it, even though he said something similar in the storage room, I still choke on my drink. "You're fucking with me." I'd let myself believe his claim of *mine* was just another shade of that scene, that it didn't really mean anything. I really should have known better.

"You heard me." He looks at me and then her. "I'm done with choices, princess. We tried that before and it blew up in our faces. It's time for something different."

Isabelle has gone very, very still, but I can't spare a thought for her because I'm too busy staring at Beast. Where the fuck does he get off putting that out there as if he's the only one who gets a choice in this situation? He decided he doesn't want her to choose so that's that. "You are such a selfish asshole."

Beast doesn't blink. "Guilty."

"You don't just get to decide for all three of us that this is what's happening. This wasn't part of the bargain."

He shrugs. "Tell me you don't want me, that the idea of the three of us trying to figure it out doesn't tempt you *a little*."

"I don't want you. The three of us doesn't tempt me even a little."

The bastard smirks. "Yeah, now try it again with some honesty."

I open my mouth to repeat my words, but they don't come. But, fuck him, he's right. I *do* want him. The last year has made it clear that my hate for Beast was all wrapped up in situational stuff. In our competition for Isabelle's love, for Orsino's favor. Without those things in play, I don't actually mind the guy. More, I respect the hell out of his ability to get the job done, out of his crafty as fuck mind, out of the way he fills out a pair of jeans.

But even that's not completely honest. If I'm being *honest*, I can admit that half my hate for him was wrapped up in thwarted lust, in a strange sort of jealousy that I can't untangle. I couldn't have him, couldn't face the fact that I wanted him, so it was easier to loathe him.

So, yeah, I want him. Maybe I've always wanted him,

It doesn't make this the right call.

As for the three of us together…

My chest aches just thinking about it. Walking away from Isabelle almost killed me. There were whole weeks I barely remember because I was basically the walking dead after that relationship ended. It took ending up in the Underworld one night and Tink ripping me a new one mid-scene for me to snap out of it.

It took another six months and change to crawl out of that goddamn hole.

If that happened after having and losing *her*, how much

worse will it be when this experiment of Beast's invariably fails? I'll fall for him. If I'm honest with myself, I'm already halfway there. Maybe more than halfway. I'll go tumbling head over heels for this goddamn heaven he's offering, and then when he gets bored or Isabelle gets spooked, they'll walk. And I'll be left worse off than before.

My voice is rough when I finally find the words. "It'll never work."

It's Isabelle who turns to look up at me, all wide brown eyes filled with hope. "But what if it does?"

CHAPTER 24

ISABELLE

*T*his has to be another trap, another mind-fuck, but I don't care. I'm terrified by how much I want what Beast offers. The three of us. Something I never dared hope for, something that feels so right, I could weep.

But Gaeton doesn't look convinced. Someone else might look at his expression and think he's furious with Beast for even speaking the words, but I know him better than that. He's just as terrified as I am.

I carefully move to my knees, putting me at eye level with him. I wish with all my heart that there was something I could do to banish the uncertainty from him, but it's circling my chest, too. Making this decision, going forward with this I'll lose the one thing I once valued above all else. I can't be free while I'm owned by these two men. They're too domi-nant, too protective, too determined to put their stamp on my very soul and ruin me for anyone else. If I say yes to this, I'm giving up the hope of one day leaving Carver City.

I close my eyes. It was a false dream, anyways. I have to admit that to myself, even if I haven't been able to admit it to anyone else. I am Orsino Belmonte's daughter. I was never leaving this city, was never having a life outside the responsibilities of the territory. I was never going to be *normal*.

When I open my eyes again, it's to find Gaeton looking like he's torn between throwing himself at us and leaving the room as quickly as possible. I can't dredge up a smile to comfort him, not when I'm so unsure myself. Not when there's still so much burned and salted ground between us. "It's okay if you can't forgive me, Gaeton. It's …" It's so hard to get this out. Setting him free is the last thing I want, which makes me a bigger hypocrite than I can ever say. I swallow hard. "I know what I did was unforgivable."

For a second, he seems like he's in actual physical pain. He slumps back against the headboard. "It makes a funny kind of sense. If there's a god, that fucker is laughing his ass off at us right now." He drags a hand over his face. "You're not the only one to blame, Isabelle. You were never the only one to blame."

"But—"

"No." He shakes his head. "You were right before. We agreed to that fucked up situation, and we both failed to be honest with you. I don't know about Beast but I just wanted to be good enough for you." He laughs a little, the sound jagged and sharp. "He calls you princess, but that's the fucking truth of what I thought. You were a princess and if I just compressed myself enough, I could be your Prince Charming."

It's a truth we've touched on again and again in the last few days, but hearing him admit to it shakes me to my core. I reach out a tentative hand and place it on his chest. "I don't know if you've noticed, but I don't *want* a Prince Charming."

"No, you want two monsters." The words hold no venom.

Beast shifts closer, not quite touching either of us. "Monsters are more effective than princes when it comes to

216

keeping what you care about safe." His blue eyes flare. "They're better at playing dark games in bed, too."

I can't quite fight down a shiver as the memories of the night crash over me. "That's the damn truth."

Beast seems to make an effort to bank the heat in his gaze. "We were missing something before. Several some-things. None of us were honest about what we wanted." He finally looks at Gaeton. "And none of us were getting every-thing we needed out of it. Closing the triangle will solve that."

Gaeton's already shaking his head. "You say that like it's that easy."

"It *is* that easy. I might not have recognized that my hate for you was thwarted lust, but hindsight is twenty-twenty." Beast takes my hand, his fingers playing against my wrist. "And Isabelle will never be happy in a monogamous relation-ship. That was our first sign to get creative, and we would have noticed if we weren't so wrapped up in competing with each other."

I pull back. I can't help it. Beast holds on to my hand a second longer than necessary, as if reminding me that he chooses to let me go. I pull the blanket more firmly around myself, but it doesn't do a damn thing against the possibili-ties beating against the barrier around my heart. "Is this an extension of the scene? Some kind of playing pretend?"

"No." Beast shakes his head. He doesn't have his cold mask on. Instead he looks almost vulnerable. "An unconven-tional solution, maybe, but not nearly as unconventional as some people think. I want both of you. There's not a single fucking reason we shouldn't be able to make this work."

I have admitted so many dark truths to these men over the last few days, but somehow this feels like the deepest, darkest truth yet. I lick my lips. "I want you both, too. I *love* you both. I never stopped, even when I was helping us burn things to the ground last time."

Gaeton still won't look at us directly. "What happens when Isabelle gets skittish? Or you get bored? It will fall apart just like it did before."

"No, it won't. We're not trying to have a conventional relationship like we were before." Beast leans forward. "We're not *lying* the way we were before. Something doesn't work, we talk about it and figure out a way to fix it. There will be some uncomfortable conversations, but it's a small price to pay."

Gaeton crosses his arms over his chest. "Uh-huh. And what happens if your long-lost love shows up in Carver City? You're going to drop us like yesterday's trash to run off and retake Sabine Valley with him."

Beast flinches. Actually *flinches*. "Cohen is dead. He's *been* dead for nearly a decade."

"And if he isn't?"

I should jump in, should derail this line of questioning, but I'm holding my breath because I want an answer, too. I know about Beast's ex, of course. I know that he never made it here to meet Beast and that the loss haunts him still. It never occurred to me the man could show up, or what would happen if he did. "Do you know something we don't?"

"No. But it's a question that needs to be asked." He's staring hard at Beast. "We're his second choice. Or second and third."

"No, you're not second choice. And neither of you is *third*." Beast looks like he wants to shut down this line of conversation, but he finally sighs. "I'm not the same person I was nine years ago. *If* Cohen is still alive, he's not the same man I fell in love with. He's my past. You—both of you—are my future. Together. No one above the other."

I slip my hand back into his. Talking about this can't be

easier than hearing it. He's trying to lead by example, and as much as I don't like the idea of Cohen showing up to put it to the test, Gaeton is right. It had to be asked. "This might blow up in our faces."

"It won't."

How can Beast be so sure? None of us have an excellent track record with relationships, let alone one as complicated as trying to juggle three people's needs. "You don't know that."

"And you don't know it won't work until we try." He gives my hand a squeeze. "Try with me?"

I might be questioning this, but there's only one answer. It's there in the weightless feeling in my chest and the endorphin buzz in my head. "Yes."

We both look at Gaeton. He doesn't seem any happier about this than he was a few minutes ago. "If we try and fail, the entire territory will bear the cost of it."

"We won't fail." Beast sounds so confident, I'm being won over despite myself. I've seen him when he sets his mind on something. He won't give up just because things get hard. He wants this, and I do, too.

Gaeton gives another of those long sighs that make me ache for him. "I don't trust how good this feels."

My heart wrenches in my chest. There was a time when he would have trusted it, when he would have the same confidence in this that Beast does. *I'm* the reason he's doubting now.

If we do this, there will be no traditional white wedding like he had pictured in his head where I walk down the aisle to him. Saying yes means robbing him of that future

Unless it doesn't.

If we're going to be *unconventional* about our relationship, why not do it with our marriage, too? Maybe a marriage like that wouldn't feel like a trap.

I give myself a little shake. We're barely agreeing to this in the first place. Looking that far into the future, to a moment where I might walk down the aisle to *both* of them, is a bad idea. I sit there and wait for my normal panic at the thought of being tied down permanently to hit, but my only answer is the steady beat of my heart in my ears.

Beast touches his chin, bringing them face to face. "Do you trust me?"

Gaeton tenses like he wants to argue, but finally gives a jerky nod. "Yeah. I trust you."

"Trust me to take care of us until this feels real."

The sheer scope of what he's demanding leaves me breathless. Or maybe it's hope that has my lungs seizing and my body shaking. When Gaeton finally nods again, it feels like every bone in my body goes liquid in relief. I catch his hand with my free one and he gives me a tentative smile. "You know sealing this with a kiss won't cut it."

"Whatever you want." I still lean forward and kiss him hard. *I love you. I love you both so much.* I've said it. I can't keep saying it, can't apply gasoline to an already explosive situation. I can't expect us to all be there. Not with me. Not with each other, either. I have to be patient and let this play out, but the buoyancy in my chest has me feeling just as drunk as I felt coming down from our scene. "Anything you want."

"What *I* want is both of you naked." Beast climbs off the bed and starts stripping. He does it in short, economical movements that aren't designed to entice, but leave me enraptured all the same. He's beautiful. He's *always* been beautiful to me, scars included. They just show his strength, his will to survive despite everything he's gone through. Knowing that determination will be focused on progressing this relationship makes me feel warm and tingly.

I nudge Gaeton. "You heard him."

"Just enjoying the view," he rumbles.

Beast takes off his pants and I can't help licking my lips at the memory of that piercing against my tongue. Gaeton huffs out a laugh and climbs off the bed, which has my gaze dragging helplessly to him. His big body, thick neck and thighs, the hair dusting his chest and lower. These two men could not be more different, but I want them so much, I practically quiver with desire.

The concept that I don't have to choose, that they're both mine and I'm both of theirs, hasn't really sunk in yet. Maybe it will later. Maybe I'll spend the next five years waiting for the other shoe to drop. Either possibility leaves me dizzy. It doesn't matter. Tonight is a way of stating our intentions, and I won't let my fear hold us all back.

I let the blanket fall as both men climb back onto the mattress. Part of me expects the three of us to fall on each other like starved creatures, but that isn't what happens at all. Beast slides his hand through my hair to cup the back of my neck. Then he does the same to Gaeton. The slightest pressure urges my mouth to Gaeton's and the feeling of Beast guiding this is just as intoxicating as Gaeton's lips parting and his tongue sliding against mine. He tastes like home. I don't think these men will ever *not* feel like home to me.

The pressure of Beast's hand on my neck eases a little and I pull back as he leans in and takes Gaeton's mouth. Their kiss is tentative and so filled with yearning that I feel like the worst kind of voyeur for witnessing it. I don't care. I soak up the sexual tension rising between them, luxuriating in the fact that there will be no choosing tonight. We get it *all*.

Beast kisses me next. It's nowhere near as tentative as the one he shared with Gaeton. No, this is like him reminding me who owns me, body and soul. By the time he lifts his head, I'm shivering against him, gripping his arm with one hand and Gaeton's with the other. Beast nips my bottom lip, and then I'm kissing Gaeton again as Beast moves to my back, reaching around me to run his hands down Gaeton's chest to grip his cock.

There's no talking, but there really doesn't need to be. Not for this. It feels like the most natural thing in the world to be pressed between these men, our bodies getting tangled up in our need to touch each other, to stoke our desire until it threatens to consume us whole.

I don't care about the danger.

I want to burn.

CHAPTER 25

GAETON

*W*ith every touch, every kiss, my trepidation fades. Beast is right. I hate that he's right, but it doesn't change the truth. The three of us *fit*. Physically and otherwise. Our strengths complement each other; with three of us, our flaws feel less pronounced. I don't understand how it works, I just need it to work.

They topple me back onto the mattress, Isabelle ending up astride my stomach and Beast between my thighs. I arch up to press her breasts together and tongue her nipples even as she bends back to kiss him and his hand closes around my cock again. It's an assault on the senses, but in the best way possible. I never want it to end.

Isabelle pushes me back down and kisses me, writhing against my chest in a way that leaves me with no doubt that Beast has his fingers in her pussy. She breaks the kiss to say, "I need your mouth on me. Please."

As if my woman has to beg for something I'm just as desperate for. I drag her up my body and then lift her to straddle my face. Her ass must still be sore from the spanking, because she winces a little when I grip her, but her sharp inhale turns into a moan on the exhale. She loves that spice of pain, and I love that she loves it. I drag my tongue over her pussy, savoring the feel and taste of her. A dark, savage part of me loves that she's begging for *my* mouth after she had Aurora going down on her like the other woman never needs to breathe. It's not jealousy, exactly. Just a heightened possessiveness in the aftermath of that kind of game. It makes my cock so hard, I almost come the second Beast's mouth closes around me.

He sucks me down, pleasure damn near making me black out. I growl against Isabelle and pick up my pace, as if fucking her with my tongue has any effect on the slow blowjob Beast is currently torturing me with. Slow, steady, wet heat and the drag of his tongue along the underside of my cock with each retreat. Fuck, it's good. Too good.

I suck hard on Isabelle's clit. Harder than I mean to. I wanted to draw this out, to tease her until she's sobbing through an orgasm, but I left my control on the floor with my clothes. Her hands hit the wall at the head of the bed and then she's grinding against my face as she comes. Too hard, too fast. It won't satisfy her for long, but that's okay.

Beast lifts his head with a dark laugh. "Got you."

"Shut up." I give Isabelle one last lick and then lift her off my face. He's there to catch her, dragging her down my body to straddle my hips. It's his hand that fists my cock and guides me into her pussy. He grips her hips as she rocks slowly, still winding down from the fast and dirty orgasm.

Beast climbs off the bed and moves to dig through the nightstand, coming up with the bottle of lube. My whole body goes tight with anticipation. This, this is what I need.

Not doubt, not reality, just us.

He urges my legs wide. "Up." I lift my hips and Beast slides a pillow beneath me, and then shifts Isabelle a little to make room for him. Both me and Isabelle go completely still as Beast spreads the lube, and then his cock is there, pushing into me slowly but inexorably. My breath hisses out at the sensation, and I can't help my grip flexing on Isabelle's hips. "Fuck."

"Mmm." He sinks the rest of the way and gives a little pump. He cups Isabelle's breasts and then grasps her throat with one hand and slides the other down to stroke her clit. The position bows her back, and then I can see him looking down at me and, fuck, my heart about bursts out of my chest from the wave of emotion that cascades over me as I drown in this man's eyes.

Beast gives Isabelle's clit a little slap. "Ride him, princess."

She jumps and moans and then obeys, her hips finding a smooth rhythm as she seeks her own pleasure from my cock and Beast's fingers. It's so good, I could die. And then it gets better, because Beast starts moving, fucking my ass in a nearly perfect mimic of Isabelle riding my cock.

My brain shorts out. I know I should do something, should move, should do more than just take it, but it's too good and it's everything I can do not to blow right here and now. None of us are moving fast, as if we all agreed that we want this moment to last as long as possible, the threads tying us together tighter and tighter as our pleasure rises in a steady wave.

Isabelle tips over the edge first. She comes with a cry that forms into my name, into his. "*Gaeton*. Oh fuck. *Beast*." Her pussy clenches around my cock and it's too much. I fuck up into her, chasing my own orgasm, pumping her full of me even as I hold Beast's eyes.

He topples Isabelle onto my chest and braces his hands on either side of me. He was playing nice before. He isn't now. He fucks me roughly with deep strokes I swear I can feel in the back of my throat. Taking me like I'm his, like I've always been his and he knows exactly where my limits are and has no concern about crossing them.

It feels so fucking good, my cock twitches inside Isabelle, hardening against all reason. She moans and writhes and then we're off again, caught in something that feels bigger than any one of us. I can't stop. I don't want to ever stop. I want this forever. I want it so fucking bad, it might destroy me, but what a way to go. I kiss Isabelle with everything I have until we are forced to come up for air. "I forgive you."

Her eyes go shiny even as she works herself on my cock. "Promise?"

"Promise." I kiss her again, framing her face in my hands and releasing that last bit of anger that's resided in my chest for so fucking long, I feel a hundred pounds lighter.

Beast curses and then he's coming. Isabelle follows him a moment later, the combined pleasure taking me with them. We lie in a pile on the bed, the only sound our labored breathing. Isabelle shivers. "Do you think a person can die from pleasure?"

Beast gives a rough laugh and pulls out of me. "We're nowhere near that threshold."

"Speak for yourself." She nuzzles my chest, her body boneless against me. I wrap an arm around her and watch Beast disappear into the bathroom. A few minutes later, he returns and we take our time cleaning up.

I frown down at the bed. "I know I said we'd stay here tonight, but I've changed my mind." Especially when we have one last promise to fulfill, one last fantasy to play out. Beast may think I've forgotten, but fuck like I'm going to let this night end without doing what I promised.

Doing what we should have done two years ago on that sunny afternoon in Isabelle's room.

"Yeah, agreed." Beast pulls on his clothes, already steady on his feet. "I'll get the car. Meet me downstairs in ten."

"Sure." It takes me a little longer to dress, my legs still feeling wonky. I dig through the dresser to find the clothing the Underworld keeps stashed in all the overnight rooms—and quite a few of the playrooms. Things have a habit of getting torn or otherwise ruined during play, so there are backups available. For a price, of course.

I find a pair of leggings and a shirt and take them to Isabelle. "Here." It feels like the most natural thing in the world to dress her, and though I expect her to argue that she can do it herself, she passively allows it. I end up on my knees before her, but this time the position doesn't sting the way it did before. "I meant it."

She looks down at me with so much vulnerability on her pretty face. "It's okay if you don't yet. I—"

I take her hands. "I meant it. I forgive you." I hesitate. "I hope you can forgive me, too, given time. I was a fucking asshole."

She presses her lips together. "I forgave you a long time ago. I think there was more than enough of us being assholes to go around on all sides." Isabelle tugs on my hands and I let her guide me to my feet. She gives a tentative smile. "Do you think he's right and we can really make this work?"

I look at the door. "I wouldn't bet against anything Beast puts his mind to. If he's decided we can work, there's a damn good chance he's right."

"I really want him to be right."

"I do, too." I squeeze her hands and start for the door. "Let's go home."

It's not until we're in the car driving back to my apartment that it dawns on me. This won't be home for much longer. We're headed back to the proper territory, sooner rather than later if we're all in agreement in the morning. I had braced for another week and change of uncertainty, so the realization leaves the ground feeling a bit unsteady beneath my feet.

I glance at Beast as he parks. "You didn't just come up with this plan a few hours ago."

"No, I didn't."

Thought so. I frown harder. "When did you decide that this was what you wanted?"

He gives me a strangely soft smile. It will take some getting used to the man beneath the hard edges. Beast reaches out and drags his thumb over my bottom lip. "Somewhere around the time you had your mouth all over my balls. Or at least that's when I finally admitted it to myself."

I grin. I can't help it. "Liked that, did you?"

"You know I did." He gifts me with a wider smile. "I like everything the three of us do together when we're too caught up in fucking to get in our own way. So I decided that none of us needed to choose."

"Just like that." I should probably be irritated, but I'm mostly amazed by his audacity. This fucker sees something he wants and goes after it with a single-minded intensity that blows me away. I never thought *I'd* be one of the things he set his sights on.

"Just like that." He kisses me, quick and possessive. "I used to hate you, but that saying that hate and love are two sides to the same coin?" He shrugs without moving away. "There's some truth to it."

I can barely believe what I'm hearing. My heart is beating too hard, nearly drowning out the rushing in my ears that his words bring. "What the fuck are you saying?"

He grins against my mouth. "I'm saying I love you and your big cock, Gaeton Thibault. It's not the same as what I feel for Isabelle, but it's all tied up together the way we are. I love you and I'm keeping you."

"It's too fast to feel that shit."

He finally moves back and gives me a long look. "Take your time with your own feelings, but you don't get to tell me what I feel."

Anyone else would seem vulnerable or nervous to start spouting talk of love after less than a week of fucking, but Beast is just ... Beast. I stare at him. This isn't anyone else, and this situation is hardly what someone would consider *normal*. I've known this man nearly a decade, and he's infuriatingly right in this just like he has been about other things. Now that my anger and hate is gone, there's a warm feeling in my chest that might be something akin to love. It's not the same as what I feel for Isabelle, as it is more thorns than roses, but I hold the sensation close all the same. "There's going to be no living with you if I tell you that I love you, too."

He kisses me again. "I fuck harder when I'm smug. You'll learn to enjoy it."

"You're infuriating." I huff out a laugh. "I must have a masochistic streak, because I enjoy the hell out of it."

He runs his fingers through my hair. "Let's go up and go to sleep, Gaeton. I figure we can have another couple days before we have to start figuring out the finer details, and I have plans for that big cock of yours in the morning."

"Not yet."

He goes still, but it's Isabelle who answers. "What do you mean?"

"Let's get upstairs and then Beast has a confession to make."

She's frowning as we walk to the elevator, but she holds her peace until the door shuts between us and the rest of the world. Isabelle moves to the couch and perches on it. "Okay, I'm listening. What do you need to confess?"

"Tell Isabelle your fantasy."

She looks at him sharply. "He did."

"Not the truthful one." I can't stop my smug grin. "You didn't think his wanting to fuck you on your father's desk felt a little mundane?"

"Not that you mention it ..."

"I *did* want that." Beast gives me a long look and then turns to Isabelle. "But there was a day back when we were both dating you that I walked in on you and Gaeton fucking. You didn't see me. He did." He draws in a slow breath. "I wanted to punish you both. I wanted to fuck you both." A small smile pulls at his lips. "That should have been my first indication that my needs were more complicated than I was admitting, but I wasn't ready to take that step then. I am now."

Anticipation wipes away all my exhaustion. It feels right as fuck that we're starting off our fledgling throuple by playing out this scene. "What do you say, Rose? Should we give him his fantasy?"

"As if there's any question of refusing him." She's already nodding. "Yes. Hell yes."

CHAPTER 26

BEAST

*I*sabelle walks to me and runs her hands up my chest. Her hair's a tangled mess and her lipstick is smudged. She's never been more beautiful to me. She leans up and presses her lips to mine. "I know you have some calls to make."

I don't, but I play along and nod. "Why don't you two wait for me in the bedroom?" I catch her hips when she starts to move away. "I don't suppose I have to tell you to be good."

"I will." Her sunny smile belies the wicked expression in her brown eyes. She glances over her shoulder at Gaeton, who's watching us closely. "We both will. Right, Gaeton?"

"Sure thing, Rose." He waits for her to move back and snags her around the waist. His grin is arrogant and lazy. "Just don't take too long, Beast. It'd be a shame if we got bored."

I inject a bit of steel into my tone. "Don't."

"Yes, Sir." He doesn't even try to sound like he's going to obey, and I fucking love it. That's not what Gaeton and I are. We're both too dominant to play the perfect submissive game, and the challenge radiating from him whets my appetite for what comes next. It doesn't matter that we've fucked more than once tonight. This is *my* fantasy, and they're giving it to me just like I've waited two long years for.

They disappear into the bedroom, leaving the door cracked the barest inch. I lean against the wall next to it and listen, my cock getting harder by the second. There's the soft sound of them taking off their clothes, the heavy weight that must be Gaeton sitting on the mattress.

"Come here, Rose."

"We shouldn't." Her footsteps pad in his direction. A sharp inhale. "*Gaeton.*"

I know without a shadow of a doubt that they're both pitching their voices higher so I can hear them. I close my eyes. Fuck, I love these two.

"Beast won't mind if I give your pussy a little stroke." Gaeton growls. "You don't mind, either, do you, Rose? You like being bad."

"Maybe." Her breath hitches. I know beyond a shadow of a doubt that he's got his fingers in her now, is stroking her need. She whimpers. "Gaeton?"

"Yeah."

"Maybe you could …" Another sharp inhale.

He laughs, low and harsh. "You need my tongue, Rose? Guess you don't want to be that good after all. Think Beast will notice if he comes in here and you're all over my face?" He doesn't wait for her to answer. "I don't think you give a fuck any more than I do. Come here."

She gives a little shriek and there's a thud, his knees hitting the floor. Fuck, but the man likes to be on his knees. I count slowly, listening as her breathing goes hard and the west sounds of his mouth on her pussy fill the room.

Not yet.

Not quite yet.

As if Gaeton can hear me, he curses long and hard. "I can't wait any more. I need you, Rose."

"*Yes.*"

More sounds as they shift. Gaeton's voice is deeper now, low and gravely like it gets when he's riding the edge. "That's right. Take my cock, little slut. Ride me slow. If we're going to be bad, we're going to enjoy every second of it."

Just like that afternoon two years ago, I can hear how wet her pussy is every time she comes down on his cock. I straighten off the wall. *Now.*

Pushing the door open with a single fingertip is like walking into the past. The details are a little different, but the scene is the same. Gaeton is on his back in his bed, sprawled out like a barbarian king as Isabelle rides his cock in slow, decadent strokes.

He sees me first and gives me a lazy grin. "You took too long."

Isabelle looks over her shoulder. "Sorry, Beast. We tried to hold out."

I give them a long look. "I might believe you if you weren't still fucking him while you apologize to me." She starts to move off him, but I give my head a sharp shake. "Don't stop on my account, princess. You need his cock so much? Take it."

Isabelle flushes a deep crimson, but she obeys, shifting back to her lazy fucking of Gaeton even as she watches me. I cross the room slowly, pulling off my clothes as I do. "What am I going to do with the two of you?"

"I could think of a few things," Gaeton rumbles.

"Selfish," I murmur. A thousand possibilities dance through my mind, but ultimately there's only one way tonight needs to go. We have all the time in the world to play out alternative versions. "You always were selfish when it came to Isabelle."

"Can you blame me?" He coasts his hands up her hips and cups her breasts as I round the bed to the nightstand. "Look at her."

I'm looking, but not just at her. Perfect. Tonight is so fucking perfect, I can't stand it. I grab the lube and move around to climb up onto the mattress behind Isabelle, kneeling between Gaeton's spread thighs. "Her pussy feels good, doesn't it?"

"Fucking paradise."

I trace a finger down her spine, stopping at the small of her back. "I'm going to take your ass tonight, princess. Are you ready to have both of us?"

"*Yes.*" She clears her throat. "Yes, Sir. Yes, *Sirs.*"

I move my hand up and press it to the middle of her back, guiding her down to Gaeton's chest. I hold his gaze as I spread lube over her ass. "Tomorrow, we figure out living arrangements."

Gaeton huffs out a laugh. "Plenty of time to talk about that in the morning."

"Yeah." I push a finger into Isabelle and grin when she squirms. "But we'll be spending at least half our time in the family residence."

Understanding slowly dawns in his dark eyes. "Quite a few parties on the horizon, too."

"Exactly." I squeeze Isabelle's hip and guide my cock to her ass. She's not as experienced in this as Gaeton is, so I go slow. The last thing I want is to move too fast and hurt her. Gaeton must feel the same way, because he's already smoothing his big hands over her body. "Relax, Rose. Let him do the work."

"It might be easier if you take your big cock out of her pussy," I grind out, sinking another inch into her.

"Probably." But he makes no effort to do it.

I laugh a little. "Isabelle?"

"I'm good." She shifts back, taking me deeper, and moans. "I'm really, really good."

"Next time there's a party, princess." I sink the last inch into her and exhale slowly. "Next time, wear that yellow dress Tink made for you. No panties. I want to come back to that little room and find Gaeton inside you. I don't give a fuck if it's tongue or fingers or cock."

She sobs out a breath. "Yes, Sir."

"Then he's going to fuck you." I lean down until my lips brush her ear and my chest is pressed to her back. "And I'm going to watch. I might even leave the door open a bit so you have to be particularly quiet."

"Oh, gods."

Gaeton's hands move up to my hips and squeeze. "And after you make a round of polite talk with all those assholes, you're going to go back in that room, lift up your skirt, and let Beast bend you over the couch."

"Back and forth," I murmur.

Gaeton's words begin as soon as mine end, and we both start to move. He hisses out a breath. "How long before you're dripping our come, Rose? How long before someone catches you on one of our cocks?"

Isabelle moans and writhes. "What if I want both?"

"Greedy."

"Little slut." Gaeton grins at me over her shoulder, though his expression is as pained as mine feels. "Guess you'll have to ride my cock and put on a good enough show to tempt Beast over."

It's everything I can do to keep my movements slow and controlled and not pound into her, chasing the desire of this situation compounded with the fantasy we're spinning with our words. "Wouldn't want to smudge your lipstick. Then everyone would know."

Each breath sobs from her lips. "My ass. You'll have to take it like you are now."

Gaeton curses and his hands spasm on my hips, pulling me harder into her. It causes her to writhe and clench down around both of us, which has him cursing again. "No way to pretend you're not a little slut if someone walks into find both our cocks buried in you."

"I'm *your* little slut. Both of yours." She reaches up and cups his face and kiss him hard. "I wouldn't stop, no matter who walked in. I'd beg you not to stop."

It's one fantasy we won't play out. Not exactly like this. But … I carefully pull out of her. "Gaeton."

He's already nodding. "Got it." He climbs off the bed and walks out of the room. Isabelle turns around and kisses me, pulling me down to press her against the bed.

She shivers in my arms. "You two are turning me into a sex addict."

"Lots of fantasies to work through. Lots of ways to work through them." And years to do it, if I have my way. I will. I refuse to fail.

Gaeton walks back into the room, carrying one of the dining room chairs. He considers and then sets it down a few feet from the bed, directly in line with the door. "Come here, Isabelle."

I move off her so she can obey. Watching Gaeton lift her onto his cock brings me an absurd amount of pleasure. *Mine, mine, mine.* She wraps her arms around his neck and grins up at him. "This would be more realistic if I had a dress on."

"Next time. I like you naked." He motions me forward. "Don't bother closing the door, Beast. Everyone here knows who she belongs to. How fucking *needy* she is."

Isabelle starts moving even as she glances over her shoulder at me and bites her bottom lip. "It's been too long since you were inside me."

"Like I said. Needy."

I grab more lube. Gaeton's chairs are tall enough that I don't have to squat to slide my cock back into Isabelle's ass. I kiss the back of her neck and begin to move. Gaeton does the same a few seconds later, both of us fucking her slowly, thoroughly. I nip her earlobe and then lean up and catch Gaeton's mouth. Perfect. Fucking *perfect*.

Gaeton chuckles against my lips, the sound strained. "Maybe we'll invite Aurora to one of those parties. Though gods know she'll have her tongue in your pussy the first chance she gets."

Isabelle picks up her pace, riding both our cocks. "Yes."

"So insatiable. We'll have to take both of you back to your room to let you fuck it out. Otherwise she's bound to have her hand up your dress by the bar."

I drag my mouth over the back of Isabelle's neck. "Tell him what you told me, princess." I reach around her hip and stroke her clit as she fucks us. I'm barely moving now, letting Isabelle chase her pleasure. "Tell him your newest fantasy."

She leans back, pressing both of us deeper into her, and guides Gaeton's hands to her breasts. "I want to watch Aurora ride your cock."

"*Fuck*," he breathes.

"I want …" Her breath hitches and so do her strokes. "I want to eat her pussy while you're fucking her, to have her mouth on me while one of you is inside me. Or both of you. To have her tongue fuck me while you fuck each other. To switch partners again and again and again until we can't fuck anymore. I want …"

"An orgy," I breathe in her ear.

"*Yes*," she sobs out. And then she's coming. She clenches so hard around us that Gaeton curses and starts driving up into her, following her over the edge. I barely pull out before I do the same, coming across her back in great spurts.

Gaeton looks up at me, his expression as dazed as if he's been hit by a truck. "We're really doing this."

"Yes. We really are." I help Isabelle stand and then do the same to Gaeton, guiding us to his bathroom. We shower in a daze, exhaustion a heaviness that seems to be weighing as hard on them as it is on me.

The other two fall asleep in Gaeton's bed almost immediately, but I hold out a few minutes longer, relishing this feeling of contentment. Of joy. I never thought I'd get my happily ever after. I'm not certain I believed such a thing existed even before shit went so sideways in Sabine Valley. I look down at Isabelle and Gaeton. I might have failed the person I loved most in the world once, but I sure as fuck won't do it again. It doesn't matter who I have to remove to ensure our future is secure. I'll do it, and gladly.

Tomorrow.

Tonight is for dreams and joy and *love*.

CHAPTER 27

ISABELLE

I wake up to the bedroom door crashing open with a violent bang. Beast and Gaeton are already moving while I'm trying to figure out what the hell is going on. It doesn't make any difference. They barely get an inch before a familiar voice says, "Do not move. I would truly hate to shoot you, but I will."

I shove Gaeton's arm out of my way and sit up. "Muriel?"

My sister-in-law stands in the doorway, a handgun held easily in her strong hands. She's a curvy Dominican woman with long black hair pulled back from her face, wearing one of her favorite dresses—one with kittens printed all over it—looking as fresh as a fucking daisy. There are three men on either side of her, also with guns. I blink again. "I told my sisters I had things covered."

"Cordelia thinks otherwise." She raises her brows at the bed with the three of us. "Get up. Get dressed. Now."

"No."

"Do we really need to resort to threats to get you to move, Isabelle?" Muriel sighs. "I have permission to shoot one or both of these men. Shall we cut through the song and dance of convincing you that I'll do it?"

I already know she will. Cordelia will make hard calls and do what needs to be done, but at the end of the day she might feel some guilt over it. Muriel won't. It doesn't matter that she's worked with Gaeton and Beast for years. She has her orders and she'll pull the trigger, wash the blood from her hands, and go back to deliver my sister her report and a kiss.

"Don't even think about it," Gaeton rumbles.

I'm already moving, carefully crawling to the edge of the bed and climbing to my feet. I'm naked, but acting bashful will only undermine me at this point. As I stare down my sister-in-law, it doesn't escape my notice that all six of the men behind her are focused *very* hard on the men and not on me. I glance back at the bed. At the two of them looking like they're ready to fight their way through the room to me. "I'm holding you to what we agreed to last night. Come to dinner tonight. We still have living arrangements to iron out."

Muriel snorts. "Cordelia will love that."

I ignore her. "Promise me."

Beast nods first. "We'll be there."

"Yeah." Gaeton is still staring hard at the guns pointed in his direction. "Consider it a date."

It has to be enough. I hate that our time has been cut short, but if everyone meant what they said last night, we're looking down the barrel at forever. And *forever* means we have to deal with my sisters eventually.

I pull on the T-shirt and leggings from last night. The only shoes I have here are ridiculously tall heels, but I put them on all the same. I want to kiss the guys goodbye, but Muriel grabs my arm and nearly hauls me off my feet as she drags me to the door.

As much as I want to rip her a new one, I save my arguing

for my sisters. Muriel wouldn't come here on her own, and damn it, I wish Cordelia trusted me enough to let me handle this. The men file out of the apartment after us, three taking position ahead and three behind.

I don't speak again until we're in the back of an SUV, now flanked by two identical vehicles. "There was a better way to go about that."

"Maybe." She shrugs. "We got the point across, didn't we?"

"That's bullshit and you know it."

She gives a dry laugh. "If Cordelia called you under the same circumstances as forty-eight hours ago, would you have sat back and waited for her to work through things? Or would you have done exactly what she did?"

I would have trusted my sister to have things covered, and to communicate if she didn't. Because Cordelia is a grown ass adult, just like I am, and more than capable of handling herself in a variety of situations. *Just like I am.* I start to cross my arms over my chest, but it feels like pouting. "I have it under control."

"Good. Tell her that." She leans back against the seat with a sigh. "She's been difficult as hell to deal with for the last week, and that's *your* fault. You fix this."

Cordelia is the one who sent me to the Underworld in the first place. I press my lips together to prevent myself from yelling it. I'm not going to win Muriel to my side. She supports Cordelia, and if they ever disagree, they do it behind closed doors. I've never seen them as anything other than a united front, and I sure as hell won't see it for this situation.

We finish the ride back to our territory, back to my father's house, in silence. My breath grows thick as we drive through the gates protecting the property from the outside world. Once upon a time, this area was a train yard, but the company went under and my father bought it for pennies on the dollar. It took years and a small fortune to convert it to his own little stronghold at the edge of Carver City, but now that's exactly what it is. Thick walls surround the main house and half a dozen other buildings, including barracks for his people and a lab for Sienna. For all that it's basically a military base, the house is a study in sheer indulgence. It's not quite Victorian, but you can see the influence in the lines and slopes of the building.

My father always did appreciate a good first impression.

I close my eyes for half a second, striving for control. I wish Gaeton and Beast were here, but this is something I have to do on my own. By the time I have my shit together, we've climbed out of the car and stopped in front of the broad stone staircase leading up to the front door. Muriel matches my pace, and it's impossible not to notice how something in her unwinds the closer we get to my sister.

Cordelia, being Cordelia, doesn't meet us in the foyer. She makes me go hunting for her in her study. I'm tired. My feet hurt. My *whole body* hurts. The last thing I want to do is go a round with my older sister.

I walk through the door and stop short. *Both* of my sisters are here. Because of course they are.

Muriel slides past me and pauses to give Cordelia a kiss before she takes up her usual position to one side of the bay window on the other side of the study. Sienna lounges on the small sofa situated to the side of the deck in an informal kind of sitting room, a book on some advanced scientific theory I've never heard of open across her stomach. She gives me a finger wave. Cordelia leans against the massive desk at the center of the room, as tense as if she's ready to charge into battle.

She sweeps a look over me. "You're walking. I wasn't sure you would be."

That's about enough of that. "I had everything under control."

"Did you?" She crosses her arms over her chest. "I sent you there to *talk* to them, and the next update I get is you in Gaeton's bed, obviously having been fucked with. I don't think you had a single damn thing under control. I think they saw an opportunity and they took it, and you felt too guilty to do anything but go along with it."

I love my sister. I do. I would take a bullet for her. But sometimes I want to shake her until some sense falls into that big head of hers. I give her a long look. "Oh, were you done? I was really enjoying you telling me how *I* felt and what happened with *me* even though you weren't there."

"Don't take an attitude with me, Izzy. You would have made the same call if our positions were reversed."

I shoot a look at Muriel. "Funny, your wife said the exact same thing in the car. You're both wrong. I would have trusted you to tell me if you needed help."

"I couldn't afford to make that mistake." She runs her fingers through her long dark hair and grips it briefly before letting it go. There was a time when Cordelia dealt with stress by pulling out her own hair, but years of therapy have helped her acquire healthier coping mechanisms. She seems to forcibly lower her hands. Muriel moves up behind her, clasping her hands gently. Cordelia leans back against her wife, but accepting that comfort doesn't make her appear any less fierce. "We just lost him. I can't lose you, too."

Just like that, my anger drains out of me. How can I be mad at her about this when we're all so messed up for the loss of our father still? Short answer: I can't. Muriel moves out of the way right as I walk around the desk and pull Cordelia into a hug. "I'm fine. I'm here. I was never in any danger." Not in any physical way, at least. The jury is still out on my heart.

"I'd kill them myself," she murmurs, hugging me hard enough that I have a difficult time drawing in oxygen. "I don't care if he loved them, too. If they hurt you, I'd kill them slowly."

I pat her back. "No need for killing. I'm here. I'm safe." I lean back and look at her. "I'm *safe*."

"You're safe," she finally agrees.

"Just really well-fucked," Sienna calls from the couch.

Cordelia narrows her eyes. "I'm still pissed that you didn't tell me you were in contact with her." She turns that look on me. "And that you were taking *her* calls and not mine."

I shrug. "It was for science."

"For the love of—" She walks to the couch and drops on the cushion near Sienna's feet. "You two are terrible for my blood pressure."

"The role of younger sisters worldwide." Sienna sits up a little, her dark eyes alight. "Want to know the results of my algorithm? I was going to email you, but Cordelia had you brought in so this is so much simpler. It's fascinating really."

If I let her get going, we won't be leaving this office for hours. I hold up my hand. "I don't need the algorithm. I—"

"Choose them both," Sienna finishes for me. She grins like a kid on Christmas morning at my dumbfounded look. "That's what you're going to say, isn't it? That you're going to be a delicious little throuple?"

"I ..." I motion vaguely at her. "How ..."

"I told you." She looks so smug, I want to hit her in the face with a pillow. "Science and math and a little bit of finesse."

I shouldn't ask. I truly shouldn't. "Your algorithm said I would choose them both?"

"No, don't be absurd. That wasn't a possible outcome." She waves that away. "But every time I ran the information, it came out a little differently, and no matter what tweaks I put into place, the percentages were startlingly close. Either there's something wrong with my work—highly unlikely, but I can't ignore the possibility—or the best decision is *both*." She stares off into the middle distance. "I *do* need more information for the components to allow for multiple partners in an accurate way."

"You terrify me."

She grins. "Thank you."

Cordelia narrows her eyes. "You're choosing them both."

"Yes." I take a slow breath. "Things didn't work how we had them before, and there's a reason for that. I think they can work now."

"If you're wrong, you're putting the entire territory at risk."

I know that. The entire territory and my whole heart. I swallow hard. "I'm not wrong."

She considers me for a long moment and then sighs. "Well, this is going to make things awkward after this morning." Cordelia lifts her chin. "I'm not apologizing."

"I doubt anyone expects you to," Sienna says as she picks up her book. "We all know better."

"What's that supposed to mean?"

"Hmmm?" She turns a page.

Cordelia looks at Muriel, but her wife is studying the ceiling as if it holds the mysteries of the universe. "You're all assholes."

I clear my throat. "They're coming for dinner tonight, and then they're staying." Actually, I don't know what the plan is for living arrangements, but I have a permanent suite here in the main house, so as Beast said last night, we'll likely spend half our time here. Or I suppose I'll talk to the men and see what they think. Because we're communicating now, and that means we all get an opinion and will work through each complication. The thought makes me giddy. *We can actually make this work.*

Cordelia looks like she wants to argue, but finally sighs. "I'm not going to say good job at getting them back here, because I think the cost was too high."

"The cost of my happiness?"

"You don't know if you're going to be happy. It's too new."

I have to fight not to roll my eyes. "The three of us have known each other for nearly a decade. I dated them separately for *two years.* We have plenty of foundation, and none of it is *new.*"

"Fine," she snaps. "Forgive me for giving a fuck."

"Consider yourself forgiven," I snap back. I open my mouth and then burst out laughing. "This is the most ridiculous fight."

"Only because you're ridiculous," she grumbles. Cordelia waves a hand. "If they're coming to dinner, we're making a thing of it. A statement."

I have to fight down a blush thinking about the *statement* we made last night. "I'll leave that to you."

"Go take a nap and get your head on straight. I need you on your A game tonight, Izzy."

"Consider it done."

It's only when I get up to my room and strip out of my borrowed clothes that I have a chance to wonder if this short time of forced distance will be enough for cold logic to set in with the men. It's easy to agree to a throuple when we're all naked and fucking. Will it hold up to the cold light of day?

I turn on my shower and walk back into my room. It's only then that I realize I left my phone at Gaeton's. I have no way to call them, no way to reassure myself that they still want this, still want me.

If they show up, I'm going to feel like the biggest asshole

for having doubts. I should trust them, should trust the connection I know we all felt.

But I can't help the shadows creeping around the edges, whispering that this was all a game of vengeance to repay me for the harm done.

CHAPTER 28

BEAST

*I*t feels strange walking into this house again. Strange to know that this time, if things go as planned, we won't be leaving in any permanent way. I glance at Gaeton, but he's got his arrogant grin in place. That tells me as much as anything. He's not comfortable, and he's not sure how this is going to play out. Saying that we want to be together is all well and good, but if Cordelia decides that she isn't a fan of the idea ...

Then we're left with two options. Take Isabelle and run, cutting her off from her remaining family. Or walk away for good.

I hate both those fucking options, so I'm invested in ensuring no one has to make any tough choices. I brush Gaeton's arm. "Steady."

"Steady as a fucking rock."

The door opens before we get to it, and I nearly miss a step at Sienna Belmonte grinning at us. *That* expression never means anything good. She stands back and opens the door wide. "Come in, come in. You're nearly late."

I exchange a look with Gaeton and we walk through the

248

door. The house looks nearly the same as it did a month ago, which is strange to me. Orsino's passing from this world should have more physical consequences. There should be more in evidence here. It's an odd thing to expect; it's not as if Cordelia's priorities right now are on redecorating.

Sienna strides down the hall, leaving us to pick up our pace in order not to be left behind. She gives another of those unsettling grins over her shoulder. "I don't think I have to say it, but I'm a fan of clearly marked action and consequence. As such," She slows. "If you hurt my sister, I will take you into my lab and make you wish for death before I finally let you cross over. I'm very good, and I can make it last a very long time. Do we understand each other?"

She's not bluffing. Sienna is incapable of bluffing. I hold her gaze. "We're not going to hurt Isabelle."

"Then I suppose we'll never have to worry about it, will we?"

I expect her to take us back to the private dining room the family uses on a daily basis. Instead, Sienna leads us down the wide hall meant for entertaining. To the banquet room. There's no other description for it. Orsino knew how to put on a show when the situation called for it, and everything about the dining room is designed to impress, from the size of the table to the paintings hanging along the walls of the room. The table is large enough to fit twenty people easily, and it's already half-filled when we walk through the door.

Cordelia sits at the head of the table, Muriel standing at her shoulder. The latter watches every person in the room with an intensity that says if anyone steps out of line, she'll strike first and ask questions later. Sienna takes the chair at Cordelia's right hand, the seat on the other side of her occupied by a plus-sized dark-haired man. David. He's chatting with a man on *his* other side that I don't recognize, as if this is just as normal dinner. David's always had that skill, if normalcy can be termed a skill. He puts everyone around him at ease.

I should be clocking the other people at the table, but my attention snags and narrows in on Isabelle. She sits at Cordelia's left hand, her back to us. Her hair's been piled up on her head, leaving her long neck bare, and she's wearing a cheery yellow dress that should look out of place in this gathering where everyone is dressed in muted colors. But no, she's a beam of sunshine in this room and I take a step toward her before Gaeton nudges my shoulder.

"Focus," he murmurs.

Right. There's a song and dance to perform, and we can't afford to skip any steps. I glance at him. "After you."

He gives a faint smile. "You're just looking for a shield."

"Cordelia likes you more than she likes me."

Now his smile broadens. "*Everyone* likes me more than they like you. It's my winning personality." He moves in front of me, leading the way. I can't see the head of the table with Gaeton's broad back in the way, but I'm conscious of the attention of everyone *else* in the room on us. Then he steps aside and easily sinks to a knee. I follow suit.

Cordelia watches us over the rim of her wine glass. "So the prodigal sons return. Did you enjoy your month off?"

For once, Gaeton doesn't have shit to say. It's just as well. I don't mind taking on *this* firing squad. I hold her gaze for a three-count and then drop my eyes. "Grief does strange things."

Her breath catches the tiniest amount, silent to all but those at the head of the table. "Yes, I suppose it does." She sets her glass on the table. "You're back."

It's not quite a question, but I answer it all the same. "With your blessing."

"That's not all you've come to ask my blessing about, though, is it?"

At this, I look at her and then at Isabelle to my right. They want to do this publicly? I don't know why I'm surprised. Cordelia will want to lock us in, no matter what needs to happen to ensure that result. I study Isabelle. "Is this what you want?"

She nods, slowly. She, for one, doesn't look unsure in the least, just quietly watchful. "If you two are okay with it."

"Of course we're okay with it." Gaeton gives his cocky grin, though it's a little strained around the edges. The only sign that this situation is stressing him the fuck out. He turns to Cordelia. "We want your sister. Both of us."

Her brows rise a fraction of an inch. "She's not an animal to be bartered."

Oh, so it's going to be like this? I give her the look that statement deserves. "That didn't stop you from sending her to retrieve us, no matter the cost."

She narrows her eyes. "Something you were only too happy to take advantage of. Don't think I'll be forgetting *that* anytime soon."

"Cordelia." Isabelle shakes her head. "This is what I want. It's what they want. It's what *you* want. Stop fighting for my honor when it was my choice to begin with."

Cordelia grimaces. "I still don't like it."

"You don't have to like it. You just have to give your blessing."

She turns that glare on her sister, and her expression instantly transforms to a sickly sweet smile that isn't the least bit sincere. "If karma exists, it's going to take the form of a herd of daughters from these two men that will give you a head full of gray hair."

Isabelle gives a choked laugh. "I don't know why you and

Sienna are so obsessed with the idea of me having babies. You first, Cordie. *You first.*"

For a second, it looks like they might start tussling right here in the dining room. Muriel leans over and touches Cordelia's shoulder and that is all it takes for her to get her game face back in place. She spares us a glance. "You have my blessing. Next time you decide to take a *vacation*, get permission first."

"Yes, ma'am." Gaeton rises easily to his feet and gives me a hand up. I don't need it, but I like that he offered. I like it even more than he doesn't drop the contact immediately. We turn to Isabelle as a unit.

Before I can say a single goddamn thing, one of our men bursts into the room. He checks his stride so he's not quite running, but there's no hiding how frazzled he looks. He hurries around the table and murmurs in Muriel's ear. She leans down to whisper to Cordelia, and the woman's face goes still. "She's early. Yes, let her in. Give us a few minutes and we'll meet her in my office." She stands and gives a bright smile to the table. "If you'll excuse us for a few moments. Duty calls." She lowers her voice. "Sienna, Isabelle, bring your men."

Isabelle rises and moves to us. She gives a tight smile. "Thank you."

"You have nothing to thank us for." Gaeton slips his free arm around her shoulders and gives her a squeeze. "Let's go see where the fire is."

We end up in Cordelia's study. It's not the same one Orsino used, and something inside me relaxes at that. I know I'll be faced with memories of him, again and again, but this is a welcome reprieve. Or it would be if I knew what we're walking into.

Cordelia sits on a chair that aspires to be a throne, Muriel in her customary place at her right shoulder. Sienna lounges on a fainting chair, her head on David's thick thigh, reading a book on some kind of theoretical physics, as if we weren't just about to sit down to dinner.

Gaeton and I exchange a look and he drops to sprawl on the empty couch to the other side of Cordelia's chair, pulling Isabelle down to tuck against his side. If shit gets heavy, he'll use his body as a shield to protect her. I move around to stand behind the couch, close to the metal lamp that can be used as a weapon in a pinch. I'd prefer guns, but we both knew better than to show up armed to this meeting.

We don't have to wait long.

The same frazzled man from before enters the room and stands aside to hold the door. I'm not exactly *surprised* to see Ursa come through the door next, but I honestly expected her to wait longer to make her move. She's got her hair piled in a crown on her head and she's wearing golden gown that shimmers as she walks. She looks around the room. "Good, everyone is here." A glance at the man. "You can leave."

Cordelia arches a brow. "Don't give my people orders, Ursa. It's rude." She sounds cold and perfectly in control, the nerves I glimpsed earlier nowhere in evidence.

"I'm sorry, darling." Ursa laughs. "I'm so used to being in charge. I'm sure you understand."

"All the same."

"Hmmm, yes. Of course." Her attention lands on Isabelle and then slowly moves to Gaeton before settling on me. "I see the three of you have made things official. Congratulations."

I tense. This is no meeting of congratulations, not when we were teetering on the brink of war before the three of us got our shit together. Not when we're *still* teetering on the brink of war. This isn't my show, though. It's Cordelia's, and I have to keep my fucking mouth shut and let her run this.

With that in mind, I lean down and grip both Isabelle and

Gaeton's shoulders. I might have the control to stay silent, but if Gaeton lets her rile him, this will be all over.

Ursa clocks the move and her red lips curl. "Cute."

"Ursa." Cordelia doesn't shift, doesn't seem to so much as breathe. "I intended to save this for an official meeting, but since you're here, now is as good a time as any."

"You want me to cease and desist with our little border skirmish."

Border skirmish?

The gall of this woman. I might be impressed if she wasn't threatening the very people I care most about in this world.

"It's a waste of time and resources. You must know you can't win."

Again, Ursa's gaze glances on the three of us. "A woman can dream." She flicks fingertips with nails as red as her lips. "Ah well, not every plan comes to fruition. I am willing to, as you put it, cease and desist. For a price."

"Are you fucking kidding me?" I don't realize I've spoken until Isabelle's hand covers mine and she squeezes my wrist. Hard.

Cordelia flashes me a look and then refocuses on Ursa. "I'm listening."

"I have business with Olympus, which is troubling because I'm no longer welcome within the city limits." She shrugs. "I'm sure you understand."

"Explain it to me."

"There is a girl there, an unfortunate soul if you would like to put it that way, who is in desperate need of my assistance. I require her."

Now it's Isabelle's turn to tense. "We are not going to *kidnap* some girl from Olympus for you."

Cordelia looks like she wants to strangle her youngest sister, but manages to get herself under control before Ursa looks back at her. "We have no issue with Olympus, and I fully intend to keep it that way. What my sister says stands."

"I'm not in the business of stealing princesses." Her smile doesn't dim in the slightest, as if we've amused her. "I simply need a message delivered. I can't send my people for obvious reasons."

"Then send a text. An email. A goddamn letter. I don't see why you need *my* people to play messenger."

Ursa sighs. "It needs to be in person. She's under lock and key so the normal modes of contact won't work." She looks at Isabelle. "She will, however, take you as a visitor."

"No." Again, I don't mean to speak.

Gaeton's protest echoes mine. "Fuck that."

Ursa ignores us both. "Orsino's precious youngest daughter. You've been to Olympus before, little Isabelle. You've even spoken with this princess of sorts. No one would think to bar you from her."

Isabelle leans forward a little. "Who is it?"

The Sea Witch's dark eyes light up. "Zurielle Rosi."

"Triton's daughter?" Gaeton murmurs. "What the hell do you want with *her?*"

"That's my business. I simply need a messenger girl."

"No." I shake my head. "Absolutely fucking not." Going to Olympus is a special kind of dangerous, but I've never had the authority to tell Isabelle it was a bad idea, not when Orsino gave his blessing. Doing it for her own amusement is one thing. Doing what could potentially come down to an act of war? Fuck no.

Isabelle squeezes my wrist. "I deliver a message and there are no more 'border skirmishes.' You stay in your own territory and stop bothering with ours."

Ursa's grin widens. "Consider it a deal."

"No," I say again, but Isabelle isn't listening to me.

KATEE ROBERT

"I want to know the full message before I agree to anything. And your promise that you won't hurt the girl."

Cordelia's shaking her head. "You don't have to agree. We can find another way."

"You know better, Cordie." Isabelle tenses like she wants to say more, but finally refocuses on Ursa. "The message."

"Simple, really." Ursa touches her hair almost absently. "Tell her that I know where her precious Alaric is, and that I am only too happy to assist her reuniting with him." Her smile is far too satisfied for my peace of mind. "And I have no intention of doing anything to the girl that she doesn't want. She'll remain unharmed."

I narrow my eyes, but Isabelle speaks before I have a chance to. "Deal."

"I knew you were a smart girl." Ursa looks around the room. "A pleasure doing business with you." She turns and sweeps from the room.

And then all hell breaks loose.

CHAPTER 29

ISABELLE

*A*s soon as Ursa leaves, everyone in the room starts arguing. Sienna thinks this deal is a good idea. Cordelia doesn't want to agree, but she's in a crappy position of having to worry about me versus worry about the entire territory. Neither Gaeton nor Beast wants me anywhere near Olympus.

They *especially* don't want me there when my sister rises to her feet and levels us with a look. "It's decided. Izzy is going and she can take *one* of you as escort." She holds up a hand before either of them can get a word out. "You just got back here. You can absolutely not leave again. I'll allow you to pick which one will act as escort and which will stay behind." She motions to Muriel, Sienna, and David. "We'll let you discuss it amongst yourselves, but don't take long. Dinner's going to get cold."

Gaeton is on his feet before the door shuts. "This is a shitty ass idea."

Beast moves around the couch to glare down at me. "You shouldn't have agreed."

I feel a little silly sitting here while they glower down at me, so I join them on my feet. "There wasn't another option."

"You keep saying that, but you didn't give us a chance to *find* another option."

They're right and they're wrong, all at the same time. All afternoon, in between worrying about whether or not they'd show up for dinner, I listened as Sienna lounged on my bed and posited scenarios to get us out of this conflict with Ursa. Eighty percent of those scenarios ended in a conflict that could cause the death of one or both of the men I love. I won't let us get to that point, not if there's another option.

"I just found you two again. I don't want to lose you."

Gaeton takes my hands. "And what the fuck do you think is going to happen if Triton figures out you're delivering a message to his favorite daughter from the fucking Sea Witch?"

Nothing good. Those two have a long history, and I want no part of their war, either. "I know Zuri. Or at least I've met her before. No one will have any reason to suspect me."

Gaeton shakes his head. "It's too dangerous."

I give a choked laugh. "Funny, coming from you." I glance at Beast. "*Either* of you. What happens the next time there's a fight and you're needed? You're *generals*. Danger comes with the territory. I—" I wish I could keep them safe, could guarantee that they'll always come home to me without injury. I've grown up this world. I know it for a lie. "I will not stand in your way or prevent you from doing what you need to do. I need you to give me the same respect."

Beast's hands land on my hips and he leans against my back. "I think you can understand why we're having trouble with this."

Of course I can. This life isn't easy under the best of circumstances and this hardly qualifies. I release a shuddering breath and relax back into him. "I know. But you understand why I have to do this." Anything to protect my family. *Anything.* I lost my father. I can't lose anyone else. I won't.

Gaeton sighs, his shoulders dropping. "Yeah, we get it." He meets Beast's gaze over my shoulder. "Who goes with her?"

"You do." He doesn't hesitate. "I'll stay here and help ensure Ursa keeps her word. Isabelle, can you get in contact with Zurielle and set up a meeting or however you want to go about it? Once we have a time frame, we can get the finer details down."

And, just like that, they shift gears from arguing with me to spending their energy on ensuring this goes off without a hitch. I should be relieved. If Ursa keeps her word, it means we avoid the threatening war. It means I keep the people I care about safe for a little while longer.

It means I throw Zurielle Rosi under the bus to save myself.

No one questions that part. I shouldn't, either. If there's a choice between this girl I barely know and my family, I will choose my family every time. I know what my father would say, what he would do. *Family first. Always.* It's one of the few rules I've always followed. This just doesn't feel right.

"This is wrong." I don't realize I'm going to speak until both my men look at me. "We shouldn't have agreed to this."

"Isabelle—"

I shake my head. "I don't know if Zurielle trusts me, but she's naïve and sheltered, and she hates it. She's not going to look for the poison in this offer. She's going to jump at it with both hands." I don't have to know her well to know that. I might not have always loved living under my father's rules, but Zurielle *hates* it. I understand her feelings in a way only a youngest daughter can. "She's going to take Ursa's deal."

"That's her choice." Beast frowns. "She gets a choice, which is a better offer than I was expecting."

It's Gaeton who seems to understand. He crouches down in front of me. "You can't save everyone, Isabelle. Sometimes you have to choose who's worth your blood and sacrifice, and let the other pieces fall where they may."

"She's so young, Gaeton." I don't know why I'm still arguing this. Because it could have been me a few years ago? "She's like twenty-one. Maybe twenty-two. She doesn't know enough to be afraid."

He takes my hands, his dark eyes serious. "If you want to cross Ursa, say the word. We'll figure out a different way."

They would. They might question me, but they'll adjust our course and shift to figuring out how to neutralize the threat Ursa offers. If we go that route, people will die. Maybe Ursa. Maybe one of the men I love. When it's laid out like that, it seems a simple choice.

Then why do I feel like I'm selling my soul?

"Will she keep her word?"

Gaeton's gaze doesn't leave my face. "Likely. No matter what game she's playing, Olympus will mobilize if the Thirteen think for a second that we're snatching their people off the street and harming them. Hercules came of his own choice and no one died in the conflict with Zeus. Ursa's too smart to stir *that* hornet's nest. We can't guarantee anything, but I'd bet on her pulling some manipulative shit that's designed to fuck with Triton but doesn't include murder."

I look up at Beast. "Do you agree?" I'm looking for an excuse, and I know it. They know it, too.

He cups my chin. "Are you looking for permission or forgiveness?"

Just like that, I'm trying not to cry. I don't know what's wrong with me. I close my eyes for a long moment and fight for control. "This is dramatic, and I'm sorry. I know every single member of my family has had to make hard calls at one point or another and they all put us first. I know *you* two have done the same. This isn't even that hard of a call. I don't know why I'm struggling."

"Because it's your first." Beast's hand is so devastatingly gentle on my face. "For better or worse, Orsino kept you away from so much of what it takes to maintain the safety of the people in this territory. There will be other decisions like this in the future, and they'll be more complicated and won't always have a happy ending. It's the way our world works."

I know that. I truly do know that.

"I'm sorry." I sigh and open my eyes. "I'm ready."

Gaeton pulls me to my feet and envelops me in a hug. A breath later, Beast is pressed against my back, the weight of them steadying me just as much as their words did. Gaeton kisses the top of my head. "We'll be in and out and back to Carver City by morning."

We're doing this. I know we're doing it.

I just hope I find some peace about it.

* * *

ZURIELLE ROSI MEETS us in a tiny bar in a part of Olympus I've never been to. It's enough to have Gaeton on full alert, but there's no trouble as we slip through the door and make our way to the table in the back. It's bathed in shadows, but I make out the slim form of Zurielle. She's a pretty Vietnamese woman with long dark red hair, and she looks both terrified and excited when she sees me. "Isabelle."

I slide into the chair across from her and feel Gaeton take a position at my back. It's not exactly unobtrusive, but no one around us is paying the smallest bit of attention. "Hi, Zuri."

"I almost didn't believe it when I got your text." She glances at Gaeton. "I see you've worked things out."

"Yeah, it's a little more complicated than that, but we have." There's no use stalling. I lean forward and lower my voice. "I have a message for you."

She frowns. "That's what you said, but you were really vague before."

I still don't know why Ursa wants me to be *here* instead of just sending a text with the message, but the woman has her reasons and I've made my decision. I glance around the room. "You know who Ursa is?"

She flinches. "The Sea Witch? Yes, I know who she is."

"She told me to tell you..." It takes me a few seconds to get myself together. "She knows where Alaric is, and she's willing to help reunite you."

The hope in Zurielle's brown eyes make me feel like a monster. She grabs my hands, gripping me tightly enough that I have to fight back a wince. "She can reunite us?"

Even though I should leave it at that, I can't help myself. It's too big a coincidence for me to have met an Alaric at the Underworld and to have the same name thrown around by Ursa and Zurielle. "He's a tall guy, right? White, handsome, dark hair and blue eyes?"

"Yes, that's him."

I can feel Gaeton's tension at my back, but I've gone too far to turn away now. "Zuri, he's in the Underworld. You don't need Ursa to find him."

"I know where he is, Isabelle. It's not the *where* that's the problem." She lets out a long exhale. "Thank you for delivering the message."

"Don't thank me. Not if you're going to play right into her hands."

She gives me a sad smile. "Some people are worth the risk."

I can't claim that's a lie without being the worst kind of hypocrite. "Please be careful."

"Thank you for delivering the message," she repeats. She gives my hands one last squeeze and rises. "And you be careful leaving town tonight. There are strange things going on in Olympus."

Before I can decipher *that*, she's gone, hurrying out the door and into the night. I twist and look up at Gaeton. "Did I just make a mistake?"

"No." He's not looking at me, though. He's studying the room as if assassins will burst from the walls at any moment. "You delivered a message and now she's going to make a choice."

"A choice that Ursa seems to have carefully orchestrated."

"Zurielle is smart enough to see the strings. If she chooses to ignore them, that's her choice, Isabelle. You have to let her make it."

"What if she makes the wrong one?"

He pulls me to my feet, his expression serious. "Sometimes shitty things have to happen to keep our people safe, love. It's the burden your father never wanted you to have." He looks around again. "Do you want to leave?"

For a second, I think he's talking about the bar, but then his true meaning penetrates. "You mean leave Carver City?"

"I don't have to talk to Beast to know he's with me in this. We'll follow you wherever you need to be. Whether that's Carver City or somewhere else."

As if it's just that easy.

Looking up at him, I realize that for Gaeton it *is* that easy. He would walk away from Carver City without a backward glance if I asked it of him. The knowledge leaves me dizzy. "I—" I take a breath and stop. He's making a serious offer. I have to do it the honor of actually considering it.

The freedom of leaving the city tempts me. I'd have to be dead for it *not* to tempt me.

But walking away means leaving my sisters behind. Worse, it means leaving them vulnerable because I'd be taking Beast and Gaeton with me. If I stay, though, I can no longer look to the stars and hope for something different. If I choose to stay, I have to choose to be part of it.

I've already made my choice. I made it the second I took Ursa's deal.

It might take some time to come fully to terms with what that means, with what it will cost, but my choice is made. I go on my tiptoes and kiss him. "Take me home. Our Beast is waiting for us."

He studies me for a long moment and then nods. "Let's go."

We slip out of Olympus as smoothly as we slipped in. After all, no one is looking for *us*. I don't know how long it will take for the guilt to fade. Maybe it never will. Maybe that's just a burden I'll have to bear, the knowledge that my family and my men will always outweigh any allegiance I have for others. They come first. They will *always* come first. My father's voice seems to whisper to me in the back of my mind.

Family first. Always.

CHAPTER 30

I've never had a homecoming. Over the years, missions and errands might take me away from Carver City, but I'd return with as little fanfare as when I left. When Isabelle and I were together before, I didn't want to worry her, so most of the time I didn't tell her what my orders were.

We take the back door into the house, and I follow Isabelle down the hall and up the stairs to the family wing. She steps through a door to a small living room and that's where we find Beast. He's pacing, his phone in his hand, and the look on his face when he turns around and sees us ...

Fuck.

Yeah, I love this guy.

I can't doubt that he loves us, too. Not anymore.

He crosses to us and pulls Isabelle into his arms and then snags the back of my neck and tows me down for a quick, thorough kiss. "Problems?"

"No. It went off without a hitch."

He exhales and some of the tension leaves his body.

"Good." Beast leans back and looks down at Isabelle. "You okay?"

Her smile wobbles a little. "I will be."

"Hard call to make."

"I didn't think it'd be that hard." She gives him a hard hug. "Let's go to bed. I'm exhausted."

No question that we're joining her. We follow her though the halls to her room. The family suites are situated in such a way that each has their own hall to give an illusion of privacy. Walking into Isabelle's room after so long apart from her is a trip. It looks exactly the same.

That stops me short.

It's not the huge bed that she bought when we started spending the night together. Or even the complete lack of change in the other furniture. It's the photos that are scattered across every available surface. Those photographs used to aggravate the hell out of me. There were pictures of me and her next to ones of her and Beast, a mixture that never failed to remind me that I wasn't enough for her.

Now? Now, they feel right as fuck.

I would have thought they'd change after we broke up, that she'd put away any evidence of us. I glance at her. "You didn't take the photos down."

"I did." She tugs at her dress, staring at the pictures. "I put them back up this afternoon while I was waiting for dinner." She lifts her hands and lets them drop. "I missed you two so much when I put them away. But even without the pictures serving as a constant reminder, I still had the memories."

"You have more than memories now," I say

Her smile is still a little wobbly. "It's going to take some time for that to really sink it. It still feels too good to be true."

Beast sits on the edge of the bed, his blue eyes watchful. "We should probably iron out some logistics before moving forward."

"We sleep together." I don't mean to say it aloud, but the certainty settles in my chest. "Wherever we sleep, we do it together."

He nods. "I'm good with that."

"I ..." Isabelle moves to sit next to Beast on the bed and looks at me. "I'll always have my family suite, but I don't have a strong preference to where we end up."

As tempting as it is to put forth another option, there's something to be said for staying here. I look around the room. Even with all Isabelle's stuff, there's plenty of space for more. "Things are going to be touch and go for a little bit. Staying here for the time being isn't a bad idea."

"Agreed." Beast nods. "But keep your place. If we need some space, can't hurt to have that as backup."

I look at both of them and grin. "Look at us, communicating."

"What a novel thought." Isabelle shakes her head. "I guess we'll just ... talk through every issue as it arises?"

"That *is* what relationships entail." I walk to the edge of the bed and lean down to kiss her and then over to kiss Beast as well. "Let's go to bed."

We strip slowly. I don't know about them, but the events of the last few days are catching up with me. We haven't exactly had much in the way of sleep since this started, and I'm fucking exhausted. We end up in Isabelle's bed with her between us, my leg hitched over both her and Beast, his hands alternating between caressing her side and mine.

For the first time in a very long time, I don't question this. We've barely passed the first hurdle, but we *have* passed it. Isabelle's family. Ursa. The world will throw more challenges our way, but we've met these two together and come through the other side. We'll meet the rest that way as well.

I move Isabelle's hair off her neck and press a kiss to her

throat. "Marry me." I look up and meet Beast's intent gaze. "Both of you."

Isabelle gives a hiccupping little laugh. "That's not legal."

"I don't give a fuck about legal. I give a fuck about what we want."

Beast smooths his hand down my side and transfers his attention to her. "I don't need a wedding. I never did. Gaeton does. What do you need?"

She's so still, I have to concentrate to feel her breathing. Finally, she says, "I ... At one point marriage felt like something that was just another kind of trap, but not too long ago I thought about walking down the aisle to both of you. I liked the idea of it. A lot."

Beast smiles. A real smile, not his cold little tease of one. The motherfucker grins like he can't contain his happiness. "I have a few ideas about rings."

I narrow my eyes. "You just said you don't need a wedding."

"Need has nothing to do with want. I'm not a fool, Gaeton. I want you two locked down in every way you'll allow. That includes a wedding, and it sure as fuck includes my ring on both of your fingers."

"You sneaky bastard."

He shrugs, completely unrepentant. "I want what I want." Something he's said before, but I'm yet again amazed by his willingness to line up the dominoes and tip them over to accomplish the goal he has in mind. He grins at me. "Yes, Gaeton. I'll marry you."

Isabelle turns in my arms until she can lean back and see my face. I know I'm moving too fast, but is it really too fast? I've been in love with this woman for years. My feelings for Beast are newer, but I've trusted him with my life for as long as I've loved Isabelle. Longer, even. We have the foundation.

We've always had the foundation. We just required the right inciting event to get us there.

She runs her hands up my chest. "Last time you proposed, I didn't have the answer you needed."

The memory feels so much fainter now, like something out of a dream. It doesn't sting like it used to. "We weren't whole then." I grab Beast's hand and press a kiss to his scarred knuckles. "We are now."

She nibbles on her bottom lip. "I want us forever. All three of us. I want … I want the wedding. I want to say yes to both of you." Her eyes shine and her smile trembles. "So … Yes. Yes, I'll marry you." She twists to look at Beast. "And yes, I'll marry you. We might be missing the marriage license, but I don't care about that."

"Me, either." I grin. "How about tomorrow?"

This earns me a little gasp that I want to eat right up. Isabelle raises her brows. "If you think for a second that my sisters wouldn't hunt us down, hog-tie us, and then build a dungeon to throw us in if we snuck off to get married—"

"Good point." We just got back to the territory. Plenty of time to aggravate our new sisters-in-law later.

Isabelle gives a soft smile. "But I think I'd really like a spring wedding. *This* spring. You're right. We've come this far. I don't want anything holding us back from our happily ever after."

I kiss her temple and share a look with Beast. He laughs in response. "I pity the circumstance or person who thinks to get between us and our forever. You're ours, Isabelle Belmonte. And we're yours. Always."

* * *

THANK you so much for reading Geaton, Beast, and Isabelle's story! They're very special to me, and I hope you enjoyed reading them as much as I enjoyed writing them. If you did, please consider leaving a review!

Need more Gaeton, Beast, and Isabelle in your life? Sign up for my newsletter and get a BONUS short giving a glimpse of what happens after the events of THE BEAST... and what happens when Isabelle finally walks down the aisle to her two men.

The Wicked Villains series continues in THE SEA WITCH, which begins with Zurielle arriving to ask Ursa for help. The only bargaining tool she has is herself, which leads to her agreeing to a virginity auction to raise the money to buy Alaric's freedom. Except nothing is as it seems... Including Alaric.

Looking for your next sexy read? You can pick up my MMF ménage THEIRS FOR THE NIGHT, my FREE novella that features an exiled prince, his bodyguard, and the bartender they can't quite manage to leave alone.

ACKNOWLEDGMENTS

We're still going strong! My endless thank you to all the fans of this series who have read the books, loved them, and told others about it. That word of mouth has given these stories legs, and I cannot thank you enough.

Big thanks to Jenny Nordbak and Andie J. Christopher for always being ready to give me a "hot or not" meter on things I'm considering for this series. This can be such a solitary road, and it feels much less lonely knowing that you two are as invested in seeing what kinky shit my brain comes up with!

Endless thank yous to Manu from Tessera Editorial and Lynda M. Ryba for helping me get this book into the best version of itself.

All my love to my husband and family. The last bit of editing done on this book was done during week 3 of self-isolation, and I am so incredibly grateful for the support offered by everyone to allow me to keep putting words to paper. Love you!

CPSIA information can be obtained
at www.ICGtesting.com
Printed in the USA
BVHW031135160721
PP12417800001B/2

9 781951 329051